Sins of Survival

From Darkness series Book One

Roxanne Ward

Go Go Self Publishing VW

First Edition Publication by Fulton Books

Fulton Books, Inc., Meadville, PA

ISBN 978-1-63860-484-6

Second Publication by

GO GO Publishing VW, Idaho, USA

Second Edition

Published April 28, 2023

Cover illustration by Bella Leonard

Cover design by RG Graph X Design

ISBN paperback 979-8-9880010-1-0

ASIN Kindle   B0C3XVHBS7

Genres: Science fiction, speculative fiction, post-apocalyptic fiction, military fiction, romantic fiction, mystery fiction.

NOTICE: This novel contains adult sexual encounters, unethical behavior, offensive language, and military violence.

file 14

Other Books

By Roxanne Ward

FROM DARKNESS series

Sins of Survival Book 1
Lion's Creed Book 2
Reclamation Book 3

HIGHMINDS series

Somewhere Else Book 1
New Haven Book 2
Journey to Cali Bantu Book 3

Dedication

*To my loving husband
for his steadfast belief in me,
and to my father for
making literature my passion.*

Sins of Survival
From Darkness

Roxanne Ward

"And what he greatly thought, he nobly dared"

Homer

Prologue

Leland Delano walked into the run-down coffee shop and nodded at the barista behind the counter. He waded through the empty tables and headed down the hall with the bathrooms and the offices. Standing before the maintenance door with the "staff only" sign, he punched in his code and made his way to the back. After passing through another locked door which lead to an elevator, he hit the button for the fifteenth floor. He watched the lights blink through the levels as he rose ever closer to his destination. It would be another sobering meeting, and once again they would beat their unsolvable issue to death. The issue that would mark their souls forever.

Leland Delano walked into the run-down coffee shop and nodded at the barista behind the counter. He waded through the empty tables and headed down the hall with the bathrooms and the offices. Standing before the maintenance door with the "staff only" sign, he punched in his code and made his way to the back. After passing through another locked door which led to an elevator, he hit the button for the fifteenth floor. The lights blink through the levels as he rose ever closer to another sobering meeting where once again he and his partner in crime would beat their unsolvable issue to death. Their worst crime yet, one that would mark their souls forever.

Banner Vogel and Leland had knocked the problem around again and again, but the same unacceptable solution presented itself. They realized all the arguing could not change the reality, and no brilliant plan could solve it. The dilemma arose when a determined young man with brainless ambition stumbled upon their lethal secret, setting in motion an irreversible course of action. He was a threat to civilization, as well as the plans of two very powerful men, and now, murder as a solution swirled in their minds.

Leland had pondered the ethical dilemma a thousand times. The question of murder, he found, was fought on the battleground between morality and survival. While morality is the endeavor of enlightenment and compassion; survival is the pursuit of knowledge and perseverance. It is science that fuels the war between them, and it can also still the waters. Yet when survival is threatened, even the moral will turn feral.

"Okay, so have we've decided?" Banner's face was pained at the grim conclusion and completely done with the rehashing of it.

"All our work will be lost, and the already dim future of humankind could be as well." Leland shook his head wearily at the thought of forsaking his life's work and its lofty potential for mankind. "These innovations and formulas could end our air pollution and waste problems. It has the potential to increase food production ten-fold. It could profoundly improve life on earth. Since the meteorite disaster, this world has been reeling in oligarchy hell. We could change that."

"And we will, but right now, we have no way to control it, manage it, or protect it. As benevolent as it is on one side, it is dark as night on the other, Tyson, I mean, Leland. Shit," Banner cursed himself for calling his longtime friend by his true name. When Tyson came to him for help, following the murder of his wife, Banner set up an alternate identity to protect, him and his children, and his discovery.

He continued with his thought, "Look, it's time will come again if not by us, by another. Who knows how many times we invented the wheel and the lever?" Banner was attempting to lighten the mood, but he realized the comparison was overly simplistic, and the mood was far too morose for levity.

"And the boy, Ket. Is there any way his life can be spared?" Lealand pondered the irony of struggling to grab a mental image of his beloved wife when this boy's face was eternally burned in his psyche.

"Right now, we have to protect our families," Banner stressed," *and* our world. If you can find another way, I'm all ears."

Leland let out a long weighty breath. "My daughter should have been more careful. I'll never know what Ariel saw in Ket. He's arrogant and self-indulgent. He was going to turn me in, and that would have endangered Ariel, his girlfriend, and her younger sister too."

"It's indefensible. He's an asshole, for sure, but he's just a pawn. He has no idea what he'd be turning over to the Neighwah. And he has no clue that they will kill him the moment they secure the information." Banner felt sorry for the young man too, but their solution, as brutal as it was, was clear. "He may be naïve in his intent, but he is set on his course, and his actions are destined to cause countless deaths. The choice is to sacrifice our morality or let hundreds of thousands, perhaps millions die."

"My girls need protection. They are innocent and completely unaware of who I am. They think I'm a history teacher, for God's sake,' Leland pleaded.

Banner stood tall and resolute. "They will have it, and so will you. But we must talk about what to do with Ket."

"It seems more abhorrent every time we discuss it. We will surely drown in emotional anguish, but even a lifetime of remorse will not serve as fair penance. We are taking his life because we can't, or won't, divulge our secret. He may be guilty of selfish ignorance, but we are committing premeditated murder." Leland rubbed his eyes, restraining the tears that pooled behind them. He took several deep breaths, but it didn't help. "Before you say it, yes, I know the alternative is worse. Our duty is bigger than this moment. I know this."

This whole thing felt like a Greek tragedy to Lealand. A judgement that was passed down for his hubris act of stealing knowledge. He believed himself to be an ethical man, but he had harnessed a dangerous power and put it within reach of humankind. Holding it back will only delay the inevitable and make targets of them all. "Oh Banner," Lealand sniffed and let go a shuttered breath. "If it must be done, we have to do it. We cannot burden another with it."

"Agreed." Banner held out his hand with grave remorse, vowing to the final verdict.

Leland paused and stared at Banner's outstretched hand. With a weary sigh, he grasped it, and a solemn shake sealed the fate of a critical discovery and an overzealous informer.

Chapter One

Jillian Delano sat in front of her father's aging laptop. Gunfire and shouts from the street below pounded out an all too familiar rhythm. She read the subject line, "Invitation A," as she scrolled through her emails. Scams were beyond rampant, and she had more reasons to delete the mysterious message than she had to open it. But open it she did, with quite a bit of trepidation. Is this the contact message she was waiting for? Praying for? It had been so long, she'd given up on the whole idea. For a moment, her heart flooded with that rarest of feelings—hope. The message disappointingly read:

Acknowledge your resolve;
Assert your values; Assess your life.
Summerhill High School;
April 6; 3:00 p.m.; room 203

She rolled her eyes at the gimmicky, cryptic pitch, and initiated the dump and purge she learned from her dad, hoping it wouldn't corrupt her software or alert the Neighwah. Just in case it was the message she had longed for, she immediately wrote down the meeting details on her fingerboards. Paper was a luxury and rarely used for simple memos, but it would be risky to use it for secrets.

Her father told her of a time when every purchase came in multiple layers of disposable wrappers, and people would discard them, allowing the wind to send them sailing around on the streets. It got so bad that laws had to be made to prevent people from tossing unwanted paper and other items on the ground. She couldn't get her head around throwing away things that could be burned for heat, reused, traded, or used to fill the cracks and bullet holes of dilapidated dwellings. Today, there was no clutter on the streets, just the stench of filth and the crumbling decay of a dying city.

The write-and-swipe fingerboards, greatly improved from a child's toy, saved a lot of time, and when you erased it, it was truly gone. It was given to her by a teacher, Ms. Fuller, as a gift. The sisters were allowed to go to school even though their status didn't qualify them to go. It was believed their dad set it up from the extra jobs he did, but they wisely never questioned it.

Jillian thought back to the day she was approached by her college anatomy teacher about joining a team determined to create a secret sanctuary away from the decaying cities. She spoke of a place with security, mercy, and the basic comforts of life. Jillian was more idealistic back then, and believing it was possible, she expressed an interest. Truth be told, she was more than interested. She thought about it obsessively. She craved it, needed it.

As the world turned uglier, the government stopped funding colleges, and their father lost his teaching job. He was shot during a shootout at his new position as a ticket collector. Though he survived the wound, he died from a superbug infection. Then Jillian's teacher and mentor, Elaine Fuller, moved when Jillian was beginning the last year of her nursing degree. It was her worse year.

Jilly missed her father and needed his strength and guidance, but, now they also needed more credits. Both of them were counting on Jilly getting a nursing job to make up those credits, and now there was no way to finish. She tried to find her teacher, but to no avail. Maybe she was at the town she talked about, and she decided not to include her. One more disappointment in a world wrought with absolute sadness.

Jillian pondered the mysterious sanctuary plan from time to time and fantasized about a day that didn't involve dodging the desperate, the diseased, and the crazies. But worse were the mercenaries called Drangers. The term morphed from rangers and dangerous persons. After the great meteorite disaster, the police were disbanded, and gangs became widespread. Since then, they have developed into organized evil-for-hire bands across every city and town in the Colorado territories.

The Neighwah were more lethal because they had the best weapons. They were backed by owners of large corporations called Corporates and had access to vast resources. They executed "justice" with a swift, malicious hand, and more often than not, they attacked the poor workers, not the perpetrators.

The Drangers were organized exploiters getting paid for deeds, but the Neighwah soldiers were given steady pay and lived on the middle rung of society with the Uppers. They had nice places, plenty of food, and credits to spend on luxury items. And then there were the Elites. They were at the top of the food chain, but no one knew much about them, nor had anyone ever seen them.

Dailys didn't tend to engage in violence. They were just survivors going about a simple, scrounging existence at he lowest rung of society. When they weren't at their assigned jobs, they hid in their dwellings, and when they went out, they stayed in groups.

All Dailys had to work, and for that, they were issued enough basic supplies necessary for them to continue working. If Dailys couldn't work for an extended time, they often had horrible accidents or were assigned toxic tasks. When Dailys are taken to the hospitals, they don't tend to leave, so many died at home.

Reporting a death was immediate, so the body could be taken to the local freezers. They told the people it was to manage disease, so not reporting a death was a crime. A truck came every week to gather the dead and take them away to the crematorium. There was no time for grieving.

She thought back to her childhood and shuddered at how brutal and uncertain the times had become. How soon before she or her sister became one of the many forgotten victims, like their mom and dad? She and Ariel, Ari, were so young when their mom died, she couldn't bring up a clear memory. She was hit by a vehicle, her dad said, but that's what parents told kids. It was code for the awful things adults hide from them.

The whole world was mean, tumbling into anarchy, and there was no hope of better days; in fact, there was a certainty of worse. As the civilized world plunged deeper into chaos, so did her expectations for it. And like the slow-cooking frog scenario, she adapted to each new horror. Yet this desperate dream rang in her head too loudly to be drowned out by logic or fear.

Motivated by more shrieks of violence outside, she decided to check out this "invitation" and bring Ari. It didn't say "come alone," "bring ID," or any other nefarious inference, but she had been warned about the high level of secrecy expected by the group. She didn't care. She'd never leave her sister behind.

"Leave a message," Ari's voice stated plainly and directly when Jillian paged her sister's work band. Ari was always straightforward, pragmatic, and guarded. Being three years older, she was able to finish her engineering degree before riots shut down their campus. Jillian still had one year left to complete her training for her nursing certification.

"Call me," mocking her message with the same tone. Within five minutes, Jillian's phone played her space-age ringtone, and she quickly picked it up.

"You rang?" Ari stated.

"Hey, want to go on a date tomorrow night?"

"A date? With whom? Where?"

"With me, and where is umm, it's a surprise," she said, knowing even the sparsest details would have Ari ranting, and the call listeners questioning.

"Oh, goodie. Love those," came the answer with palpable sarcasm.

"Please. It's kind of a mystery to me too."

"Geez, Jilly, what dangerous crap are you messing with? What, where, and when is it? Who contacted you?" Jilly's overly trusting nature was of constant concern to Ari.

"Summerhill High at 3:00. There are still guards there because the school's still open for training. It's only five blocks from our place. I think it will be okay. It was just a general message." Jillian knew she was stretching the truth all the way to a lie, but it was kind of true.

"What is it about?" Ari asked, feeling very skeptical of the plan.

"My old anatomy teacher, you know, the one I've told you about, it's a lecture she set up a long time ago. I want to go and talk with her. I miss learning and being in a classroom," adding more strands to her expanding web.

"How long will it last? I don't want to leave in the dark," Ari warned.

"I promise we'll leave at 4:30, no matter what."

"Ughhh," Ari groaned with annoyance. "Fine, be ready at 2:40 because when I get home, there won't be time to dink around." She'll be five minutes late, thought Ari, but it shouldn't take more than ten minutes to ride their bikes there and secure Dranger parking.

Jillian waited for Ari in the apartment their dad arranged for them. Shortly before their dad was killed, he sold his home. He secured them an apartment near the Vogel building. It was highly patrolled, and he set up a fund with a trusted friend to supplement their expenses. It seemed tragically coincidental, but what didn't these days? He constantly gave the safety advice and warned them to be unnoticeable, as if it needed to be said.

To stay unnoticeable, the women became efficient at conserving resources. They heated their small upstairs one-bedroom home with a corner woodstove installed by their father. They burned the trash and debris they collected at abandoned sites under the protection of hired Drangers.

When summer the months became unbearable, they opened the hidden skylight also designed and put in place by Dad. With the chameleon-painted bars he fitted on the doors and windows, the place was like a secret fortress. For a short while, he lived there with them, and he taught them how to survive. He was wicked smart for a high school history teacher and sorely missed.

All those conversations are exactly what gravitated her to Elaine Fuller's offer. She even said she knew their dad from his lectures. Jillian often wondered what lectures a high school history teacher could offer to interest a college anatomy teacher. More conspiracy theories ran through her head.

Even though her older sister constantly questioned her trust in others, Jillian believed herself to be a good judge of people. The only time she had been scammed was when she trusted an ad online. And though she knew this person, and no credits were on the line, this situation could be more costly.

The bike ride was quick but long enough to witness the ruthless arrest of a Daily and two bodies being loaded on a Neighwah trailer.

The smell of death and fear saturated the street. It was reflected in the eyes that peered from every dwelling and corner where the forsaken Dailys tried to hang on. Like hunted prey, they clung to the illusion that the looming predator would be satisfied with its current kill.

They secured their bikes by paying the Dranger protection fee. Keeping their heads down, Ari and Jillian made their way to the second-floor classroom. The scurrying rats, bashed lockers with missing doors, and street art displayed a common theme.

Wire-embedded windows peppered with bullet holes left sparkling, exploding stars that radiated outward. How wrong to be beautiful when it's likely they marked a deadly tragedy. Jillian looked straight ahead, worried she wasn't as shocked as she should be.

There were about fifteen people already settled into the dilapidated desk and chair seating. It was oddly quiet while everyone waited for the presenter. Then Jillian saw the message printed on the battle-weary whiteboard, "No talking, no note-taking, no note passing, no pictures." The unkempt classroom was draped in ripped posters dangling from the walls among the graffiti expressing the heartbreak of its artists.

Six more people came in before the speaker arrived and closed the door. It wasn't Ms. Fuller. Her nerves tweaked and dire scenarios danced in her head. The man stood in front of a table and set down his briefcase and a small thermos. Everyone was silent, as he meticulously, he unscrewed the lid and set it aside. He opened his thermos and poured an orange beverage into the small lid. Jillian's mouth watered at the thought of real orange juice, any juice. He surveyed the room and stopped at Ariel and then at Jillian.

"Yikes," Jillian whispered.

"Yikes? Why yikes? I thought your teacher was a women. And why did he stare like that?" Ari whispered back. A couple of people made hushing sounds, and the sisters mouthed, *We'll talk later*. The speaker ran his hand through his dark auburn hair. Jillian watched the curls curve around his fingers. He removed his rumpled sports jacket and drank down the liquid like a shot of shine whiskey. Jillian wondered if it was indeed more than an innocent beverage.

He was tall and handsome and probably in his late thirties or early forties. His eyes were the color of cold steel, but his look was kind, if not weary. She could tell he kept in shape, but as he adjusted his wedding band, Jillian reeled back her sensual observations. Rolling his shoulders and correcting his posture, he began speaking with a low gravely voice.

"If you are here for enlightenment, you will be disappointed. If you are here for salvation and acceptance for the end of times, that meeting is in room 215. This meeting is about reality. The reality of what it is to be human. This meeting is about accepting our nature and using it to be our best, our wisest, and to survive.

"Humans are a strange species. We are in constant conflict with our world, other humans, and especially ourselves. We are full of promise and dread at the same time. We can imagine globally, but we tend to act selfishly. We can envision who we would like to be, but we just have not evolved enough to act on our own expectations, at least not when it really counts. Sure, we have our heroes, but that only proves how uncommon selfless acts of dire sacrifice are rare. I am excluding those crazed persons, who cause chaos and destruction with the goal of posthumous fame.

"Our curiosity has propelled us to great heights of achievement, but our predatory nature uses our creations with tragic immaturity. So, is our curiosity to blame for our shortcomings? Or are our primal instincts at fault? I say one begets the other. They are inseparable; each being ineffective without the other.

"Everyone in this room is concerned about the same things. We want to avoid those cornered situations that debase us. We want to do more than survive. We want to live without fear and be with our loved ones in peace and civility.

"It's relatively easy to maintain these things when our world offers them. We become charitable and kind, and we smile at one another and enjoy happiness. But these are not those times! Some say these are the end times, 'the last days,' Armageddon.

"True, there is unrest, and we are fearful. But there has always been unrest, and fear is a necessary component of survival. The end of times depends on the power to escalate this unrestful era into a near or total extinction event. As with every dark era, the technology has the power to destroy, but it can also protect. The ingenuity that brought us here is the key to our salvation.

"Thank you for listening and braving the trip. Our 9/11 is upon us, but I call you to rise up, reassess your material needs, and together, we will bring back civility."

The man closed his thermos and began to gather his papers.

"That's it?" Ari was exasperated. "That wasn't even five minutes. Did you see how intense he was when he said those last lines? And why use an antiquated term like 9/11? There have been quite a few graver events since then." Ari shook her head. "What is this about, Jillian? Tell me you know."

"Maybe, just a minute, I need to talk to the speaker. Did he ever say his name?" Jillian scrunched her face and tipped her head, searching for the answer.

"Actually, no, he didn't. Weird." To Ari, everything about this was weird but mostly concerning.

Jillian walked over to the speaker and got his attention. "Mr. umm, I didn't get your name."

"I didn't give it, Jillian. I see you brought a guest."

Jillian turned two shades of red. "I'm sorry. I didn't see where it said… How do you know…?"

"You will be contacted," he calmly stated, interrupting her sentence.

"Wait! What is…is this…"

He put up his hand, telling her to stop. And then he promptly left the room. Jillian stood dumbfounded. It was interesting but overly enigmatic and strange. Very strange. "Oh man, Ari, do I ever need to talk to you when we get home." She whispered to her sister behind her cupped hand.

"Uh, yeah, I'd say so," Ari replied with an obvious attitude of pure frustration.

Walking into their apartment, they saw an envelope had been shoved under the door. *It just keeps getting crazier*, Jillian thought. *Is this from them? So cloak-and-dagger. How did they know we attended? How do they know where we live, and what did they do here while we were gone?*

With a quick walk-through, nothing appeared altered. Ariel eyed her sister, forming many conclusions, none of which were good. Maybe Jillian had gotten involved in something awful, or maybe she had finally lost it.

Jillian realized it was high time she confided in her older sister despite her vow of secrecy. She was getting anxious and scared. She knew she had to tell Ari everything, but the danger to her was real, and the contents of the envelope, irresistible. So, before she uttered a word, she ripped open the envelope. Ari watched her sister while various alarm bells rang in her mind. *So many ways this could go wrong,* she thought.

Inside were two half-sized sheets of paper. One was a short letter, handwritten, in their dad's all-caps style. Jillian reviewed the improbability of the last hour, as Ari looked over her shoulder to see what alarmed her sister. They sat down and held it, so they both could read together.

My dear girls, if you are reading this, I'm sorry I've left you alone. I was involved in a very obscure group of businesspeople with the hope of providing us with a better life and the promise of a future. I secured this letter with them, so they could contact you when it was time to act if I wasn't here to do it myself. I hope you have fared well.

If this is the same group with the same goals, it is your ticket to a better life. Remember what I used to tell you before you went to sleep? It's still good advice. Follow it! I ask that you trust them. There is little hope the world will repair and return to civility any time soon. This is your best shot at happiness and peace. I love you so much, Dad.

Tears welled up in both women's eyes. "Do you think it's really from him?" Jillian asked, her voice high and squeaking like it did when she was feeling vulnerable and wanting to be told those happy lies.

"It would be mean if it wasn't, but the world is mean. He did tell us that Shakespeare quote every night ad nauseam, as I recall. Who else would know about that? Let's look at the other note." The next slip read:

Thank you for listening and coming to <u>Summerhill.911.com</u> seminar. Our 9/11 is upon us, but together we will move up, dig deep, and civility will find you. Keep the faith—stay the course. Please dispose of all refuse responsibly.

(It is not the stars to hold our destiny but in ourselves.)

"That's the Shakespeare quote Dad always said, but what if they got it out of him? What if this 'group' betrayed him? And what a strange note. Why can't they just talk like normal people?"

"I think you better start talkin' normal, missy. And without the squeaking. I'm emotionally done right now."

They talked about the few details Jillian knew and decided to open the site on their laptop due to a multiple of apprehensions. Ari was nervous about what she might be opening. Was it truly the hope of a new beginning or a can of vipers that would destroy their security, minimal as it was? The website address included led them to an undecorated, white-and-black site. Ari was encouraged by the straightforward approach. The material presented was typical of the prepper sites that had bloomed on the net, feeding on present fears, but too often they swindled their patrons.

But this site lacked descriptive details and was devoid of anecdotal endorsements. It was oddly missing the bells and whistles of persuasive rhetoric to produce the characteristic sense of urgency. It was simply a tedious list of items and weirdly worded advice. She couldn't imagine anyone would invest their time or resources in it.

Both sisters decided the answers to their questions must be coded or hidden on this site. She questioned Jilly about everything Ms. Fuller said that related to this topic. The detective nature in Ari was intrigued, and while Jillian scraped their dinner together, Ari puzzled out a guess. As they sat down to stale bread with cheese and reconstituted lima beans, Ari explained her reasoning.

"Okay, here's what I believe is going on. This isn't a site for the random public. Its dull amateur format is meant to cause visitors to quickly move on. Assuming it's your group, it gives directions in a series of steps. One, 'Move UP to Breckenridge to be safe from the dangerous populations," I believe means you need to be acclimated to living at a high elevation. Breckenridge is 9,600 feet."

"Shit, that's high! Here in Denver, we're already above 5,000," Jillian reflected.

Ari nodded. "Two, 'assess your current supplies' means gather the items on this list, which seems rather lacking, so there may be another list or some kind of fee later."

"What if we do all this and can't pay the fee?"

"Well, they seem to know an awful lot about you, and probably us, so I assume they also know our situation. And if it falls through, we'll have some sensible supplies, most of which we have. Three, 'if you seek civility, civility will find you' means wait for further information; they will contact us. And 'be careful, keep the faith, and stay the course' means keep doing what you're doing. Don't talk about this; don't look for us, and be patient."

"I'm not sure I like the part about not bringing or buying any electronics devices that gather or store information, but not to dispose of them either. They will be picked up those items. Our laptop is old, but I like having one. I don't like giving away trading credit. They also advise against packing or buying any kind of electrical appliances."

"How do we keep warm, cook, or stay alive?" Jillian was squeaking again, so Ari droned on in her calm, confident tone, though she felt neither calm nor confident. She knew committing to this could end up anywhere on the safety continuum.

"It would make sense to provide those on a community level rather than to each individual. I'm intrigued by the 'containers are provided.' I wonder what kind of containers they are talking about. It will take a lot more than the items on this list to survive up in the mountains at that elevation. Man, I don't know. They seem well-organized in the big scheme so far, but they're being very careful with the complete picture."

"It's all so ambiguous. I don't know what to do. Should we be interested? I mean, it's both of us or neither. I wouldn't go without you, Ari. You're everything to me and the only family I have left! What if it turns out to be a labor camp? It would be all my fault." Jillian's squeaking was getting higher.

"Down, girl. The letter from Dad is our best evidence, it looks legit. Along with your teacher, that's two people we trust have approved this. Look, evidently, they are going to eke out the information at a need-to-know pace, which is smart. I say we start gathering what we can without causing suspicion, and the rest will just have to wait," Ari replied with a long sigh. "I think the other bolded text in the email, 9/11, was a date for...I don't know, a deadline for these items, or moving to the site?" Ari sighed before continuing.

"As obscure as the information is, it is a plan where we have none. It offers a little hope where the other choice is to exist until we slowly fade away with the rest of the Dailys or succumb to violence. It's a big gamble, but if you're in, I'm in." *If I'm allowed in*, Ari thought.

"We need to move soon. The more time spent getting acclimated, the better," Jillian advised, remembering her paper on altitude sickness. It was a topic that had been interestingly more than just suggested by Ms. Fuller.

They copied the list on a fingerboard, then destroyed the note and deleted the email and website history as instructed. They were troubled about destroying the letter from their dad, but in the end, they did. They knew their dad wanted them to be safe, so in his honor, it was burned, and its crushed ashes scattered out between the window bars. They began researching their new hometown where harsh winters had a whole new meaning.

Chapter Two

Bannon Vogel stood in front of the full-length window of his high-rise Denver office. He peered down at the twenty-year-old amber liquid swirling over the rounded ice cubes in his priceless tumbler. All his father's influence could not ebb the tide of darkness rising and consuming what was left of humanity. He repetitively reviewed the sequence of catastrophes that brought civilization to this precipice.

Perhaps it was the aftermath of the clustered meteor strikes that caused raging fires, enormous scars, and all manner of destruction worldwide. Though none of the meteorites were large enough to cause an extinction event, they pounded the globe for seven days, and together they were devastating. Initially, countries worked together until the reality of the loss stirred their primal survival instincts.

Terrorist leaders from the Middle East recouped their losses by putting on daily displays of public executions and torture to extort resources from others in power. The extremists attained stockpiles of goods that way, including a plethora of war paraphernalia, the command of six strategic satellites, and eight nuclear missiles with state-of-the-art guidance systems.

But people became numb to the painful displays and stopped paying attention. The death of the innocent became an accepted tragedy, and when their suffering ended, it was a blessing. The world shrank as people cocooned in their decreasing communities while unthinkable brutality exploded, and the tolerance of it became increasingly pervasive.

Then came the med wars. The occupation and subjugation of medical supplies and facilities by foreign-owned super-corporations left millions without even basic care. It certainly was to blame for the mega pandemics, which included illnesses of every kind, begetting third-world conditions throughout Europe and eventually the world.

More battles evolved over food, shelter, and other critical supplies. It shattered what was left of civilization, leaving the carrion of humanity to the greedy and the wretched.

At first, the chaos was confined to Europe and a few nations in Northern Africa. The countries in the Asian continent sealed themselves off. North America had not suffered as much as other nations, but it was a shadow of its once prominent self. The worse devastation was overseas. The diseases and shortages eventually spread to the Americas and ravaged them with heartbreaking resolve.

The community and state police were a thing of the past. Most officers left the job, and the rest were fired or murdered. The National Guard turned into a militia for the super elite in each state. Every duty they performed advanced the Corporates' agendas.

There were no juries or trials to decide cases, and if they visited a neighborhood or an individual, it wasn't to save them. It was to invoke some decree and deliver messages via punishments.

Then came the Neighwah, an offshoot of the Neighborhood Watch program. It began honestly enough. But soon, as predicted, the Corporates took them over and used them to fight over territory and resources, causing the Region Wars to escalate.

The national scene was no better. The president was replaced by unelected officials who gained power through violent assassinations.

The international scene was worse. Nuclear missiles were imminent, though it was reported that "talks" continued.

Banner, Bannon's father, was elected to the US Senate with his sights on the presidency. He was a good-hearted, moral man. He wanted to be an agent of change and believed the tide could be turned. But the tsunami of human brutality caused cascading failure at every level. Banner's political interventions, though considered brilliant, were like throwing pebbles at a tornado. All it got him was sorrow. He died violently and maliciously, along with his wife and daughter-in-law.

Bannon felt too young to feel this old, and too old to be so alone. He missed his parents and, especially, his wife. But it only fed a determination to see his plan through. Numerous columns of smoke billowed forth from random areas in the city.

It was August, and the Dranger's lessons had become more common and violent, while the people became increasingly numb to the chaos and suffering. Dailys hid from the battles. They didn't have the energy or the strength to fight while the Uppers isolated in their safe communities.

He thought back to a gentler time. He was just out of high school, but he still remembered when people had a voice, an unfiltered voice without punishment or fear. A time when lively discussions precluded actions, a time of law and order, and compassion, genuine compassion. A time when his wife smiled sweetly at him, cradling her pregnant belly.

Then came his plummet into hell. He lost his parents and his wife in a bombing while driving to meet him at a restaurant. He had lost so many people to violence. The only family he had left was his four-year-old daughter, Ellie, and his younger sister Dana. Dana wanted nothing to do with running the business, so Bannon said he would buy her out.

He went from being an executive in his father's multibillion-dollar shipping and supply corporation to the sole owner of Vogel Enterprises. He still remembers the day he and his sister cried and talked into the night about happy childhood memories, and how they wished to secure a better future for Ellie.

They joked about the idea of a secluded town, a place where people could pursue their lives with freedom and dignity. A place he could raise Ellie in safety. A place where she could dream, play, learn, and grow up.

The more they talked, the more their fantasy morphed into an actual plan. At that moment, Dana wanted to be a part of it. He was overjoyed that she wanted to remain his partner. He trusted her more than anyone in the world. And so began the complex scheme to create a sanctuary. Having a shipping business gave them incredible access to selling, purchasing, and transporting goods and services.

He had established an extensive network system with like-minded business owners, and many went to him as their businesses failed or were threatened by other Corporates with more access to the Neighwah armies. He felt bad about taking over their inventories for mere pennies, but it allowed them to disappear before they were conquered and executed.

On the fifteenth floor was his fortified secret office with elevator access hidden in a dilapidated coffee shop on the basement floor. In this undetectable room, he and Dana worked on their secret mission, hoping to beat the timeline of their own corporation's demise. It held the piles of documents, maps, and contracts, and they attacked the details with an addictive determination.

The official government collapsed, and the rebels in charge could no longer maintain its assets. The political machine needed capital, so he was able to purchase the Eisenhower Tunnel and many other critical supplies. They used an untraceable corporation to acquire the tunnel as well as the materials and manpower to repair and improve it.

The Eisenhower Tunnel provided the perfect location, and most importantly, the needed infrastructure was already in place. At 11,000 feet above sea level, it was too high for most people to access or want to. Life at that level was expensive and difficult, but in the tunnel, they would be well protected from the elements and attack. Though high, life at that elevation is viable if the residents are properly acclimated.

They worked tirelessly and enjoyed each triumph. But the long hours and the year and a half of stress had left them both fatigued, and there was no rest in sight. Putting the plan together may prove much easier than holding it together. It was a giant tapestry with so many diverse pieces and hundreds of individuals holding threads that could unravel the whole plan.

He longed for a simpler time or even a weekend off, but he knew this was not the time to ease up their efforts. He looked down at his hometown city, sighed, and mumbled, "How did everything get so bad? It happened so fast, within a couple of decades, everything just turned so..."

"What? I didn't catch that," Rand said, looking up momentarily from his laptop.

Rand Lewis was the right-hand man of Bannon's father, Banner. Rand was incredible on computers, extremely efficient, and most importantly, he was loyal. When the plan was shared with him, he was ecstatic. His sense of purpose and devotion to nailing the details was invaluable. The other man sitting at the table was Gray Takota, the head of his security.

"We're running out of time. We need to finish up the inhabitation process. I know we had the tentative 9/11 date, but we're going to have to move that up. It was more of a code than a hard date," Gray said as Bannon turned from the window to face him.

"Yeah, I agree," Rand answered. "But it's still good as a deadline, and we kind of put it out there already. And deadlines are absolute. That's why they have 'dead' in them."

"Very cute," Bannon said sarcastically, though he appreciated the attempt at levity.

"Okay, back to serious," Rand answered while still tapping out a steady rhythm. "There are a few last-minute details, important details, that need to be in place before we load up and close up. We've had to slow-walk the rest of the supplies to avoid suspicion, which took more time and manpower than anticipated. I believe all the supplies are at the tunnel now, just not in their permanent spots."

The logistics of this operation were difficult, to say the least, but the demand for intense secrecy threw difficult over the edge. The ruse of repairing the badly decaying I-70 tunnels was funded by marketing the expansion of the western half of the state to the imperialist Corporates.

It also allowed Vogel Ent. to build hundreds of shipping container homes and business structures and store them near the tunnel entrances without suspicion. When the accident was staged and reported, Bannon promised to refund his customers and use the containers to seal in the fabricated toxins.

"Yeah, I have to admit it went smoother than I had thought. I had serious doubts whether the Neighwah would buy the nuclear accident story, but with everything going on, it appeared to be just one more bad act in the shit-show of the times. We secured the Eisenhower Tunnel without much drama," replied Bannon.

"I know," said Rand. "It was pure luck that the Neighwah liked the idea that no more tunnels meant they were protected from other territories invading. When we heard them talking about collapsing the tunnel, we moved up the nuclear waste spill story. The timing was genius because it had their suspicions pointed at each other. They also bought the story of using shipping containers to block the radioactive gases from escaping.

"We not only secured the compound, but we also got over 70 percent of the containers and tons of supplies in there within a couple of weeks. We confiscated ten nuclear generators from the military for nonpayment, though we only needed four for the tunnel. They release a small radiation signature near the entrances of the tunnels, well below dangerous levels, which validates the story."

"We haven't heard of any leaks from our sources about the town," added Gray.

"It couldn't have gone more perfectly," Bannon stated rather proudly.

"That's what scares me," said Gray, as the security naysayer he was paid to be. "Nothing goes perfectly, ever. We're still in major danger of discovery. So, what is our timeline for beginning the moving-in process for the rest of the residents? I need time to move the first group into the town and to settle the next group into the Hold."

"Yes," Bannon said as the sound of a new explosion shook the window, sending another plume blossoming in the distance, "a timeline is needed."

Rand interjected with more logistical facts. "The directors of each occupational category are moving in now, along with eighty workers and twenty Defenders. But the last container homes are within a couple of weeks of completion. We are currently delivering the residents' belongings to each house. The inventory of their crates took some time because we did it as they arrived at the drop-off facility. The facility is all but closed now.

"We still have some security there to ensure we don't leave any clues, and no one is tracking our movements. The first resident group is at the Hold, where they go through contagion screening, training, and final vetting. We're doing that in two stages. Each group takes four weeks."

"So, the timeline for closing it up is..." Bannon raised his right eyebrow, awaiting the answer to the question he had to repeat.

"Five to six weeks," Rand responded. "I mean, if all hell broke loose, everyone in security knows the drill, and we could get people settled pretty quickly. That's not the issue. The power grid is still giving us problems regarding the air regulators. We've had to modify the connections to the nuclear generators we got from the military.

"The good news is we have decades of power secured from the ten nuclear power generators we acquired. But it definitely will be fixed in...say...two weeks." Rand's voice rose at the end of his answer as if it were a request, if not a plea, for forgiveness.

"Try to move it up if you can. Of course, that issue is critical, but we could ration power if we have to until we have it fully operational. Make this a high priority. Some of the other town facilities can wait. I have a bad feeling about the Corporates. Something's coming. I can feel it. It's gotten way too quiet. Word on the street and Net make me think we're next on the Corporates' hit list. We need to move the rest of our operation into the tunnel tonight." He thought about the almost one hundred employees he would leave behind.

Bannon paid his employees, while most Corporates gave minimal lodging and supplies instead. He had recently scaled down his operations considerably, but he still had ninety-three employees left, few of whom would be included in the town. It just wasn't possible. He couldn't even warn them, but he would send out a notice of his resignation in a week. Some would leave immediately before the takeover, others would be absorbed by other Corporates, and a few might be allowed to go to another town. It was a time of unbearable choices, and he was the unfortunate one to make them.

Gray rubbed his forehead knowing it was his turn to pick apart the final stages of the plan to ensure there would be no leaks or casualties. He sympathized with Bannon's position. He could not save everyone. That was just a hard fact. He knew his employer and friend could be stubborn, and he worried about the secrets he may be hiding from him to avoid being told no.

If the Corporates found out about their deception, everyone involved, which was nearly five hundred people, would most certainly be tortured and executed. Many of Bannon's favorite amenities and Rand's technological ideas had been shot down as too dangerous, but feelings and pet plans had no place in a project this complex and secretive.

"We need to keep up the image of the radiation hazards. For instance, we need to order more protective gear because if we run out and no one gets sick, then they will take a harder look at us. Also, the existing plan of transporting people to the Hold has to be rethought. The Corporates recently issued a new shift schedule at our high-elevation transition sites," Gray added.

He watched Bannon nod his head while leaning over and holding the back of his chair. Gray wanted to believe, as Bannon did, that everything would settle into a calm paradise at some point, but he knew making it there safely would morph into keeping it safe.

Bannon felt the familiar tightness in his chest and the rumbling pain in his stomach. He shook his head, hoping to regain control of his anxiety as he grabbed a couple of downer tabs before he experienced a full-on panic attack. His life had an absolute purpose now, but that purpose had absolute control over him. His world had become utterly dubious and convoluted, and he prayed his vision wasn't evolving into a blind obsession.

"Bannon, come back. You're spacing out again." Rand waited to get his attention. "So yeah, in a pinch, we could make it work. Tough way to settle in, but it won't be the last time they—we—will be asked to make sacrifices."

Bannon sighed at the daunting tasks before them. He trusted the men in front of him absolutely, but this complex plan had millions of working pieces all rattling around his head. "Please let it work," he whispered to himself.

Chapter Three

The expected knock on their door arrived early one morning, just as the sun was trying to stretch its twilight rays across the broken city. They were called Defenders and were so geared up that the sisters could not tell what they looked like. In the last briefing, they were told the Defenders would be in combat gear and shown how they'd look. Though the women weren't surprised, they still were intimidated.

To the public, most of whom were still sleeping, it looked like an all-too-common Corporate robbery, and people avoided getting involved. The uniforms were black with numerous zippered pockets and straps that held equipment and ammo. A holster on each side held black weapons, and another long gun was slung over their shoulders. The black helmet fit in a trim, sleek fashion with wide reflective black visors that allowed them full peripheral vision.

While the other two held the hand trucks with the crates, the last one delivered a paper to be signed by them. He was waiting down the hall for their signal. Jillian worried that if they took too long, he would probably leave. Jillian and Ari reviewed the paper they were required to sign before they could go to the next step.

It was called the Town Creed. It stated that belonging to this town meant not being able to leave, not being able to contact anyone on the outside, having an assigned job that one must attend and address with fidelity, and that their supplies would be allocated. It sounded a lot like how they lived now.

"I'm kinda scared, Ari," Jillian whispered in a small voice.

"Well, look at it this way," Ari said, "it can't be worse than what is out here now, and we don't have anyone we need to stay in contact with." Ari put on a good face as she always did for Jillian, but there was much to be afraid of. They signed the paper and gave it to the Defender, and the other two loaded the crates into their apartment.

Many an agonizing moment had been spent purging those items that would not fit in the 3x3x4-foot box each person was allowed. Most of the suggestions made sense, but some gave signs that their lives would look different. For instance, it was highly suggested, but not mandated, that each person bring a bicycle or some form of transportation that did not require power. These would be packed separately from the crate.

They expected an extensive list of warm clothing for such cold weather, but the suggestions focused on clothing in good shape. Some personal hygiene items, even make-up, were allowed but listed in the unnecessary column.

They laughed at some of the supplies they were warned would be limited or unavailable, like coffee, tea, alcohol, and recreational drugs. They wondered what kind of people hadn't already given those up. Chancing the black market was bad enough to get necessary items, but those things were costly and perilous to attain. It also put a target on your residence. Jillian's favorite suggestion was an additional box no bigger than 2×2×1 tall of decorations, including seasonal items.

"We're gonna have holidays, pretty festive holidays," Jillian sang while dancing around the room. "Ari, can I pack that box? Can that be my job, please?"

"Absolutely," Ari smiled at her sister's childlike joy. She was questioning the wisdom of unnecessary junk, but it had been almost a decade since she had seen Jillian look so happy.

The list of unacceptable items was just as interesting. No furniture, aerosol cans, or any kind of flammable substances were permitted. No kitchen supplies whatsoever were permitted. Anything motorized, requiring batteries, or electricity was also not allowed. The next morning, the crates were picked up by another darkly dressed Defender.

They were also instructed to pack two small travel bags with supplies for a week. These would be picked up just before they leave. It was the night before leaving day, and they checked their carry-on bags one final time.

It was a beautifully clear and starry night in the almost abandoned ski town. They had moved to Breckenridge, Colorado, with the help of a friend with an SUV. They, in turn, sold him their high-tech apartment and all their furnishings. It had taken a few weeks to not feel out of breath from common tasks, but they acclimated rather quickly, according to Jillian's studies on the subject.

They expected their stay in this town to be short, or at least that was their hope. The summer was beautifully warm during the day and crisply cool in the evenings, but that would change to just brutally cold soon. At least they got to keep their old jobs and work remotely from their new home. Back in Denver, Ari had been an assistant and gofer for the engineering department, and Jillian did data entry for the medical facility.

Though they were aware their dad had set them up before he died to be financially stable, they didn't know how he had managed it on a teacher's allotment of credits. Even if he had resources from before the takeover, as a Daily, those would have been confiscated. They concluded he must have had a powerful friend, but not powerful enough to make their added comforts obvious to others.

Five weeks had passed since they left their Denver home. They flopped down on the old couch, sending a slight plume of dust into the air. It came with the apartment and was comfortable enough. They sat with anxious impatience waiting for the Defenders to pick up their totes with one week's worth of gear as instructed.

It was a "be careful what you wish for" moment, and the irony had not escaped them. Just as the sun began to drag itself over the hazy horizon, two military-looking people came and collected their bags. It was too dangerous to walk about town with totes and luggage. They only had to walk four blocks to the transport site at Johnson Elementary.

As short as the walk was, they still risked being attacked by desperate individuals and Drangers. But boarding and leaving in a transport would cause too much attention and arouse suspicion. They were nervous and highly alert, but they tried to act as if it was just another day in hell. Inside, they prayed, hoped, and wished to make it on time without being hassled, detained, or worse.

Everything they had was invested in this do-or-die gamble, and they were counting on it being worth it. The streets were empty, and with only one more block to go, Ari and Jillian started to relax.

Suddenly, Ari jumped when she felt a rough, twisting grip on her arm. Someone from behind was pulling her toward a broken-out storefront. She came out swinging and kicking with all her might, but she was easily overpowered. Jillian attacked the large man with the dirk she always carried. He let go of Ari and delivered Jillian a brutal uppercut punch to her ribcage and tossing her down and yanking her upright again by her hair.

From out of nowhere, two Defenders tackled the perpetrator and shoved him in a van, driving off and leaving the two sisters stunned and stumbling toward their destination.

Adrenalin surging through them, they made the rest of their journey quickly. Shaken and rattled, they made it to the first-floor room as instructed. Ari found a way to compose herself, but Jillian was quietly sobbing and holding her belly. The look of pain on her face was intense.

There were other people in the room, and they watched silently as Ari and Jillian sat down. Everyone seemed frozen in place while Ari rocked her sister. They no doubt worried about what kind of trouble these girls brought with them.

"Calm down, Jilly. It's okay, we're safe now," Ari whispered.

"You know that's not true," she sobbed quietly. "I'll get myself together. I will. It's just all been so much, but I'm fine. I'm fine," she continued the chant under her breath. She took a couple of deep, pain-filled breaths to control her emotions and looked up to see how much of a spectacle she had made of herself. Just lifting her head had her spinning.

A little girl around four stared at her from under a woman's cradling arm. As the child started to tear up, Jillian immediately got herself together. She mouthed the words *I'm sorry* and wanted to explain, but the rules said no communication until given permission. *Well, we just broke that rule...again*, she thought, remembering the lecture.

She wasn't her best in such austere environments. She hoped this "sanctuary" didn't turn out to be some kind of severe military camp. She vowed to avoid the Defenders, so she wouldn't mess up. She had to try for Ari. *I got her into this*, echoed the familiar burden in her head. Serious doubts bubbled up again, and she tried to hold back the tears, but clenching her stomach sent stabbing pains all through her. She slowed her breathing and calmed down the way she had been taught in nursing school.

A Defender motioned for them to go down the hall, and another one pointed outside to a large box trailer that was outfitted with rows and rows of bench seats. It reminded Ari of a passenger airplane. She struggled to recall the memory of a trip she had taken as a child. The bench seats were secured to the floor, and four sets of seatbelts lay lazily about the benches.

It surprised both women that everyone was so quiet and disciplined during the whole process. Even the children didn't make a peep. What was this world going to be like? Jillian's imagination ran wild, and she envisioned a mining camp with a meager, starving existence under the eyes of evil overseers. Or maybe they just took their credit codes, and this was their last drive to the wasteland.

But she kept going back to the idea that her dad had pretty much set it up for them, and her teacher was someone she had known well and trusted completely. She just couldn't believe they'd be fooled so badly and put them in harm's way.

The door rumbled closed. When it was secured, a Defender pressed a button on his shoulder and, in a robotic voice, told the passengers to buckle up. Some were so young they weren't familiar with how to buckle them, but others offered help while remaining silent. Ari remembered seat belts, but Jillian had to make a couple of agonizing attempts, yet she figured it out before help could be offered.

Then the four Defenders positioned themselves at the walls of the container and popped open small round slots with guns ready while watching the targeting monitor on the side wall. One in the front turned toward the passengers and held his pointer finger against his helmet to remind them to be quiet. Ari looked at Jillian with wide eyes, and the sisters reached for each other's hands. They were saved or trapped now.

All they had was a dull light from the ceiling and no view of the outside. A Defender in the front made a motion with his hand, and another took a different position. A clatter of shouts and other noises came from outside. Objects began hitting the container, but none got through.

The Defender in the new position leveled his gun through the slot and fired. It made more of a clicking and a *woosh* sound than a bang, and Ari realized it must have a suppression device. Ari strained to hear noises from outside, but even the normal dull rumble had ceased. Bullets have a way of scattering Drangers and Dailys alike.

They were jolted in their seats as the transport abruptly took off, picking up speed and rocking around turns and over aging roads. As their injuries set in and the initial numbness faded, they understood it would be a painful journey. They made several more stops, and the seats filled up until there were only a couple of vacancies left. Still, no one made a sound, except the random fidgety infants.

The transport's silent electric engine was in stark contrast to the container as it creaked and groaned along the bumpy road. Ari thought about the lack of technological infrastructure sending so many advancements back into the past. Innovation had not been completely discontinued, but the infrastructure for producing new machines and devices was focused on weaponry.

Still, Ari noted the wisdom of using electric models over fuel-driven ones. For one, they're inaudible; her father would approve. Another reason was that carbon-based fuel wasn't easy to come by for Dailys, but whoever was heading this operation was no Daily. The brilliance of it was their superior performance at high elevations.

The excursion dragged on mile after mile, and the children's restlessness began to emerge. At the signal of the person obviously in charge, one of the Defenders walked over to a box. Jillian suddenly wondered if the parents or the children breaking the quiet rule would be punished or drugged. Her anger started building, and her head filled with protective retaliation plans, causing the crushing pain in her abdomen to increase.

But the Defender simply opened the box and passed around water and meal bars, and they provided bottles to the infants. When the passengers were settled, he casually went back to his station, and the transport plowed on.

Sometime later, the transport stopped, and everyone wondered where they would put more passengers, but no new travelers arrived, and the engine stopped. Wide eyes looked about, searching each other, hoping to see if anyone might be aware of what would happen next. Was it another attack? A couple of little ones began to cry, and tension pulsed through the people like a bass drum. Jillian wanted to scream, but she felt too awful, weak, and scared, very scared.

The Defenders, almost in unison, pulled off their helmets, and the man in charge addressed them. "Sorry for the weirdness, everyone." Then he turned, looking straight at Jillian and Ari. "Are you okay, ladies?" Both women nodded, and he continued to speak. "We noticed that guy following you, so we followed him. Sorry, we couldn't avoid what happened or give you a ride, but you're okay, right?" Again, both women nodded, but it was a gesture of obedience because the truth was neither felt even close to okay.

Another Defender addressed the rest of the group. "Y'all can talk in a minute," he drawled, "just watch your step as you exit and grab your bags from the transport parked outside. When ya get your stuff, look at the tag on your bag, and go to the line with those numbers."

Jillian unbuckled her seatbelt and stood up. Pain ripped through her, and she fell back to her seat. Again, her tears welled up, and she fought her way back from the downward spiral. "Come on, Jilly. I'll help you."

Ari put her good arm under Jillian's and helped her up. Her feet faltered as she walked, leaving Ari to bear the brunt of her weight. Ari was also feeling the full extent of her own injury now. Biting through the throbbing pain, she pressed onward. Ari stared at their bags, trying to come up with a plan to carry them and her sister.

The commanding Defender saw them struggling and jogged over to them. "Whoa, just stay put for a moment," he ordered.

"Why? We haven't done anything. Are we going to get kicked out now? Here in the middle of..." Jillian looked around and realized she was far from anywhere she had ever known. Her racking sobs kept pace with her raging pain, and it consumed her. She couldn't even finish her sentence before she began to slide down Ari's side. The Defender caught her and lifted her into his arms.

"Jesus! Okay, okay. Hey, wake up. We're gonna get you taken care of," he exclaimed. "I need a wheelchair here, and someone grab this luggage," Grayson Takota barked the orders, and soldiers scurried about to complete them. Jillian looked up at him.

He was intently watching his soldiers, but she could see his deep green eyes, kind eyes. His rich brown skin was lightly shadowed with stubble. He was strong and confident, and though she shouldn't trust him, she felt herself give into the protection of his arms until he settled her into the wheelchair. He crouched down, assessing her condition. She was thin and pale and clearly in shock. She looked so vulnerable. He cursed himself for not realizing sooner how badly hurt she was.

"I'm Grayson. What are your names?"

"She's Jillian, and I'm Ariel. We're sisters. Where are you taking her? I want to go with her," Ari demanded.

Grayson ignored her demand, thumbed through the papers on the clipboard, and pulled one out. He bent down to talk to Jillian. "Don't worry about a thing. You're going to the infirmary, and they'll patch you all up. Hey, I've taken a few gut punches. They're miserable, but they turn out okay."

He handed the Defender Jillian's papers and waved him toward the registration tables. Grayson immediately got in front of Ari, blocking her path. "Nice to meet you, Ari. Don't worry about your sister. They have to examine her before anyone can visit. I'll personally bring you to her when she's deemed stable."

Ari stood watching her sister being rolled toward one of the large industrial buildings and disappearing around the corner. The separation made her even more anxious about her sister's condition and this whole place in general.

"So, how are you? Do you have any injuries that need attention?" Grayson asked.

"My arm hurts, but it's fine. I can walk on my own in case you're thinking of picking me up too."

He laughed with an easy-going manner. "Let's just see your arm."

"So, you're a doctor *and* a Defender?" she snapped, not meaning to. She was grateful for his help, but worrying about Jillian and the drama of the day left her feeling irritated. "Sorry, I think I've had my fill of trauma today." She removed her jacket and winced at how painful it was. Her arm was quite swollen, with the outline of a hand turning a deep shade of purple. He gently moved it up and down, and she cringed at even the slightest movement. Her skin felt hot, and he figured it was probably broken.

"Well, I guess you get to go to the infirmary sooner than you thought," he said, carefully returning her arm to a resting position by her side. She submitted to his decision, though doctors and hospitals weren't known for pleasant or quality care. At least she would be going where Jillian had been taken.

Grayson and Ari followed Jillian's path. The building seemed ominous. Jillian was all alone in there, but soon they would be together. There was a sea of people flowing from the baggage trailer, which carried the luggage for all five passenger transports. They stood docilely in lines along a row of tables that stretched across the parking lot.

Three-digit numbers were propped on poles, instructing the robotic crowd to line up according to the last three digits of their resident codes. There was a soft mumble of voices, but the crowd seemed very submissive. They were surrounded by four large buildings, and groups were being led to them, lugging their children and all their possessions.

Why did it seem like everyone else was so calm? She felt so fearful and out of sorts. *Have they done this before? Do they know of some accepted inevitability of which I am completely unaware?* She knew her imagination was running wild. She looked around, really looked around. She saw the people's faces as they trudged across the pavement. They looked beyond weary. One woman was on her own with three children plodding after her with heads down.

Another had a young girl with her, probably around six years old. The woman had only one small suitcase tied with a cord that she looked ready to fight for. Gangly arms hanging out of oversized clothing and unkempt hair told a story of harsh times and poverty. The woman stopped for a minute and locked eyes with Ari. There was a look of recognition, and she held her attention for an extended moment, then quickly turned and walked away.

They all were too thin and rolling their luggage behind the Defender as if dutifully walking their last mile. On a day that should have involved rejoicing, they trudged along with dejected faces, and no fight left in their bones. They weren't calm; they were broken. She was broken. She didn't know how broken until this moment. She thought she had remained above the fray, not like the other Dailys dragging through each day. The revelation was the first sign that she belonged here; she was one of them and woefully aware of the lie she had been living.

While the crowds headed through the two main doors in the middle of the structure, Grayson and Ari entered through the left side of the building. The interior room was small and clean without any furnishings. The corrugated metal walls made it look more like a factory than a medical facility. The room was empty, and it compelled its visitors to proceed directly to the wall with a single sliding window. A woman approached and slid it open.

"Hi," Grayson greeted the pretty receptionist behind the desk. He gestured to Ari, "She was attacked and has an injured left arm. I think it's broken. She's not registered yet, but she was on my transport. I don't have her papers because Axle turned them in. Her name's Ariel..." he turned and looked at Ari for the rest of the info.

"Delano," Ari stated.

"No last names here. What's your resident code?"

"Oh yeah, sorry. NH2SW#091A."

"091A" the woman was staring at a monitor. "Yeah, there's another 091 here."

"That's my sister."

She nodded and turned to Grayson. "Thanks, Gray, I'll take it from here." She looked down at her workstation and continued typing on some device hidden by the wall below the window.

"Okay, I'll take care of your luggage, get your ID bands, and deliver your stuff to your home in the Hold. See you gals later."

Gals? Ariel thought. *That's an old term.*

Two hours later, Ariel was released. She had a hairline fracture of the humerus that was expected to heal within two to three weeks of bone growth meds and physical therapy. She had never received medical attention before because Dailys used home remedies, but she had to admit that her arm felt much better.

She sported a sling and a bubble cast that secured her arm to her torso. She was instructed to wear it for the first week, even as she slept. They brought her back to Jillian's room. She had two cracked ribs and serious contusions on her abdomen, but they could find no internal bleeding.

Grayson was called to pick up Ari, but Jillian was to spend the night as a precaution. He had registered them in the Hold but needed to give them the briefing they missed. He soon showed up and stood at the foot of Jillian's bed.

"So how are my sister gals doing? Are you on your way to being healed up?"

"'Healed up? Gals?' Where are you from?" asked Jillian.

"I come from a small town in Idaho. It's an old-fashioned place. Lots of people say gal, don't they?" Grayson said with an impish grin and a relaxed tone. The women shook their heads.

"No, seriously, I started saying gal instead of formal titles or first names because it's always awkward trying to figure out how to address a woman I've just met. Some want formal, some want casual, so I go with the quirky and unexpected. It tends to get a laugh, and the ice is broken. So, where are you gals from?" He was teasing them now.

"Is this a test?" asked Ari. "Are we even supposed to be talking with you about our personal information?"

He smiled. "I know, I know. We take our security pretty seriously, especially out there, but we can drop the covert subterfuge now. This is a safe zone."

Ari wasn't falling for his charm right now. This place had her swimming in unanswered questions. She stood next to her sister's bed with her arms crossed. "It seems a bit militant to me. Besides, there is no such thing as a safe zone. This place will be found," she quipped as she sat down on the edge of Jillian's bed. She paused, and with a more serious tone, she asked, "Is this it? Is this the sanctuary?" Her disappointment was evident.

"Yeah, that's why you shouldn't miss briefings," he quipped, folding his arms and mimicking pretentious authority. "No, this is a holding area. I know you've been kept in the dark and subjected to severe military protocols. It was necessary, but that's over now. Things will get better from this point on. This place is just a stop on the road to your real home. We keep you here for about a month until we know you don't have any contagions or issues that could threaten the 'sanctuary' which we call New Haven."

"You already know I'm Ariel, and my sister is Jillian, but most people we know call us Ari and Jilly. We both grew up in Denver. I'm thinking we are still in Colorado based on the drive time, but it's been so long since I took a trip in a vehicle. So, where are we, or can I ask that?"

"You can call me Gray. And yes, we are still in Colorado, but that is all I can say for now. You gals missed your Indoctrination Part One: Welcome to the Hold," he scolded with his finger and proper instructor voice, "so I'm going to walk you through it."

He proceeded to tell them the schedules for meals, sleeping, laundry, showers, medical exams, counseling, recreation, and job training. "I secured your sleeping quarters and put your belongings in the locker of your Hold home, which we affectionately call your curtain. It's decorated in what I like to call a minimalistic style."

The women laughed at his animation and exaggerated gestures. "There are two cots, each with clean white sheets, blankets, and a pillow. Two small nightstands on the outside edges with reading lights are elegantly positioned next to each slender bed. A demure desk sits on one side of the door and accommodates two wooden folding chairs. The desk has two thin drawers, and positioned on top is a binder with protocols, schedules, and other information."

"A secure storage locker on the other side of the door neatly holds your belongings in four drawers, a couple of shelves, a small closet with hangers, and a full-length mirror tucked inside the closet door. To open your locker, simply hold your wrist badge up to the scanner. A small clock displays the oh-so-chic military time since we have no windows to distinguish between day and night.

"The whole arrangement is enclosed by a tasteful, medium-weight gray curtain secured to the poles on the bottom and top to all sides except one. That side is your doorway, complete with an easy sliding curtain for your entries and exits. Last but not least, there is a broom, dustpan, and trash bin standing against the locker by the door. And there you have it, your new community and your little curtain home," he finished with a bow.

The women applauded with sophisticated claps and then laughed. It felt good to meet someone new and joke around. *It had been so long since they had done that*, Jilly thought.

"That was awesome. I think you're right; things are already getting better," replied Jilly with a big smile. It was the first time he saw her smile. She shone warmth and kindness in a world of villains and victims. Her teeth were straight, white, and pleasantly healthy for a Daily. But it was her eyes that pulled him in. The center was light blue, but the edges were rimmed with dark blue, and it had a surreal effect on him.

Her hair was a rich auburn with golden highlights that danced in the bright lights of the infirmary. He hadn't seen her stand on her own two feet yet, but he could tell when he carried her that she was petite but toned. His thoughts turned to beating the holy shit out of the Dranger who hurt her and simultaneously to holding her in his arms again.

"It's mealtime and the end of visiting hours. Time to go home, Romeo," remarked a snarky nurse as she brought Jilly a tray with all kinds of bland-looking food. "You'll get a better meal tomorrow when the doctor upgrades your status," she said in a firm, all-business voice to Jilly.

"Well, if you knew what I'm used to, you wouldn't apologize." Outwardly, Jilly sounded kind, but she didn't like this nurse. She studied her with more scrutiny than medical observation required. It felt like she was sizing her up. She wasn't nice, but she wasn't unkind either. Yet, under the surface, Jilly detected a disapproving edginess in her voice.

"Come on, Ari, I'll take you to the mess hall. Everyone gets dinner early tonight. Then I'll show you where your curtain is. Good night, Jilly," and he and Ari left.

Dinner was served cafeteria-style and tasted amazing. There was so much food, and she wasn't used to three-course meals. Ariel was overly tired before she ate the big meal, so she asked Gray to save the tour for tomorrow. He dropped her off at her curtain. She was anxious to see it, settle in, and go to sleep.

Their new home literally was a curtained-off area. The room was about eleven feet square. The furnishings fit so well in the allotted area, there wasn't much opportunity for other arrangements. *It had been well-described by Gray,* she thought. She looked at the clock, which read 1920 hours. *How can it only be 7:20 p.m.?* she said to herself. She was weary, and her arm was starting to throb, so she took one of the four pain pills she was given.

She turned toward the beds where their two bags were set. She grabbed her gear and walked the short three steps to the lockers and opened the left side with her band. She thought about unloading them but changed her mind and tossed her bag in the bottom of the closet and her take-along tote in the drawer. She left Jilly's on the empty bed.

Ari lay down, drawing the blankets around her with her one good arm. She was too drained to dress for bed or get between the sheets. She looked at the empty bed across from her. This was the first time they had spent a night apart for as long as she could remember. She hoped she was okay and wondered if she was scared. As worried as she was, the pain meds began to dull her defenses. She barely remembered closing her eyes.

Chapter Four

Jilly was released in the afternoon of the next day, and Grayson took them on a tour, insisting Jilly use a wheelchair. He explained the Hold property had four sections, each one just like this, housing forty to fifty residents and staff. Curtain homes came in five sizes to accommodate singles, couples, and families with one to three children. There were three unisex restrooms and utility rooms built from combining shipping containers. They were parked on the edges of the curtain area. Each provided six toilet rooms with full doors and six sinks on one end. The other end had five private shower stalls with connected changing areas and two small baths raised on pedestals for bathing infants and small children.

"There will be lines at certain times, so plan your shower and other hygiene habits to avoid the crowds," Gray warned.

Ari already knew about the mess hall and the medical stations where everyone's vitals were taken daily, but Gray reviewed it for Jilly. They were interested in all the recreational activities. He explained movies were on a big screen in the mess hall twice a week, and everyone would bring their folding chairs or blankets. He took them to a large open space that was called the yard. It was bordered by benches where parents could watch their children play with the provided toys.

The sides next to the curtain homes and the mess hall had ten-foot fences with gaps for walking through. The bottom of the fence was made of a sturdy material, which he said was a barrier for sports equipment and other items from causing issues. Ari recognized it as a weapons-grade protection wall. It didn't shock her, and she wasn't gullible enough to completely buy into the safety pitch so far.

Only two children seemed to be taking advantage of the opportunity to play in the yard, for it was something one could only dream of on the outside. Like themselves, no one felt that safe. Gray continued. Games such as badminton, beach ball volley, bingo, and foam Frisbee games were played a couple of times a week in the same area. Board games and cards could be played during the day in between meals at the mess hall or checked out to play at your curtain. There was also a library with hundreds of books to check out for recreational reading. The schedule for all four weeks could be found in their binder and was also posted in the mess hall.

"And tonight is Meet-and-Greet night at the mess hall."

"Oof, we don't feel up to that," Ari said out loud while Jilly was shaking her head. "Do we have to go?"

"Yeah, you do. All the counseling sessions are mandatory, but the M and G is especially important. But if you are too fearful, you can attend a private session over there." He pointed to a door with a sign that read Dr. Haru Abar. "But don't worry Haru, the director, knows that everyone has a certain level of anthropophobia, so they play games that help you navigate that. In the briefing, you *missed*," He emphasized the word *missed* to tease them. "Haru discussed the need to start 'calming down that guard dog in your head. It's time to remember or learn what civility and community mean.' That's the point of this whole project—regaining our compassion and humanity so you can be part of a community."

"Anthropophobia?" Jilly inquired.

"Fear of people. You'll hear that word a lot this week."

"Ohhhh yeah, probably true."

"We'll be there," said Ari, resigned to the task. "I want to be a part of a goal like that. I know feeling safe enough to happily engage with others will be hard, but it is why we joined."

Jilly was a little surprised by her sister's willingness to join in. Jilly held up her hand and said, "I'm in too."

They made the rounds, and Gray dropped them off at their curtain. "I'll take this chair back unless you think you need it," he said.

"No, but I probably would have faded during the tour, so thanks for insisting." He waved and left, heading toward the infirmary.

"Do you think we'll see him again?" asked Jilly. "We're settled now. He has no reason to visit."

"Huh. Yeah, he'll be back," Ariel quipped and rolled her eyes at her naïve little sister.

The M and G turned out to be fun. They met many people, and Ariel and Jilly set up future meeting times with their new favorites. Ari tried to find the woman and the little girl from their transport site, but she didn't see them. *They must be in another building*, she thought, and she suddenly realized how big this project was.

They went to bed but couldn't sleep from the excitement of the day. "Thank you, Jilly, for including me."

"No way would I have left you, but so many nights, I worried about what I was getting you into. I'm still afraid the outside world may destroy this dream, but I'm glad we get to be a part of it now."

They talked and talked until exhaustion overtook them.

Ari woke up at 1:30 a.m. to Jilly groaning on the floor. She ran out of her curtain and yelled for the Defender on duty. A medical team quickly arrived, loaded Jilly onto a stretcher, and headed her back to the infirmary. Ari was told to wait in her curtain, and they would send news. Worst-case scenarios swirled in her head. *Was she bleeding internally? Was she going to need surgery?* All her outer world experience told her surgery was, more often than not, a death sentence. Billie heard the commotion and peeked in the curtain and saw Ari alone with her head in her hands. Billie put her arm around her new friend. Billie sat with Ari while she let down her steely guard, trying to assure her it would be okay.

In the infirmary, the doctors and nurses buzzed around the exam room like ants on a popsicle. Jilly was unconscious. Monitors beeped, a ventilator swished up and down, and the sono-resonator view rolled about on the screen.

"Her abdomen is stable, but her vitals are dropping. What did the blood and urine tests show?" Doctor Maya turned and asked the orderly coming in with a tablet.

"It appears she's been poisoned with some form of a slow-sunset drug," the orderly said as he walked up with the results.

"Poisoned? Damn! Okay, most SS drugs take five or six days. They are blackmail drugs used to get something from the victim in exchange for the antidote. The symptoms are showing up in less than three days, so we can assume her injuries sped up the delivery of the drug."

Dr. Maya began to look for injection evidence, starting with her abdomen, using the magnifying overhead light. "There, look, a pinprick in the middle of her injury. We missed it, but to be honest, I'm not sure why we'd look for it."

At that moment, Gray walked into the facility and went up to the receptionist. He was unaware of what was going on. He just knew there had been a disturbance. Yawning as he approached the check-in window, a nurse slid the window open and filled him in on the attempted murder case using a slow-sunset drug in the emergency room. Alarm shot through him when he realized the victim was Jilly.

"I need a secure line," he ordered and buzzed himself through the door. He walked down the hall toward the Defender Operation Room and key-punched his way into the technology room. Computer-lights blinked, and a noticeable hum filled the space. The technician turned. "Hey, Gray, what cha need?"

"Give me a secure line to the off-site jail at location Kappa." The technician heard his all-business tone and quickly snapped into duty mode. Handing Gray the phone, he asked if he needed privacy.

"I'll let you know." And his attention returned to the call as it was answered. "Eddie, it's Gray. Hey, how's that prisoner from yesterday morning? Did he say anything?"

"Yeah, we got some intel from him, but he was just a foot soldier. He died last night. He said he'd been attacked, and they gave him a note with instructions. It explained that he'd been poisoned. If he didn't get the girl to the rendezvous and get the antidote, he would die. We found an injection ring, and we were able to identify the poison, but it was too late. What's going on?"

"He attacked a resident at the transport site. He punched her with that ring."

"Shit! I'm sending the antidote info. Man, he was a big brute, but not a professional. He said they told him the ring was a sedative and to punch her to subdue her. Whoever hired him had access to SS drugs. That's definitely Upper-level shit. Did it come through?"

"Getting it now. Got it. Thanks!"

He ran it himself down to the emergency room, handing it directly to Maya. The doctor looked relieved and sent a nurse to retrieve the pharmaceutical supplies for the formula. He gave her the intel Eddie told him.

"That ring may very well have included some kind of sedative in it. She was pretty out of it when she came in the first time. I think the pain of her injuries kept her from passing out." Maya contemplated her initial diagnosis and treatment of her patient. She would have taken the appropriate tests, but checking for such a cutting-edge drug in a Daily made no sense.

Maya Toriyama was the chief physician for the Hold and New Haven. She had a high-security clearance and was in direct contact with Bannon. She had access to resident files and other highly classified information, but she was unaware of why this patient was such a high priority for the outer world. She started to wonder. *Did Jilly disclose or unknowingly leak information about New Haven? Was she involved with infiltrators? Was her past more complicated than the vetting process revealed?* She needed to talk to Bannon immediately about what security breach they may be dealing with.

"She gonna make it?" Gray asked.

"She has a good chance if we caught it in time, but she will have a rough night while the SS drugs and the antidote cocktail play havoc with her body. It's better to get the antidote before the symptoms emerge," Dr. Maya answered. "We won't have a clear prognosis until she comes out of it. If she doesn't come out of it in a couple of days, it could indicate the drugs have already caused too much damage."

Gray used his radio to call his second, Axle, and informed him that he was staying to stand guard over the victim. But he knew it was more than duty that kept him there. He held her hand, and she whimpered from time to time. Once, he thought she was regaining consciousness, but she was hallucinating and thrashing her head back and forth. "Drowning," he thought she said over and over, but it was so slurred he wasn't sure. He touched her forehead with a cool cloth periodically and gently tucked her hair away from her face when she tossed and turned.

Her vitals were still critical, and there was no improvement by the next morning. He realized hour by hour, this girl had seized his heart. He longed to see those eyes, those intoxicating eyes. She had to be okay. He felt his gut clench, and he fought against releasing the dam of his emotions. Exhaustion was taking its toll as day two marched at a steady pace toward the next. The nurses began to comfort him more and had that consoling look when they stopped believing in recovery. The clicking and beeping machines seem to mock his desperation with absolute cruelty and indifference.

He closed his eyes, bowed his head, and prayed. He hadn't done that in a long time. But he poured out his heart, and it was then he knew he would always protect her. He swelled with rage, wishing he could exact his revenge on the one who set this up, but he calmed himself back down when her discomfort reflected his mood. He felt connected to her.

He befriended the snarky nurse, AnnDrea Channing, from Jilly's first visit. Making her rounds, she saw Gray kneeling with his head bowed, and she got on her knees beside him, and they prayed together. Finally, the next afternoon, Jilly opened her eyes. Gray was passed out with his head on the bed, holding her hand.

Jilly peered through blurry eyes and tried to figure out where she was. She looked down at Gray and vaguely remembered being carried by him. He was holding her hand like they were close, but she could barely remember him. She needed to make her brain focus. She wasn't sure what to do with this connection, but eventually, she moved her hand, and when she did, Gray woke up.

"Hey," he yawned, "welcome back. How ya feelin'?" Gray spoke with a tender voice, trying to keep his joy from revealing his feelings.

"I'm, I'm, where am I? I can't think, my head, my head, it hurts." She sat up, winced, and lay back down. Memories of the attack abruptly and vividly returned. "Gray?" It was coming back to her in waves now.

Working his best to keep his emotions in check, he tenderly brushed her hair behind her ear. "Yeah, I'm here."

"He hit me—Oh my God, Ari! Is Ari okay? Where's Ari?" she gasped, struggling to get up and shuddering with pain. It was obvious she had lost some time, but he'd seen this often in newly conscious patients.

"Careful, Jilly. Just lie still. Ari's fine. You just missed her visit. I'm going to get the doctor." He got up and added, "Just lie back and don't move," in his commanding tone, and ran out of the room.

"She's awake!" Gray said with more excitement than an officer watching over a victim. Yet the whole staff had watched him suffer at her bedside, and the level of his devotion was unmistakable.

"Yes, I was on my way. The station nurse informed me her readings kicked up on the monitor. This is great news." The doctor personally checked her vitals while Gray stood by. "Well, you have certainly turned out to be the most interesting case we've had here so far. I'm glad to see you've improved from yesterday. How are you feeling?" the doctor said, looking at a clipboard she collected from the bed rail.

"My head is pounding, and my belly is on fire."

"I'll see what I can do about that," she said sympathetically, "but in a short time, you've had a serious cocktail of drugs. I'm hesitant to add to the list. However, there are some things we can do to lessen your pain. Can you tell me your name?" the doctor asked.

"Jilly, he just told me," she smiled and pointed impishly at Gray. She was waking up more.

"Okay, check off the humor question," Maya shot back. "Why don't you tell me what you remember?"

Gray decided to let Dr. Maya finish the exam, so he gave them a wave, saying he'd be back later. He needed to report back to work, but first, he had to tell Ari the good news.

Chapter Five

Jilly spent another day at the infirmary. They ran more tests, and the counselor came to check on her before she was cleared to leave. They were on day five before she came back to the curtain. Grayson became a frequent guest, and Jilly lit up every time he visited. That first week was mostly scheduled around counseling, group activities, and time to connect with the other residents. Jilly had missed most of the interactive activities, but she did assignments to keep up on a tablet the counselor, Haru, brought her. Though she missed physically being with the residents, the outpouring of support made her lots of new friends.

Monday was day eight. Ari and Jilly woke up at 8:30 to the announcement, "Welcome to Week Two. Today, we will be issuing job assignments for New Haven. The meeting will begin at 10:00. Parents, please drop your children off at the yard where Defenders will watch them. It's a short meeting, so please be on time."

"Man! Has it already been a week?" Ari stretched upward with her good arm and straightened the covers on her cot. Looking in the mirror, she began brushing her wavy, brunette hair and deciding what she would wear. "Jilly, get up."

"Ahhh," Jilly stretched and exclaimed in yawn talk, "I slept so good last night. It was the first time I didn't need to get up and drink that awful detoxer sedative." She tidied her area and went to the closet by

Ari. "I hope we have a little more room than this in New Haven," she said, turning sideways to grab her clothes.

"Wow, haven't we become spoiled by three meals a day and a safe place to live?" Ari hip-checked her gently. It was true, what they lacked in space, they gained tenfold in safety and happiness. It was contagious. People smiled and waved at each other as they passed by. Children's voices could be heard shouting and playing in the yard. Women hung out at the mess hall tables and yard benches. They shared stories with tears and laughter. Men, too, hung out together and talked of their pasts, both distant and recent, and they laughed out loud at their favorite jokes they finally could share.

Ari had expected a lot more tension and mistrust, but it had not happened. She had cynical expectations for cynical times. Maybe it was being managed by the counselor, or maybe people were changing. She, like everyone else, still had an apprehensive view of the future, but she was trying not to live that way here. Maybe human nature *is* to be civil, and they have been waiting to be true to that.

Everyone attended the mandatory counseling meetings on Mondays and Thursdays in the mess hall. The residents were given activities and questions to discuss in rotating groups. New communication techniques were taught, and activities were assigned to practice them as well as the ones from previous sessions. Some people also attended private sessions and or joined small groups at the counseling office to cope with more severe traumas.

"This isn't a cure, " Haru Abar, the counselor, often said. "Everyone here has been a victim of violence, everyone. But we must walk the path from knee-jerk fear to compassion and trust. It is not a short journey, but employing these skills will help you manage your emotions in healthy ways. You are now members of a community where you can move about safely with freedom. You can develop friendships and build support systems to strengthen your community. It isn't a cure, but being a part of a caring community is powerful medicine."

Jilly saw evidence of that firsthand. She looked at the cards she'd received from well-wishers during her ordeal. They were filled with kind messages and children's scribbles. A cup with marker-infused napkin flowers sat on the desk. Their new friends had been kind and helpful throughout their recovery. Not only were they recovering with their loving support, but the whole Hold group felt good about the pent-up kindness they finally were able to give.

They still had emotional healing to do, and it was not uncommon to witness bouts of hesitation all the way to full-blown panic attacks. But day by day, they improved physically and emotionally. There was a seed planted in each heart with the hope of growing into love for their fellow human beings.

The sisters ate a quick breakfast and rushed to the bathrooms to get a spot to brush their teeth. It was crowded, but getting used to being near people and sharing had a cathartic effect. They were becoming a family. All the resident adults sat in the mess hall at the dining benches. The children could be heard playing in the yard, overjoyed to have the Defenders be their playmates.

Haru, the director, asked for the residents' attention and began the meeting. "Today is job assignment day. This week is all about introducing you to your new careers. You each were tested and shown the results of your strengths. You applied for positions, and today, we have those assignments."

"Okay, listen carefully. This is a test to see how well you have gotten to know your community. I will set a stack of large, sealed envelopes on each table. Everyone will grab one and read the name, look around without getting up, and pass it toward its owner. When you get your envelope, do not open it. If at any time you feel uncomfortable with the energetic chaos, just move to the outer area and wait to retrieve your envelope. Any questions? Okay, get ready, go!"

Pandemonium ensued. People were shouting names, crawling under tables to retrieve dropped envelopes, and belly-laughing the whole time. Ari was slow at passing the envelopes due to her arm. Her tablemates grabbed them from her, which got her laughing so hard she was even less help. Jilly was not allowed to participate due to her injury, but it was astonishing to watch. The exercise had most in a euphoric state, but a few individuals pulled out of the fray. Jilly noticed Haru jotting down things on his clipboard, and she realized this was more than just a game. It was a treatment as well as a test.

Most of the citizens in this rag-tag group of downtrodden souls were now laughing uncontrollably with the emotion they had held in for so long. Some even cried, but their friends comforted them. They were changing, flourishing. It was baby steps for sure, but the change was unmistakable. Finally, the chaos slowed down, and Haru resumed.

"Well, that looked fun. Does everyone have an envelope? Okay, good. I'm going to ask you to go to your curtains and open them there. Inside, you will find instructions on how to begin your job study. Please give this opportunity a true and honest chance. We ask that you take a full twenty-four hours to go through your packet, regardless of your initial opinion about it. Learn what your job will involve and all the possibilities it can offer. If you still have questions or doubts, we'll work it out with you tomorrow.

"Be sure to keep your packet secured in your locker when you aren't working with it. Again, lock them up. It's critical to protect your information and the information of your new team. We will meet again as a group tomorrow. Please don't forget to collect your children from our brave Defenders, as tempting as it may be to extend your freedom. Thank you."

Ari and Jilly considered staying to talk with their friends about how much fun the pass-about game was, but they were more anxious to open their envelopes. It appeared they were not alone in that desire. The residents swiftly dispersed to their curtains. Ari and Jilly were opening their envelopes as they slid their curtain door open. Ari expected to be given an engineering position, but she was eager to see which section she would be assigned to. Jilly broke the silence before Ari could make her announcement.

"I'm a nurse! I thought I would be given a receptionist job or something because I don't have my degree, but... Oh, wait a minute. I have to be supervised by another nurse until I finish my studies. Oh, look, we have a college, and I can start working on it now! This place is more than incredible; it's heaven. Maybe we are in heaven; we should look for Dad." She was manic with joy and rambling without a filter. "Ari, what is your job? Engineer, right?"

"Yes, I am an engineer," she answered, looking dumbfounded by her news.

"What kind? Are you okay? Is it bad? You can petition to—"

"Jilly, shut up! Sorry, yes, it's good. It's better than I thought. In fact, it's more than I deserve; I may be over my head." She was trying to stay calm despite her increasing anxiety.

Jilly locked her gaze on Ari and waited for the other shoe to drop without saying a word.

"I applied to be a maintenance engineer because I don't have much practical experience. But I'm on the innovation team," she said with more apprehension than pride and contentment.

"Sooo, is that good, or..."

"It's incredible. It's a dream job where I can spread my wings and try new things. But it comes with a teetering pedestal and a lot of responsibility, the life-and-death kind. I don't think I'm ready." She sat like a statue, holding the paperwork in front of her. That she was over-accessing her brain couldn't be more obvious if it emitted a hum like a computer.

"I think you're the most responsible, dedicated person I know. I believe they knew exactly what they were doing when they chose you. I'm sure you'll have a mentor. Look, I have one, though I don't know who it is yet."

"I'm going to go through every detail of this packet, and I'm also going to ask them why I was chosen."

They began poring over their packets. They stayed up late making diagrams and lists on their fingerboards. They shared their insights and pointed out the gems found in the material, and then they'd go back to reading their study packets. They continued to peek in and out of their solitary worlds, like the sun on a cloudy day until, like that sun, they eventually faded.

The next morning, the meeting was a swarm of activity. People shared their new jobs and discussed their excitement and concerns. Jilly and Ari sat with their new friends and shared the news of their new positions. Jilly had become quite close to a woman named Billie, who would be assigned to the farm and livestock area. Those who had concerns about their job assignments received assistance at a side table while the rest of the residents were directed to tables related to their sections. Jilly went to the medical table while Ari went to the engineering/maintenance table.

An electronic notebook connected to a closed network was permanently issued to each new employee. At each table was a monitor that had a video ready to introduce the new employees to their section. Soon, a murmur of videos hummed around the mess hall. Residents watched intently as the director from each area explained the career basics. After the video, the new section members discussed the assigned topics.

A common surprise was that the videos were filmed in New Haven. The videos didn't show many details, but visual proof of its existence caused much enthusiasm. They were dismissed to complete the assignments loaded on their notebooks.

Billie pulled Jilly aside. "I need to talk to you," she said, sounding worried.

"What's wrong? Are you okay? Is it your job assignment?"

"No, Jilly, stop. It's none of those." Billie paused and took a breath. "I think I'm pregnant."

"Oh, I didn't know you were seeing someone." Jilly noticed the amount of time and the close relationship she had with a man named Gabe, but they insisted they were just friends. "Who's the father?"

"Gabe, we've known each other for a while. We met at the first lecture meeting. We're just friends, but one night about a month ago, we got intimate. We decided the next morning it was a mistake, and we should just remain friends. He doesn't know."

"Well, you can think about him any way you want, but this connects you in more than just a friend way, and you can't leave him in the dark. He's a good man. He doesn't deserve that."

"He'll hate me. This ruins everything he wanted to do with his life." Billie started crying. It was the first time she had cried since—actually, she didn't remember the last time.

"Well, he'd have to hate himself, too. It's not like you did this alone. It sounds like he means a lot to you. You're more concerned about him than you are yourself."

"I do, I love him. But we decided, he decided, not to have that kind of relationship. He doesn't feel the way I do. I don't want to obligate him. And besides, I now can't be in a single dorm house in New Haven. What if I get kicked out?"

"Look, I don't think they *can* kick you out at this point. You know too much, and I refuse to believe they will off you and an unborn child. Billie, I will help you in any way I can. You can count on me, but...there are some things you need to do before making any decisions. First, get tested, then if you are, make a with or without him plan. But no matter what, you *must* tell him because he's going to find out, and then he *will* be mad."

"Yeah, maybe it's just nerves."

Jilly noticed her looking a little green and led her to the bathroom.

Chapter Six

Week three's tasks were about the practical application of new jobs. Maintenance personnel practiced troubleshooting and fixing machinery, a triage simulation was set up for the medical personnel, and educators worked on lesson plans. Everyone was busy with their assigned tasks, and the mess hall teemed with activity.

But the news that had everyone buzzing was the mini farm. Chickens and rabbits had arrived at the Hold that morning and were being kept in another section of the building. The animals were also in quarantine before going to New Haven. The tiny livestock would be used in conjunction with a new bio technique that took an ounce of protein and increased it by ten times, so a few animals would go a long way to maintain protein in the New Haven diet. The farm and ranch employees were eagerly engaged in on-the-job training and working with the animals. The residents bombarded them with questions when they returned.

The least favorite tasks for the week were the formal assessments of current knowledge from the notebook lessons. Each lesson on the notebook had a test at the end, but you could start the lesson over if you didn't pass the first time. But the formal assessments were turned in and scored, so tensions were high. Ari aced hers, of course, and Jilly got a 95 percent, which she was very happy about.

Billie barely passed hers, and Jilly knew she was struggling to focus since her pregnancy test came back positive. Billie was sitting on a yard bench watching the children play. She always wanted to be a mother, but surviving in the world had become too hard and dangerous. Now she had the better world, maybe, but she was alone. It would be difficult, but many parents were alone these days. She saw Gabe coming her way, and it was too late to pretend she hadn't noticed him.

"Hey, Billie, how's it going? I haven't seen you around much."

She looked up at him with big brown eyes.

"Uhh, yeah. I've been busy with my studies."

"Uh-huh, yeah. What's up with you, Billie?" Gabe asked. "You've been avoiding me for over a week." He stood in front of her with his arms crossed, waiting for an answer.

"I did horribly on my test," she answered.

"Oh, sorry... wait, we just got our results this morning. That ain't it. Are you pissed about something?"

Billie lowered her head. "I gotta tell you something, Gabe."

"I'm listening." He uncrossed his arms.

"I'm, I'm sorry I can't see you anymore." She lost her courage and couldn't tell him. "I just need to figure out some stuff."

"Oh, really?" he snapped back. "Is it because you're pregnant? What, did you think I didn't notice you going to the bathroom every morning, heaving your guts out?"

She stood frozen with shock.

"I've been waiting for you to tell me yourself. Don't you trust me?"

"I... I just didn't want you to, to hate me."

"Hate you? Jesus, Billie, I'm crazy about you." He had loved her from the first time he'd seen her. Her dark chocolate skin, big brown doe eyes, and luscious lips made him impatient waiting for the right kissable moment. He liked to tease her by running his hands through her braided hair hanging in a sexy cascade down her back, while she'd warn him not to mess it up. Everything about her was his type. He knew the first day they met, he'd find a way to make her his own.

"I didn't know. Why didn't you say something?"

"I *did* something. I was so glad we made love because I thought it meant we could actually be a couple. I thought we had finally crossed the awkward friend barrier. I hate being friends. But maybe you feel differently, do you?"

"I love you so much. I was afraid that if I said it out loud, you'd feel uncomfortable and leave me."

"Well, apparently, we need to work on our communication. I'll start. Marry me, Billie. I want to be with you always, and I'm overjoyed about the baby, my baby, our baby."

She threw her arms around him and smothered him with kisses while whispering, "Yes," over and over.

At the next morning's meeting, Haru made an announcement. "We're going to have a wedding!" exclaimed Haru. "I need volunteers to help prepare decorations, and we have to have a dress. The event will be on Saturday this week."

Many people raised their hands, and it was amazing the items they had brought in their two-bag limit. One man said he used to help his father tailor clothing, and he wanted to design and sew a dress. The building was overflowing with goodwill and busy hands.

It was day 16 when Jilly heard a clamor growing outside their curtain. "What the hell is going on out there?" The rumble of activity and voices outside their curtain was increasing. Two parents, Rhinda and Henry, were talking to Gray with panicked voices.

"Relax, ma'am. There's no place for him to go. We *will* find him." Gray left them in the care of the counselor standing by.

"What's going on, Gray? Who are you looking for?" Jilly asked.

"Connor, their nine-year-old. He said he was going to use the restroom, and he never came back. We've made a preliminary search, but nothing yet. We'll find him."

Gray thought about the gauntlet of security the boy would have to navigate to get beyond the resident areas. The restricted areas of the building required an access badge, and to leave the building, he'd need a Defender band and a punch code after being cleared by the Defender on guard.

"How can we help?" asked Ari.

"Help search in places a kid could hide."

The sisters started looking in the bathrooms and the kitchen area. Jilly felt bad for the kid who thought he had to hide in this caring environment. She wondered what had happened to scare him.

The search barely got started before word came from the DOR (Defender Operation Room) that they had Connor. It was about twenty minutes later that a Defender came out of the DOR with Connor in tow. His parents rushed to him with frantic relief. They hugged and scolded on a repeated loop for several minutes. Axle was Gray's adopted brother and the Defender who delivered him. He whispered something to Gray, and the two of them strode toward the DOR with haste.

"We found him hiding in the storage room. He was looking for his dog. Someone told him his dog was cleared for habitation," Axle said with eyebrows raised.

"What the hell? Is that true?" Gray had a million questions, but he wanted Axle to continue.

"I haven't checked that yet. But it gets worse. Someone let him through the door. Whoever it was, wore a photo-disrupter, so the camera image is just a blur. We talked to the kid for about twenty minutes. He said it was a woman Defender. He couldn't see her face, but she was short, so he assumed she was female. The kid saw a Defender going toward the infirmary, so he ran over to ask about his dog. He's been curious since the farm was disclosed. The perp told him his dog was in the animal room, and then she locked him in the storage room."

"We know it's a woman?"

"Yeah, I'm getting to that."

He had a list of questions, like, why wouldn't she run the kid off? Instead, he urged Axle to finish his report. "I think you'd better get to the point and quick."

"We ID'd the photo-disrupter. It was from our own armory, and just before I walked him out, Deed called and said they found her in the med files, going through the resident's transport paperwork. She was looking for someone."

He handed Gray a list of names and birthdates that were on her list.

"Son of a bitch," he swore.

"We have her. She's in custody."

"For fuck's sake, you couldn't have led with that! Take me to her!" Gray was taken to an exam room where one of his Defenders, Janet, lay unconscious. "What happened to her?" he asked, exasperated at this point when he recognized the young soldier who had betrayed them. He was tempted to tell Dr. Maya to do everything she could to save her, but she'd know his ulterior motive. He didn't know what to do with her if she did survive, but he needed information.

Hannah Lopez was a Defender under Gray's command. She was his intel officer, and though short in stature, her sturdy, strong build displayed her battle-ready physique. She had Gray's highest regard, and he listened intently as she gave her report. "She had a punch ring with a quick-acting poison, and she used it before we got to her, sir. She swore she never revealed the location of our Hold site."

"Well, she was in a blind transport like the residents, so that statement makes me wonder if she said that because she doesn't know or if she uncovered that information without authorization."

"Yeah, this is a mess for sure. She got a ransom note that gave her four weeks to find one or both of the women on that list, or her dad would die. She didn't know anything regarding why they wanted them; it was just a last-ditch effort to save her dad. She started going under after that. But she had a computer hypodisk. We know she didn't use it because it was still sealed. But, sir, it was loaded with robomites. Would that have disclosed our location and everything on our server?"

"Robomites! Holy... No, it couldn't have crawled back to the owner, but I'm pretty sure it would have fucked up our isolated server. Our one outside access isn't connected to our internal network. But I'll give you this. Someone really wants this target, and they have serious resources. Until I know what they know, we're changing our threat level from 5 to 3. I need to brief the whole team on new protocols. Split it into two meeting times and set it up." Grayson's expression was grave and pissed at the same time. "And keep me informed of her condition. If she wakes up, call me immediately! Oh, and hey, good work, Hannah."

This is a pattern, he thought. It was just weeks ago that he was called by the Zeta site with a similar story. Drangers were always tasked with finding people of value for some powerful asshole. There was no reason to pay close attention to it, but now they were attacking the Hold and targeting its residents. He called the scout team off-site to look for similar crimes. He assigned the off-site computer team to search for information on the web. Who were they looking for, and what did it have to do with Jilly? Unfortunately, he was going to have to get close to her. Not close the way he wanted to be, but close so he could investigate her, even if she found out and hated him for it. But first, he needed to send a stealth drone to New Haven. He had to contact Bannon Vogel.

A few hours later, a secure call came in. "Gray?" Bannon was calling from a secure line.

"Yeah, I'm on a secure line." He proceeded to tell him the events surrounding the two poison ring crimes. And he added the 091 sisters may be involved, but he couldn't understand how or why. When he was done explaining, there was a long pause on the other end of the line. "Are you still there, Bannon?" asked Gray.

"I can't talk about this. Even on this phone. Protocol HS3, Gray. I have to go. Zip this phone. We'll talk at NH," he said, and Gray heard the phone disconnect. Gray immediately did a zip dump to scramble the phone's locator and any ghost voices. He sat back and contemplated the order. Protocol HS3? He wasn't told that very often.

HS3 is meant to protect these individuals at the highest level of security without letting anyone know, including them. The why was above his clearance and not for phone communications. HS2 was usually meant for an asset or someone with top-secret knowledge. The only level higher indicated a government or regime leader. Level 3 was for people and family members around those in levels 1 and 2. *What the devil is going on? And who are these girls? It just goes deeper and deeper into the hush-hush swamp,* he thought. He hated that crap. It always leaked out and caused something else just as bad.

He was off the personal investigation task, but he wasn't off the investigation of the crime, at least that was his take on it. He called Axle, telling him to report immediately. He needed someone he could trust to follow orders without question. Someone who could covertly trail Ari while he trailed Jilly.

The wedding day arrived. All week, items to create a beautiful celebration came trickling out of the residents' curtains. Napkins were confiscated for flowers, and someone donated a ring. It was only a costume jewelry ring, but it sparkled, and Gabe couldn't wait to put it on her finger. Grayson stood with Gabe as Jilly and Ari made their way down the aisle bordered by mess hall benches.

Billie wore a modified nurse's white dress. The V-neckline, trim fit, and sleeveless design looked lovely and fit her beautifully. It had a woven belt made of gauze that gathered just under the bodice and hung in frayed trails behind her, where a row of buttons went down her back. Her hair was tied up with scattered little braids falling around her shoulders and sprinkled with glitter, compliments of the kids' craft box. A wreath of blue-edged napkin flowers crowned her head. Ari loaned her a locket pin that was her grandmother's.

Haru, who was also a minister, presided over the ceremony. Billie was stunned when Gabe put the shiny ring on her finger. She never thought she would have a ring, let alone such a pretty one. When he told her it wasn't real, she answered, "It couldn't be more real to me."

The kitchen staff served sparkling juice and sweet pastries, usually saved for Sunday breakfasts. There was music on the speakers, and everyone danced. Ari caught the bouquet, but she quickly tossed it to Jilly. Their gifts consisted of cards with good wishes and help tickets for during and after the pregnancy. But the best gift was that a team of residents assembled a new curtain for them. The newlyweds were moved to tears when they were led to their own curtain. It was a perfect day.

Chapter Seven

Haru signaled for their attention and began. "This is our last week in the Hold, and I know I'm not the only one who has noticed our remarkable transformation. We began our journey as isolated individuals and families, fighting a treacherous world alone.

"But today, we are a caring community willing to reach out to each other. I have witnessed genuine concern for fellow members and seen the development of close friendships. We even had a wedding! I am so proud of all of you. You will soon join a much bigger community, and I know you will continue to practice what you have learned.

"Week four is all about continuing your notebook lessons and learning about New Haven. The first thing you'll be happy to learn is that the people here are your immediate neighbors in New Haven. Your resident code is your new address. The 'NH' is for New Haven, but you probably guessed that. The next number is your floor plan designation, which means the size of your house. The SW denotes you will be in the southwestern section of the town. The last number after the hashtag is your street number. So, go, walk, talk, and compare."

Jilly and Ari quickly recalled their resident codes, NH2SW#91A & B.

"Ari! We each have our own room!"

"And real walls! So, we have a two-bedroom in the southwest section of town. Since I'm A, I get to choose which bedroom I want," Ari poked at her little sister.

"Dream on, we'll rock, paper, scissors like we always do. Besides, I got this whole thing going, so I should get first pick."

Both sisters were laughing and bumping shoulders. They were delighted to have a safe place to sleep, and they couldn't wait to see what the town was like. And more importantly, how was it safe from the Corporates?

"I can't wait to put up our decorations. It will be Winter Solstice soon." Ari swelled with emotion.

"How did we ever get fortunate enough to be chosen for this?" asked Jilly.

How indeed, Gray thought while standing near them and nonchalantly watching the screens of their notebooks. Without arousing their attention, he wandered off, and Axle sauntered over. He hated this, but he justified it by saying it was for their protection, as well as the security of New Haven.

After about ten minutes of animated discussions, Haru separated the residents into those with similar family sizes and floor plans. He told everyone to find the floor plan he had just sent them. They all connected to their notebooks, and soon another round of lively discussions ensued.

"As you can see, you have no kitchen," Haru continued. "You will still use mess halls, but there will be opportunities to eat some meals at your house or have a picnic at one of the parks."

Excited voices began, and Haru signaled for their attention. "I'll address your questions later. Next, open the furnishing link I just sent you. It displays the furniture that is provided with your house. Due to the logistics of moving so many people into the site, your furniture is already installed in your home. But you may rearrange it when you arrive."

A hand went up in the crowd. "How many people are going to be there?"

"That is not a number I can tell you today, but there are definitely more. Find the neighbors closest to your street number. One of them will be the people or family you will share a small yard with. The town map is classified until we arrive, so I can't tell which it will be."

"We get yards?" an excited shout rang out.

The Worthens, Rhinda, Henry, Connor, and Meshka, lived on one side of them with the number 090. Jilly and Ari talked to them for a few minutes. While Ari discussed work designations, Jilly bent down to talk to Meshka. She was six years old and cute as could be, with blonde ringlets and blue eyes. Connor stood there, asking to go meet his friends in the yard.

He was a smart, independent kid with an outgoing personality. Jilly had spoken with him a few times about everything from the traumas they shared, schools, and people they had lost. The whole family seemed like easygoing people, and the girls looked forward to getting to know them better. But she had the feeling Connor was special. He seemed like a normal kid, and yet there was something different about this kid.

Billie and Gabe came over to Jilly and Ari. "Look, they put Gabe and me together. I thought—actually, I didn't know what to think. I was afraid to ask." Then she pointed to the smaller bedroom on her notebook screen. "It's a nursery," she beamed.

"And look at our street numbers, 091 and 092. We live next to each other!" squealed Jilly.

"Oh geez, she's squeaking," Ari teased as she put her arm around her sister and hugged her close.

Jilly smiled. "I hope we share a yard. We can sit together with the baby."

Haru called them together one more time. "I'm sure you have a ton of questions. Send them to me from your notebook, and tomorrow, I will answer the ones I can. Because it seems pointless to say work on your studies, no lesson work is due until Wednesday, but it's back to a normal work schedule tomorrow. See you then."

Later that afternoon, Jilly sat on her chair in front of her open curtain. She obsessively arranged and rearranged the furniture on her notebook. She listed the decorations she remembered packing in their box a couple of months ago. She spent hours deciding where each item would go. *This is the most enjoyable and addictive task so far*, she thought. Although she wasn't a very religious person, she closed her eyes and gave thanks for all she had been given.

When Gray stopped by, she went over each design option. He sat through fifteen or so minutes of it until he suggested they head to lunch. She asked him about New Haven, but he lied and told her he knew no more than she did. A few days ago, he would have told her he couldn't say, but now he kept everything close to the vest. He felt awful, but he was trained well enough to maintain his performance.

Jilly could tell something had changed. The way things had been going, she expected him to kiss her. She thought about that a lot and was becoming impatient. She planned on kissing him at the wedding when Ari gave her the bouquet, but he seemed to pull back. She chalked it up to her being out of danger, so he was free to return to his more urgent tasks. Maybe he had just been doing his duty, or maybe the wedding spooked him. She wondered how had she read him so wrong. And now, she couldn't read him at all. *Yet why did he still hang around so much?* She didn't see him as the fickle type, but perhaps she was just now getting to know the real Gray.

Jilly's whereabouts and vitals were transmitted constantly and directly to Gray's Defender band, or D band as they referred to them, while Axle had Ari on his. Gray knew it was very invasive and broke every level of trust between them. The only good news was that both women were rule-abiding citizens, and their daily routines were predictable. He could find no reason to suspect them of anything.

Even though they were separate from each other, all four Hold buildings had been on high security without informing the residents. All stored rings were inspected by a locker scan, and residents removed them during med scans for a fabricated mold inspection. No additional weapons were found. Most residents noticed there were more guards around, but it didn't seem to hinder them enough to seriously question it. Either they were afraid to ask, didn't want to be involved, or assumed it was about the upcoming departure.

The off-site investigations identified eight more cases, outside of the Hold, of attempted kidnappings with SS drugs and punch rings. All the victims were women who had similar features to Jilly and Ari. Either they were looking for these two sisters or women who looked like them. Unfortunately, the other women didn't survive their ordeals. The web was abuzz with encrypted messages that they either couldn't decode or didn't make sense. The one thing Gray felt optimistic about was there wasn't any indication the NH project had been compromised.

His latest theory was that the call-out was to locate women with these features because they were related to a person with a lot of power and resources. If someone could get their hands on them, they could be leveraged for a lot of whatever that leader wanted. *Pretty vague*, he thought, *but it's a start*. He was careful not to investigate the women themselves as ordered, but he was duty-bound to protect them and the rest of the residents. He hoped it had nothing to do with Jilly and Ari, but Bannon's reaction told him differently. Whoever coordinated it was well-organized, and that was extremely threatening for the sisters and everyone else too.

"Sir," Hannah called Gray on his earpiece. "She's waking up, sir."

"I'll be right there. I want to talk to her. Don't let anyone in."

"Yes sir."

Janet was in rough shape, and Dr. Maya warned Gray not to over-tax her. Through slurred speech and her fading in and out, Gray gathered a few more facts.

"Hannah," Gray called on his com, "call Axle and meet me in the conference room." Hannah was invaluable as a coordinator, and her loyalty to Gray and the project was unmatched. He took that for granted sometimes, but he didn't know how he'd function without her.

"Yes sir."

He closed the door after them and gave them what he had discovered. "The Drangers don't know who the women are or why they are looking for them, but there is a lot of pressure from way up to find them. They don't care what it takes, so the payoff must be really good. The offsite team found out Janet's father had been dead for over a month before they sent her the note. The MO was to grab anyone fitting those descriptions, and if it wasn't the right person, her body was dumped somewhere. There seems to be more than one faction after them, too.

"My suspicion is they are looking for Ari and Jilly, and not only is that unconfirmed, but it's also at the highest level of classification. I can't tell you why I think that, but I need your help to protect them and the rest of the residents. Hell, I don't want any of us to die for whatever is going on here either. I'd like to come up with a plan to step up security without raising the suspicions of those outside this room. I'm open to suggestions." They talked about the necessary tasks and split them up. Gray hoped it would be enough.

Since meeting Jilly, Gray constantly reminded himself that he was a professional, raised by his basic training instructor father. He had been brought up with strong values and was well-loved, but he was also trained to put his personal feelings aside to protect the mission. And the overall mission was always to protect the people, not the person.

That night, Janet died of an irreparable hole in her heart. They couldn't stop the poison from eating holes in her organs. A small, quiet ceremony was held with her fellow Defenders; she was only nineteen years old.

Day two of week four was craft day. Haru explained, "In your new home, the wall colors, window shades, and furnishings are all in neutral colors. Months ago, on your packing day, your family unit was told to choose a color scheme from four combinations. They included: cool grays and whites, mocha tans and off-whites, sage greens and off-whites, and smoky blues and whites. The interior of your house was painted in those shades. The exterior of your house was painted to go with the houses on your block.

"Today, you will craft decorative items to make your house into your home. The choices include pillows, rag rugs, rag-weave blankets, placemats, table flower arrangements, and wall décor. Each resident is allowed two items. You are also allowed to pick out three new outfits and a bathing suit to fit your new lifestyle.

"Although I hope you have fun creating your treasures, don't neglect your studies. The assignments are short this week, but they are still due by the end of each day." He signaled the end of the session, and people went shopping for their craft projects and their new clothes.

There were plenty of craft supplies, all arranged in kits. After deciding what they wanted to make, Jilly and Ari used their bands to get a rag rug, table flowers, a rag-weave blanket, and a welcome sign. The video directions were linked to their notebooks by the barcode found on the kits. The numerous racks of clothing were arranged by size and style. Jilly found a couple of treasures, including a beautiful sky blue sweater with tiny pearl buttons that reminded her of one her mother wore. She had found that picture and another, wedged in a drawer of her father's desk while packing. The sisters were happy they were ahead in their studies, allowing them to work on their projects.

Three days before the scheduled moving day, news came that nuclear missiles had been deployed. Washington, DC, sent one to Beijing, and the act was quickly retaliated with a hit on Hawaii. Moscow was attacked by Riyadh, and the reprisal was anticipated. None of the large nuclear hits were in their vicinity, but the fallout clouds from the smaller ones planted by terrorists and the ones that were expected could reach the Hold by the end of the week.

It was decided to put the studies and projects on hold and move up the departure day. The original plan was that the residents would leave, and the packing of the facility would be completed by some of the Defenders. But the threat of exposure from the existing radioactive clouds and the possibility of ones to come made that an unacceptable risk. So, everyone was employed to begin packing up the facility.

Within five hours, the curtains came down, leaving cots and luggage exposed and parked around the yard. The kitchen, mess hall, infirmary, and other offices were well on their way to being dismantled. The night before departure, people were instructed to wear their same clothes, so the rest could be packed. The kitchen made sacks of food for the rest of the meals before their arrival. Boxing up the toys caused the once docile children to openly complain and whine, but residents assigned careers involving children gathered them for games, stories, and fun educational activities.

Gray, Axle, and Hannah sat in the conference room with the door closed. Hannah went over her notes carefully. The world situation was becoming increasingly unstable. She took pride in providing concise briefings, and she made a detailed report with graphs demonstrating the rise in activity available on their tablets.

"Are we ready?" Gray asked his high-level security team.

"Yeah, the packing is all but done. Finishing up the infirmary is ongoing, as well as the last of the security items. This is the last group for the Hold. We also set the stage for anyone locating it," Axle replied.

"Good. Hannah, what's happening on the world front?"

"It was quiet until thirty minutes ago. Russia sent a response to MECA, which is the name for the newly formed Middle East Collation Alliance, but it wasn't nuclear. It was a combination of an FMS attack and a toxbomb."

"Toxbombs, that's bad. FMS attack? Explain this."

"An FMS attack is a frequency modulation surge attack. It identifies the modulation of a power grid and disables every electrical device connected to it. EMPs aren't as lucrative because they create dangerous levels of radioactivity. They also damage the components, leaving the devices unusable. By using the FMS, they save the devices, so they can grab technology and intel too."

"Where did they hit?"

"Tashkent."

"So, what, they couldn't make it to Riyadh or some other key city?" Gray threw his hands up in bewilderment.

"I have a theory, sir," Axle answered. "It's kind of brilliant," He added with a cocky tone. He and Gray were more than just childhood friends; they were raised as brothers by Gray's dad. He knew when to show respect for Gray's rank, but he hated to be so serious. And besides, Hannah was there, and it felt like a family gathering. Axle was remembering all the sneaking out as a kid to hang with Hannah. They would watch the Neighwah from a hiding place and belittle the underlings as they tried to convince the Corporates how smart they were. They laughed at how quickly they spilled the compliant *yes, sir, as you command sir,* and *right away sir* responses. They often imitated them in their conversations as a private joke. Hannah gave Axle a playful glare, but Gray's glare signaled an end to the antics.

"Off-site tracked a Russian convoy waiting at the Uzbekistan border last night. I bet they're planning to take the town. Nuking it doesn't leave anything to scavenge or prisoners to capture, and your newly seized town is useless. Temporarily disabling an enemy's technology and personnel cuts your casualties to a bare minimum, if there even are any. Using an FMS makes it pretty easy to repair the confiscated technology. Toxbombs to eliminate resistance may be brutal, but it's genius. When the dust settles, you have a fully functional town that's move-in ready. I think at some point they'll start using sedatives instead of deadly toxins, so they can capture high-level targets and laborers."

"Okay, Ax. Good work. That didn't occur to me."

"I've always wondered what real value abject destruction had for a nation at war with another. These weapons are cheaper, and the materials are easier to attain. It's what I would do if I were hell-bent on power." Axle leaned back into the cushioned backrest of the office chair.

"There has been no nuclear activity since, sir," added Hannah. "The rest may decide to follow that path."

"Do we know what kind of toxin they used?"

"There's been no word about that from the target or any outlying areas. The logical choice would be Serin Gas since there are numerous old stockpiles of the stuff. And it is horribly effective." Axle had seen firsthand the gruesome deaths delivered by the lethal weapon.

"Okay, well, back to our plan. So, we are all on the same page, it's a K code, level 6 with a 0 count." They all nodded in agreement.

"Okay, get the residents loaded." The K stood for kills authorized, the 6 meant the attack could come from any direction, and zero was the number of known targets that needed to be eliminated.

"Yes, sir, we know the drill."

"All right, here we go. Dismissed."

It was early morning, and the sun was still down, not that the residents were aware. They had been inside the whole three-plus weeks. But the Defenders knew and had been packing trailers and sending them off for New Haven. They were scheduled to leave just before sunrise. The residents each packed a tote with their notebooks and their projects. The children were given an e-book tablet with headphones. Notebook owners were able to choose two entertainment apps to download for the ride. There were a variety of themes, from educational activities, challenging puzzles, sports games, and RPG games.

The residents were let outside into the sunshine under the big sky. They drank in the sight of the blinding light and felt the breeze float through their hair, gently spinning it around. It was a treat they had been deprived of for almost a month. They all knew the importance of staying inside the Hold compound, not that they had a choice. There were a few who complained about being confined, but everyone knew that being locked up would be the new usual. Slowly, they lined up while soaking in every delectable moment.

The residents were instructed that once they entered the transport, it would be like the first time. They must be quiet while traveling. The engines were outfitted with sound maskers, but voices were still detectable. The Defenders knew that sound detectors could still be encountered on the road. Though most of them were in the dark about the search for two women, they knew the danger was high for many other reasons. Having something the residents could work on quietly was beneficial for everyone.

There were lots of people already loaded from the other three buildings. The three transports held sixty-four seats each, with small aisles on both sides to walk down. The seats for the first two transports were full, so Axle and another Defender closed the doors and struck the outside twice to signal the driver to go. Jilly was disappointed she wouldn't be able to travel with her own community, but Gray had held them up in casual conversation. She watched the transport with all her friends drive away. The next and last transport was across the pavement. Jilly and Ari were joined by two others heading to get in line. They were the last residents to board. Gray followed in full gear, like all the Defenders were for transport, but his helmet was tucked under his arm.

Ari and Jilly exchanged introductions with the two other residents walking to get on board. They were brother and sister who were from their building, so the foursome of siblings had seen each other over the last three-plus weeks. With the excitement of the final journey to their destination to settle into their new homes, they were giddy with excitement, and their familiarity with the other citizens made them talkative.

"Well, getting to know you guys better will be nice. We didn't get to talk with you much. I must admit we spent most of our time with the same group," Ari confided.

The woman smiled. "We did the same thing. I think everyone did."

They reached the line and were at the end of it. Gray stood directly behind them. The two new acquaintances were climbing the ramp of the transport and locating two seats, while the sisters stopped to talk to Gray. The line was quickly disappearing into the trailer, and the girls didn't want to be the reason it was held up, so they were trying to conclude their conversation.

"Well, gals," said Gray. They rolled their eyes while shaking their heads at him. "This is it. You're going home, I just wanted to say—"

Just then, two enemies covered head to toe in shabby warrior gear stormed out from the side of the building, spraying bullets as they ran. Gray slammed on his helmet and started shooting back. More bullets came from another combatant behind the other side of the building. Ari went down, and a red puddle began to pool around her. Jilly was hit while diving to help her, and she too slumped on the ground. As protocol demanded, the Defenders closed the transport and sped off. They were left with only Gray to fight off the attack.

Chapter Eight

The unaware transport holding Jilly and Ari's whole world traveled blissfully down the rutted rural highway. Though silent like the first trip, this time the passengers exchanged smiles and held up projects to share their progress. They weren't very far down the road when the Defenders became tense and were actively communicating with their helmets and shoulder controls. Gabe watched them intently.

Something had happened, and he expected them to signal the passengers, but no gesture came. He was extremely curious and wanted to probe their concern. With the security training he had so far, he knew it was not the right time, and without a need to know, it may never be. He looked over at his friend, who was also assigned to security, and they exchanged glances, denoting similar thoughts.

The third transport was tense and edgy. Though none of the passengers knew the two women or the Defender left bleeding and in harm's way, they were deeply upset and yearned to know what had just happened. They were curious; *were they dead, rescued, or captured? Was their transport in danger? Would they make it safely to New Haven?* It was in stark contrast to the mood of the transports ahead of them.

When the first two transports arrived, their travelers couldn't believe it went so quickly. Time was passing differently in the third transport. Its passengers were weary from their seemingly endless and terrifying journey. Before being let out of the first transport, the Defenders gave out directions.

"Look around and make sure you have all of your belongings. When you leave the transport, go directly with the lead Defender to be briefed." The groups were staggered to allow for a short introduction to the town and registration.

The excited residents expected to see the sky again, but the transports were backed into a loading dock. The eager sojourners were led into a large, round room with a glass-paneled ceiling. The clouds were gathering and billowing against a royal blue sky. The room was empty of seating or any furnishings, so they stood waiting for instructions.

Gabe turned to Billie and whispered, "I bet this would be an amazing place to view the moon and stars." She winked back at him and wondered when they would be allowed to spend time here.

A well-dressed woman strolled in and wandered among the new citizens. She shook hands, talked briefly with individuals, and occasionally knelt to give the children a rare treat, candy. After several minutes, she made her way to the edge of the room.

"Welcome to New Haven!" The speaker stretched out the simple statement to symbolize the lengthy journey and the moment it encompassed. "My name is Carolyn Riddley, and I am the town Recreation Director. You are at the west entrance of our town. I know you are anxious to see your homes and get them settled, but humor me for a moment. I want to describe your new town.

"For weeks, you lived with forty to fifty residents plus staff. Our town has a population of well over 400 people." Gasps could be heard from the crowd. "Around 170 of those are children from ages zero to eighteen. Everyone has responsibilities, including those children.

"We have three schools, one for 0 to K, another for first through sixth, and the last one for seventh through graduation. At night, those classrooms are used for continued education, group counseling, and other group gatherings.

"There are, as you have learned, many occupations and buildings where the employees meet. We have dining areas that are much nicer than you had in the Hold. We have mini farms at the end of each tunnel where we grow small livestock and gardens."

A hand shot up. "Can I guess your question? You're wondering what tunnel this is." The hand went down, and the questioner nodded her head. "We are in the old Eisenhower Tunnel. Now, before you get nervous, I want to let you know it is NOT toxic. That false story has allowed us to secure the structure and make improvements. It is a continuing secret that will protect us from harm and allow us to grow and flourish without outside interference."

The crowd could be seen showing signs of agreement. "The airflow systems were updated with smaller, more efficient units. The smaller units allowed us to raise the ceiling, permitting us to build two-story-high structures to conserve space. We have our own power grid and water source. Each side of the tunnel was increased in size by 33 percent. And besides the small area between every other home, we have a nice park next to each school. Three corridors connect the tunnels for quick access to the other half of town.

"Our system of government will be explained in the next week or two by your temporary district representatives. The date and time will be announced next week.

"Please follow Noah Ransom," she pointed to a young man standing by a door on the opposite side of the room.

The second transport went through the same briefing with joyful excitement. The third transport arrived, and the frightened passengers were held in their seats. They anxiously looked to the Defenders for direction. If the departure plan had been followed, they wouldn't have arrived for another ten to fifteen minutes. Spacing out the three transports caused less suspicion and higher survivability, but the attack changed the schedule. The Defenders told them they would have to wait about fifteen minutes for the second group to clear out of the skyroom, but they were permitted to talk.

"What happened out there?" asked a person from several rows back.

"I think some people died in an attack," said another.

"Who?" a voice asked.

"I don't know who the two women were, but the Defender was Officer Gray," answered a voice near the back doors.

The woman thought about how she had just had a pleasant conversation with the sisters. They made plans to meet up when they were settled into their new home. She buried her head in her brother's shoulder. "I can't believe we left them," she cried. "What are we going to tell their friends?"

"We don't know anything yet," he murmured.

"I saw Ari. She was bleeding badly, and then Jilly fell. Neither of them moved."

It was about ten minutes later that they were led to the skyroom. Carolyn didn't do her usual walk around. She waved her hand for them to stop and listen. "Usually, I lead you to this room, and you ooh and ahh at the sky. Then I give an introduction to your new home, New Haven. But the heaviness of your journey needs to be discussed first. We do not have an update on the status of the three people left at the Hold. As you know, there was an attack. Protocol demanded that the transport leave and save as many people as possible. It may seem harsh, but your lives were in danger, and the knowledge you already have could have put hundreds at risk.

"Here's what I can tell you. The two women involved in the attack were from the Southwest section, and this group is from the two northern sections.

"On the other hand, none of the residents from that section know about their friends. They will be receiving a letter on their notebooks before long. I know there will be talk, and it will be hard not to share such an experience. But I ask you to be respectful and wait for a day to allow their friends to process this privately.

"Be especially careful not to say more than what is known. Guesses will only beget rumors. While most enjoy this day of happiness, these friends will be devastated. Resist being the person who is anxious to share shocking information, to avoid being the person who brings additional sorrow to a worried and grieving citizen."

Carolyn then gave her speech on the town to a very different crowd.

While the third group received their introduction, the second transport group was led through a corridor with several tables. As they passed, their old bands were removed, and they were issued removable communication and credit bands (CCbands). The thumbprints of everyone over eight were scanned to create their door access. They received a med scan, and their pictures were taken for their work badges.

There was a bit of a line for the transportation, which would bring them to their new homes. Everyone was so excited. One by one, electric carts drove up, towing trailers with two benches that faced outward. The transportation, which they called a bus, could accommodate eight citizens at a time. Other buses collected their gear to be delivered to them. Billie wished she could have shared the first look at their new homes with Jilly and Ari, but they would be together soon enough. As they came out of the corridor, they got their first look at the town.

All the buildings were two stories and tucked against the same wall. The area in front was used for small patios and traffic. Many people were already riding bikes and walking about. The first group had arrived at New Haven a month ago. Billie knew shipping containers were going to be used for housing. She thought a lot about her own dwelling, but she hadn't broadened her vision to the grand scale of a whole town. She imagined dull industrial boxes for homes and other buildings. She assumed it would be a minimalistic existence she would be blessed to have.

As they rode, the bright, clean look of the tunnel astonished Gabe, and Billie wondered about the lighting. *Would it be completely bright during the daytime and dark during the evening hours?* The combinations and arrangements of the containers were artistically diverse. Turning twenty-foot containers perpendicular to the sixteen-foot-wide main section produced an L-shaped structure. This offshoot provided a section for the stairs and utility areas while creating an inset porch at the entrance.

The outside walls maintained the ribbed structure and added texture, complementing the freshly painted color schemes. Tasteful combinations of neutral tans or greys were painted on one building and interrupted by rich brick and cream tones on the next. Some had two containers perpendicular, forming a nice little cove in between.

One house had an elegant, abstract object in one corner to accent the entrance. It was quite large and tall and would not have fit in the precious space of the issued packing crates, curious. Billie noticed other decorative pieces adorning the outsides of houses and occupation buildings as well. It made her curious if they were available.

Chapter Nine

"Jilly, Jilly," Gray's voice echoed in her mind, like a distorted, surreal dream.

"Jilly, come on, baby. Wake up." He shook her gently. Dr. Maya told him the tranquilizer and the residual chemicals from the earlier SS drug would make it harder for her to wake up, but she was not in danger.

She was trying to reach him, but the fog kept swirling about, consuming her, drowning her, drawing her downward. She felt herself falling. Suddenly, she was aware of being grabbed, and she fought to come to.

"Jilly!" Gray yelled. "Fight it, open your eyes! Look at me!"

Sluggishly, she moaned, and her eyes, scarcely visible, emerged. "Where are we? I remember, I think Ari was shot. Is she okay? Whoa, I'm having a déjà vu thing. I think I've said this before."

"There you are." He smiled, relieved at her return, but worried about what he had to tell her. "Ari is fine."

"How? She was bleeding all over the place. Was I shot too? My shoulder hurts."

"It wasn't real blood, and your wound is from a tranquilizer dart. We staged the whole thing to fake your deaths so—"

"WHAT? Why? Why would you do that?" She was awake now, and her anger was brewing into a full-fledged storm. "What made you think of that bright idea? What about our friends? Do they know?

What do they think?" Her anger snapped and thundered. "What is going on? Why weren't we even asked? Who do you—"

"Hang on, Jilly. Just hear me out. You had people searching all over for you and your sister. They want to get a hold of the formula your dad created. That's why you were attacked by that man on the street."

"Formula? What are you talking about? He was a history teacher at a high school, for God's sake! You are such a liar. I trusted you! I thought you cared about me. Was that a lie too? Get out!" Every time she let herself believe in happiness, she was struck down by violence.

"I will after I explain."

In the next room, Ari sat up facing Bannon. Though he had never met her, his inquiries about her indicated she would find small talk disrespectful at such a moment, so he went straight to the truth. He made a brief introduction and told her his dad knew her father, and that he was the trusted friend who managed their finances. Ari couldn't recall her father mentioning him.

Banner Vogel had been a well-known public figure and a prominent multibillionaire; she would have remembered. She decided to hear him out, one, because Gray seemed to trust him by the way they interacted before he left the room, and two, she didn't have a clue where she was, or where she would go if she fled.

"Your father and mine were close friends in college. They met as freshmen in a writing class. It was the only class they ever had together, but their personalities and taste in literature meshed. By the beginning of their senior year, they'd gone different directions and lost touch."

"About twenty years ago, my dad ran into him. Your dad was at a Vogel subsidiary as a consultant. Long story short, he was in trouble. He asked my dad for help to hide himself and his daughters. Your dad and mom were working on pollution reduction chemicals, and they succeeded. But they also created a way to increase the food supply. It's incredible.

He took a hydroxyl radical and made a hybrid formula that greatly accelerated the breakdown of methane, a major contributor to global warming. However, they discovered it had serious potential for destructive uses when they created the atmospheric delivery system.

"They were working on the atmospheric delivery system when your mother was kidnapped. She was able to give herself an SS drug, hoping she could escape and get the antidote, but she didn't make it. We'll never know exactly what they learned before she succumbed to the drug, but we have good reason to believe it wasn't significant. Soon, several more of your parents' colleagues were kidnapped and killed. Before they died, we believe they revealed the nature of the project, but they were not privy to any noteworthy details.

"My dad helped the three of you disappear. When my dad died, he left me a letter with your family's information. Included in that letter was the location of you two and your father's notebook. Your father left it with him because he trusted him and knew he had the resources to keep it safe as well as provide you protection. My father hoped one day to secure your father in a place where he could complete his work.

"Back then, numerous unsavory factions were looking for the daughters of the famous Dr. Connor, your father."

"My dad is not the Dr. Connor I've read about. He doesn't look anything like him. Wait, if you're saying that's not his name, then you're saying our names are not the ones we were given at birth?"

"You're right. They changed his look and name. And Delano, as well as your first names, are not your birth names. But you're not a Connor anymore, nor can you ever be. My dad created cover stories to remove all traces of Dr. Connor's identity, and he erased you too. It has worked for decades.

"This is all so fantastical and horribly awful. So, you're saying I never really knew my dad? Why should I believe you? I don't even know you." She sat considering this handsome man with his intense blue eyes boring through her. He had dark-as-night hair and silver streaks running through it like falling stars on a night sky. She was trying not to be distracted by his looks and concentrate on this bizarre story he said was her own.

"I wouldn't say that. I'm sure he was a good father. You just didn't know he was a brilliant chemist. And I don't know how to make you believe me, but I think you know he was more than cautious, even for the times. I think a part of you is having an aha moment."

Bannon looked at her with a scrutinizing gaze. He knew she was highly intelligent and well-spoken because he vetted them after reading the letter. He learned Ari was a self-starter who knew what she wanted and relentlessly worked her way toward it. But seeing her in person, he saw her character in action.

He was quickly becoming a fan. It also hadn't escaped him that she was absolutely stunning. Her thick brunette hair was unceremoniously pulled back into a ponytail, exposing her elegant bone structure. He followed the line as it curved down, passed her ears to a graceful chin. She licked her lips, and he found the move so intimate he had to turn away.

Bannon went back to the business of explaining. He shared the letter about them with Dana, his sister, and when the sanctuary plan was devised, it was agreed that they had to include them. His sister, disguising herself and going by the alias Elaine Fuller, had sought them out after she and Bannon had fully conceived their project. She had only met Jilly so far, but she fully expected an introduction to

Ari. When a facility picture was leaked to the net because the college closed, she worried about being recognized and decided to go home.

"I'm not sure why your dad's info suddenly resurfaced, or what exactly it is they know. But it became uncontainable, and dozens of deaths began piling up due to the hunters they ruthlessly blackmailed into looking for you. We had to defuse the situation."

"And you did that by…?"

"Faking your deaths."

"Oh, I see. So now I'm a fake dead person with a fake name! What will become of us now that we're dead?" she snapped with an emphasis on the last word.

"Well, here's the genius part of Gray's plan."

"Oh, I can't wait for the genius part, which has escaped me so far." She folded her arms in front of her and raised one eyebrow.

He'd have to add witty to her list of attributes, and he gave her a crooked grin. "First of all, the residents don't know any more than what we allowed the planted witnesses to see."

"Planted witnesses! You mean the sister and brother we met in line?" she asked. "How horrible for them. They must be shocked and heartbroken to have to tell our friends."

He tipped his head in agreement and gave an expression of regret. "They don't know we planted them. They only know that you were shot and lying on the ground. They also know Gray was there to defend you. There have been no more reports to definitively say how or where you are."

"A question I feel like asking you myself here soon."

"We leaked a building security video of a 'bungled abduction.' We showed a clear view of you and Jilly bleeding out on the asphalt. Then we made it look like we killed off Gray in a shootout. We made it appear as though hired Drangers were covering up their incompetence because the orders were to take you alive.

Then the Drangers, two of our Defenders, loaded your bodies in a broken-down transport and incinerated them."

"Wow, aren't we resilient?" She patted herself down. "Look, not even a mark!"

He couldn't help chuckling at her sarcasm. "We used real bodies, just not yours," he said, breaking the lighthearted moment."

"I'm afraid to ask where you got them, and just to let you know, accessing and throwing around dead bodies isn't helping with the whole trust thing here."

"One of them was a Defender whom we caught trying to locate you in the Hold. She died of a slow sunset drug she gave herself when she was trapped by Gray's team."

"When did that happen?" She was genuinely attentive now.

"It was at the Hold building you were in. She locked a kid in the storage room to distract everyone. The other body was of a resident in a different section who committed suicide. And the one for Gray was a Defender who died in a vehicle accident while on a recon mission near the Hold."

"Well, that's sad. Did any of them have families? That would be beyond sad."

"No, none of them did. The woman Defender thought they were detaining her dad, which is why she was willing to help them, but he was already dead. The suicide victim's husband was killed a week before transport day. And the pretend-Gray's family was killed in an all-too-common battle with Drangers when he was in his teens. Believe it or not, many Defenders were recruited from Corporate security people and even Drangers. They were trained and wanted honorable work."

"I'm not sure that's comforting, but it makes sense. Did you say people were killed because the hunters thought they were us? How could all this go on in front of us, without us having a clue? Why didn't Gray tell us we were in danger?" The full extent of his betrayal was setting in.

"Don't blame him. He's good at his job, and he follows orders. That's why you're alive. Hell, it's why we're all alive, and why only six people have an inkling about any of this. They are all well-trained to protect you."

"I guess." Ari was tangled up in feelings of gratitude and being manipulated.

"And most importantly, the existence of New Haven and all its residents are safe. At least, that's what the chatter on the net tells us. We've found coded messages recalling the rewards, and everything we've uncovered indicates the searches are off too."

"So, how long has it been since that day, and where are we? You said Jilly was here but still out. Is she awake yet? I want to see her."

"Jilly is awake and with Gray. Your "attack" was on Friday. Today is Saturday, and you both are at New Haven, in the isolated contagion wing of the hospital. I'll make sure you see her as soon as possible."

Bannon said he'd give her some time alone to process everything he had told her. She lay back down and let it all sink in. She worked out the dilemma in her head. "*I guess we made it, and I should be thankful. But what will life be like? How will we resurface from our deaths? What kind of rescue lie will we be forced to tell? What act will we have to perform to maintain the secrets Gray put into action? Granted, they were for our safety and the safety of others, but did it mean lying forever to the people we cared about? They must have questions and suspicions about why we keep getting attacked.*

"I'm sorry I couldn't tell you, Jilly. Surely you can see why." Gray sat in a chair by her bed, waiting for her reaction. She had been mostly silent while he gave her the whole secret story of her dad, mom, and their dad's connection to Vogel ENT. He explained the diverted attack at Alpha Site and the performance around leaving the Hold. She knew it all now. Even that he had secretly investigated her and kept her under surveillance. He looked at her. The silence sliced through him, but he knew she'd feel hurt before she reasoned it out, and that would take time.

She closed her eyes when he finished. She leaned on the tray positioned across the bed and covered her face in her hands. Her head was reeling, and she longed for a return to the depths of that foggy, drug-induced world, but she knew it couldn't help. Nothing could help. She felt deeply betrayed.

"Okay, Gray. I'm too overwhelmed right now to know what I think. I know you did your job. I don't fully understand why you couldn't trust me, but I get it. I do. As a citizen, I appreciate what you do and what you are obligated to do. But as your"—she stopped for a moment—"But as your friend, I have to admit, I'm hurt. I don't know how to be in that kind of...friendship. I think I need some time to myself. Maybe a lot of time."

"I understand. But if you ever want to talk with me, or just hang out with me, the answer is yes." He walked out of the room. He hadn't expected her to fly into his arms, but he also hadn't expected her to be so calm. He had no idea how to read her, and reading people was his specialty.

Word of Jilly and Ari's rescue came three days after the residents' arrival. The lie wasn't as hard as they thought. The story they were told to say was that they don't remember anything. They blacked out and woke up here. It was easy because it was true. What they had to hide was their knowledge of the deception. Gray told the residents the cover story in a letter on their notebooks. He was uninjured due to his protective gear. After neutralizing the Drangers, he carried the women back inside the Hold. A doctor and nurse were securing the last of the equipment and found what was needed to treat them in the infirmary. They were stabilized and moved to New Haven at dusk on the day after everyone else's departure. The citizens were satisfied with the story and happy that the women would be okay.

Before news of their rescue was released, Gray asked Maya to create lifelike wounds in case the story was questioned, which she centered around the bruises at their dart sites. They were moved to the non-contagious ward, where they shared a room. The next day, they were allowed visitors. Gray had not visited since he coached the women on the story. Jilly met Bannon, who visited several times.

Billie was the first to come and see them. She entered the room cautiously, not knowing what kind of shape she would find her friends. She was ecstatic to see them looking quite well and happy to see her. The sisters apologized for worrying her. And knowing the truth of the account, they prayed for forgiveness. Billie was overcome with emotion when she hugged Jilly. She remembered how her friend had been there for her and hoped to return the favor.

"The houses are nice, you guys. They are all two stories. The restroom, laundry, closet, and living area are on the bottom level, and the bedrooms are upstairs. It's furnished with a table and chairs, a couch, beds, dressers, nightstands, and"—she tucked her arms to her chest joyfully—"in the second room, there's a crib and dresser with a changing mat on top."

"Oh, that's awesome, Billie. Have you put the things you made for the baby's room out yet?" asked Jilly.

"Yes, and it looks so cute in there. Have you seen the town at all?" asked Billie.

"No, we haven't been out yet, but I hear we get to leave tomorrow."

"Hey, how about I get a couple of wheelchairs and wheel you to the window down the hall?"

Jilly was stumped. *Windows? Windows to where?* She thought.

The nurse helped them into the wheelchairs. It made them feel like liars since they didn't need assistance. Billie was so overjoyed to do this favor for them, and they played along. There was no way to see any of the neighboring buildings, only the wall on the other side, but Ari was astonished to see the traffic. Bicycles, skateboards, joggers—*wait, joggers? How could they jog at this elevation? Maybe they were at a lower elevation.*

She made a mental note to discuss this with Dr. Maya. People walked together, pushed strollers, pulled wagons, and the occasional cart and trailer, which they said was called a bus, would drive by. She saw a Defender walking a large black-and-tan dog. It was a menagerie from another time. She wished she could leave the hospital now. She was tired of this room and the lies that haunted it.

Their friends visited two at a time. When the sister and brother, whom they had just met at the transport, came, they apologized profusely for having any part in leaving them. The woman's lip began to tremble, and Jilly broke down with her. Their new friend's tears were about needless regret; Jilly's tears were about needed deceit.

The next morning, they were discharged. Before they left, Axle visited to make sure they were okay and to tell them all indications on the net showed the plan had worked. A nurse wanted to put them both in wheelchairs, but Dr. Maya said they could walk and gave them a wink. She knew they were tired of playing the incapacitated victims, and walking out would go a long way toward their friends letting it go too. The nurse took them to the elevator, and they both realized the hospital building was much larger than they had imagined possible.

Billie and Gabe secured a bus to take their friends to their new home. They were more than friends; they were family. Billie and Gabe fussed over them like they were fragile, causing the sisters to check their agitation. Jilly noticed the temperature on the street was slightly chilly, and she buttoned her sweater. She took a seat on the side facing the hospital that had been her home for almost five days. She looked for the window where she watched the parade of people pass by. Locating it made the experience real, and she wasn't sure that was her intent.

The hospital was a long, two-story building. It was painted a stylish slate blue and trimmed with the prettiest light mint green she had ever seen. It was fresh, new, and lovely. As aesthetically pleasing as it was, she had no desire to return, but she would. It was where her job would be.

She saw a sign labeled "East" pointing toward the right, away from the hospital. She barely caught a glimpse of the houses in that direction before they turned into a corridor leading onto another street. She had no idea that the town would be so large. She looked both ways and wasn't sure she was seeing the end. *How can this be? Are we in a tunnel?* She thought. Then it dawned on her; they were in the Poison Tunnel.

"Is this the Eisenhower?" she asked Billie with alarm.

"Yeah, but don't worry. It was never poisoned. That was a cover story."

"Oh." A cover story, she thought. *It sounds so much nicer than a lie, but man, how they are piling up.* Distracted by the conversation, she was surprised when the bus stopped, and all their friends were waving from a small yard.

"This is your house! Isn't it pretty? And we share a yard just like we hoped." Billie was bubbling over. Jilly smiled warmly at her and gave her a side hug. She felt lucky to have her as a friend. She eyed her house as she stepped off the bus and looked up at it. All the houses were two stories with a longer perpendicular addition on one end, but they differed in length and style. The L-shape bordered a small porch, leading to the front door, and was shadowed by a delightful little balcony. On the side of the house was a shared yard, with a sliding glass door that mirrored the neighbor's side. It was charming. The soft blue color was accented with bright white, and she longed to go in and be alone. Realizing the disrespect that would involve, she turned toward the yard and walked to greet her friends.

Delicate hugs and grand smiles melted her broken heart. She would do anything for these people. Just as that thought crossed her mind, she saw Gray. He was standing apart, watching her. When her eyes met his, he looked down. She crossed the short space between them.

"Hi, Gray. Thank you for coming."

"Yeah. How are you?"

"I'm okay. I'm..." She couldn't think of an adjective to clearly describe what she felt. "How are you?"

"Been busy, lots of newbies to get settled." He instantly regretted his attempt at humor and was frustrated by all the awkwardness. It used to be so effortless to talk with her. "Look, Jilly, I just wanted to wish you well. If there's anything you need, feel free to call."

"Thanks." She meant it.

"So, I'll see you around, maybe. Bye."

She watched him go, his last words lingering in her head. It sounded so final, and she didn't know how she felt about that. Ari had opened the door, and everyone was heading inside. Jilly watched Gray walk down the street until he turned out of sight.

She stepped through the front door of her home to a noisy, cheerful crowd. The house was not intended to hold such a gathering, but she felt blessed to rub past her dear friends. The floors were a wood-like laminate, with a whitewashed grey color being subtle and striking at the same time. The walls were off white with dark grey trim edging the floor. A small white table with four matching chairs sat near the front window, and Jilly imagined sitting there and watching the town go by. The two large, open crates containing their possessions from so long ago crowded a slate blue couch, and two lounge chairs were parked against the back wall. It seemed to beckon her to come, snuggle up, and get lost in someone else's story. Haphazardly moved out of harmony were three side tables awaiting a return to their mirrored positions on either side of the sofa and between the comfy chairs.

As warned, there was no kitchen, but there was a long counter on the back wall with a water cooler. Also on the bottom floor was a reasonably sized bathroom with a compost toilet, shower, counter with an oval sink, a laundry room with a table, and a stacked washer and dryer. The shower and sink would provide plenty of water for all their needs. The two bedrooms were upstairs. They were equally sized and decorated with a queen-sized bed, a nightstand, a desk, and a reading light hung over the headboard.

The bedding in the first had a subtle design dominated by a dusty lavender hue with dark grey piping around the border. The other room's bedding had a white and navy design. Ari's tote sat on the bed. The crowd started to disperse, calling out "see-you-later," "welcome-home," and "message-me-soon" as they left. Jilly and Ari were alone. Ari came over to her sister and gave her a tight bear hug and twisted her back and forth. They both laughed at the irony of her roughness.

"How are you doing, Jilly? You haven't been the same since the whole debacle."

"I feel like"—she was tired of not being able to think and talk—"like we're being terrible friends."

"You have to realize that these people *are* our friends, and that means they would be much sadder if we, heaven forbid, had really been hurt. This 'lie' you are so worried about is what Gray and Bannon had to do for us all to survive. Survival is not a sin," she mocked the speaker from what seemed like ages ago. They both laughed, but then Jilly became solemn again.

"Maybe it is. Maybe we can move that line to fit our desires. Desires that bind us to a result of avoiding loss and failure at all costs. We can't see it when we are faced with the hard reality of it. We lose sight of what goodness is, what evil is, and we surrender to it."

Ari hugged her sister. Although she could be impulsive at times, her heart was profoundly kind and thoughtful. They complemented each other. Jilly's idealistic side softened Ari's pragmatic side, and the balance was golden.

"So which bedroom do you want?" Jilly asked Ari.

"The one my tote's on," she sassed in a big sister tone.

They laughed again and went about the task of unpacking their clothes from the crate.

Chapter Ten

Haru sat in his office, looking at the counseling schedule before him. Then he went over the sermon he was to deliver at the southwest dining hall. He was the only full-time psychologist and minister, but there were three other nondenominational ministers. They each gave one sermon a week, three days a week they were assigned to a school, and one night a week they led group sessions. He pondered the complex task of guiding his flock through this new phase. Everyone seemed to be in joy-hell, as he called it. They were so happy to leave behind the danger that they ceased to deal with the hard work of recovery and adjustment.

People made snap decisions and fell in and out of love too fast, and the more blessings they enjoyed, the more they neglected their relationship with God. Due to the violent times, the practice of arranged marriages had come back on the outside, but it had no place here. They had been guarded for so long that they forgot what it was to build a friendship before they became a lover or a spouse.

He planned to discuss these issues in his next sermon, but getting people to come early in the morning and listen in a dining hall with chatting residents was proving difficult. He was running out of patience for the church he was promised, but he also knew the maintenance team was understaffed and over-obligated. Not only was their schedule fraught with unforeseen issues, they had also suffered an unprecedented number of deaths within their workforce. Three died before transport day, and one to a virus in the Hold.

Gray was working on getting the student work program up and running, but like many plans, delays had impacted desired outcomes. Haru thought to himself *It's incredible what has already been accomplished. I can't complain.* The residents were enjoying the fellowship, even though it was held outside a church. He loved that they were feeling contentment. They deserved it, but he believed that happiness would be short-lived if the pace wasn't tempered with wisdom and faith. It's appropriate to savor the experience of safety and fellowship, but if they forget life before New Haven, complacency will eat away at the safety and the joy.

After the sisters returned from breakfast, their young neighbor, Connor, came running up to their front door. His sense of urgency made the sisters worry that something was wrong. He was very excited, but they quickly saw he was happy, not upset.

"Slow down, Connor. I can barely understand you," said Ari.

"I get my dog! She's nice and fun, and I miss her so bad." He paused briefly to add the more difficult part. "But my mom and dad say if you don't want a dog around, I don't get her. Please don't say no!"

They smiled at each other and invited him in. "Okay, Connor. Tell us about your dog." Jilly offered him a seat at the table.

"Her name is Libby, and she's a girl, and she's a terrier. She's small, only this high." He held his hand about a foot and a half off the floor. "She's over a year, but not two. I found her. She was hungry and had a hurt paw. I took care of her in secret. When the Defenders came, I asked them to take her. And I said please a thousand times. And they took her. But I didn't know if I would see her again."

"Wow, that's quite a story. Do you have her now?"

"No, I haven't even seen her. But Officer Grayson said he'd bring her if my parents and neighbors said okay."

Ari didn't want to appear too soft on Connor, knowing the responsibility would be his. "So, will you take good care of her? Clean up after her? Where will you get dog food?"

"Don't worry, I'll clean up after her and keep her from barking and not let her in your yard. And I can get food for her from the kitchen when I go to eat. That's what they told me."

Ari looked at Jilly, and they grinned at each other. "There's only one more question." Ari paused for several seconds while Connor waited with pleading eyes. "Can we walk her with you sometimes?"

"Yes, whenever you want!"

"Well, I guess we are getting a dog for a neighbor."

Connor jumped up and hugged them. "Thank you, thank you!"

He ran out the door, and Jilly yelled, "Bring Libby by when you get her."

Ari smiled. She started to wonder about other pets in town. If there were too many, they could end up with a critter problem. Did that mean there were veterinary services? They probably would be taken care of at one of the mini ranches. This certainly was an involved and complex facility. Jilly went to the couch and stared out at the yard without registering what she was looking at.

"Are you thinking about Gray bringing that puppy around?"

"No, and yes. I can't lie and say I don't care for him, but I can't live in his world. I have too many painful examples of what that world entails."

"You can't blame him for Dad's involvement in dangerous secrets. All he did was protect us from that situation. He didn't create it."

"I know, but there is always that kind of situation in his world. He's full-on in the mucky thick of it, and I need a break. I want to settle into this town and shut off all the horrible things happening beyond this little sanctuary. I want my biggest problems to involve things like allowing the neighbor boy to have a dog. I want peace."

"I wish you luck with that, sweetie. No place can remain that isolated. The world will find a way to locate the gaps and seep in. But for now, I think you do need some recovery time." She put her arm around her and let Jilly's head fall on her shoulder.

An hour later, Ari went out, and Jilly was going through the rest of the crate. The thought of not having a kitchen disappointed her at first, but after living in the Hold, she loved the idea. No dishes, no storing food, no bugs (or worse), and the space and time it saved was brilliant.

She hummed as she put her clothes away in a closet she did not have to share. She had already put the projects she and Ari made about the home. The flowers sat on the table, the rag rug was in front of the shower, the rag blanket hung over the couch, and the welcome sign was hung on a hook outside, next to the front door.

She found the decoration box and slit it open. She put the precious few trinkets that had belonged to their mom on the bathroom counter and nightstands. Ari had packed the small, framed picture of Arthur D. Little, a founding father of chemical engineering principles. Jilly had always thought her father had that because Ari wanted to be an engineer, but she knew differently now. She put that in Ari's room.

While packing, Jilly found only two pictures of herself and Ari. One included a picture of a man, who she now assumed was her dad before his appearance was altered, their mom, Ari, and herself from about twenty years ago. Jilly found it hidden in her dad's desk when she was packing. She only found it because she felt a piece of paper sticking out of the back, so she removed the drawer to retrieve it.

It was torn, and creases veined across it. He looked different, younger and happier. Her mother was unknown to her. In fact, she strained to remember ever seeing another picture of her. She knew that Ari had loaded it onto their laptop and had it printed off at the college. She meant to give it to her dad as a present, but he died before Winter Solstice Day.

Jilly thought she lost it, but she found it stuffed in the back of the linen closet. They hadn't used the extra linens because they didn't have beds; they slept on cots. They only kept them as possible sewing options. Jilly snuck it into the crate, and now, it would be a perfect gift for Ari. She looked around and realized everything about their past had new meaning now. Then she tucked it away in her closet.

She got some water and went to sit on the balcony while watching the town go by. She saw Billie coming over and leaned over to greet her. She went down, and they sat on the step and talked with easy dialogue and banter. Both laughed about Connor's enthusiasm and hoped this dog thing wouldn't be a problem.

"I came over to tell you to get ready. We're taking the town tour in an hour. Where's Ari?"

"I'm not sure. She just said she'd be back before dinner. But I'd love to take a tour. I haven't been past our dining area."

"Okay, come out when the bus shows up." Billie beamed a smile at Jilly and went into her house. She was ending her first trimester, and her sunny mood had returned.

Two other people were waiting on the bus for the tour along with Gabe. She could see they were heading east, which excited her because she had not gone that way yet. Billie asked her again if she was up to the tour since she had only been released from the hospital yesterday. Jilly assured her she was dying to get out, and this was just what she needed to feel better.

She remembered the corridor being close to her housing group as they approached it. The first new place was a medium-sized building painted the same colors as the hospital, called the Rapid Aid Station, or RAS, which also housed the dentist's office. It handled first-aid issues and, if necessary, would make referrals to the hospital. It kept the hospital space free of minor issues. Jilly rolled her eyes at the number of acronyms she had to remember.

The tour guide's name was Dewy Quince. Jilly wasn't sure if it was his real name because of something Gray had said, but she liked his rich Southern accent. Next was the recreation room, which was opening in a week. Dewy listed events and games found inside. Jilly had never played ping pong, pool, or many of the other games he mentioned, and she made a mental note to check it out.

They came to a sizeable brick-red building with off-white trim and sporting a large sign that read "New Haven Town Hall." This was where the legislative, judicial, and executive branches worked.

"Do we elect these people?" asked Gabe.

"Yeah, most of them anyway. Some 'er assigned by the people y'all elect. In fact, there's a meetin' comin' up. It'll 'splain everthin'," answered Dewy.

Jilly enjoyed his take on the language and thought she could listen to him all day long. He was handsome, though slightly unkempt. His sandy blonde hair had not seen a comb that morning, of that, she was sure. His unshaven face wasn't thick enough to be left on purpose—she hoped, anyway. Of course, his Defender uniform was neat and spotless. Gray ran a tight ship. Though he answered each question with a colorful flair, he gave smart, quick, and clear answers.

They passed more houses, and he told them they were in blocks of eight with varying sizes. They came to the daycare with a little toddler playground in a fenced area. Billie and she looked at each other and smiled with giddy gestures. Jilly was stunned at the rest of the park next door. It had grass and a couple of trees, which must be artificial. There were swings, slides, and other things sized for preschool children. Benches lined the back edge, a three-foot fence ran the perimeter, while the front section was kept as pavement for traffic.

"This place is amazing!" Billie exclaimed, and Jilly nodded in agreement.

They continued and saw another kitchen and dining hall, followed by a storage building. Jilly saw the "Maintenance" sign on a sky-blue building with black-and-white trim. The bottom section was walled completely off with large windows above, so they could see the rows of plants with a little stream.

"That must be the water source for the garden," suggested Gabe.

"That an' the fishin' river that I ain't gonna get to fish in," answered Dewy. He went on to explain the hydroponic system. The fish swam in an artificial current in an oval-pattered stream around the whole farm. Their waste was filtered through various sizes of gravel and filters in levels at the bottom. The fertilized water fed the plants, while freshwater was fed into the stream. They went through the corridor to the northeast end of the tunnel and saw a mirror image of the southwest farm with different species of fish.

"This place is an absolute feat of engineering," Jilly proclaimed with evident admiration.

Suddenly, Gabe spoke out excitedly, "Sweet heaven above, tell me I'm not dreaming. Does that say, 'Bar coming soon'?"

Dewy laughed out loud. "Yeah, but it ain't quite open yet. Now that ever'one is here, I 'spect they'll get on that. Hope so anyway."

They passed security, and Jilly looked up, wondering if Gray was up there, but Billie was checking out the two-story building labeled

Museum. "That's not open either," added Dewy. "We're still sortin' stuff like that out. While we were waiting on you guys, we were movin' stuff into buildings, 'round the town, and settin' up the farms and mini ranches. We're just now gettin' goin' in our jobs."

He explained there were plans in the future for a church and a movie room. More houses preceded the food storage, dining hall, and kitchen. Each dining hall was decorated differently with plants and attractive centerpieces on various-sized tables. Gone were the picnic benches from the Hold mess halls. Residents were assigned a dining hall, but they could go to different ones as long as they signed up in advance. There was a menu for the month posted on the wall and sent to the tablets. All the dining halls followed the same menu, but it would be nice to go to dinner with friends and have a change of scenery.

The next park was twice the size of the first. It was simply a plain, open field with sports equipment stored in a fenced area. As they passed the largest school for seventh grade through graduate school, Dewy explained the schools would open next week and begin practicing for team sports. During practice and future games, this part of the street would be blocked off, and traffic would be detoured to the corridors.

"Nice! Do they need coaches?"

"Yeah, all that will be worked out at the meetin', I'm told."

"Why so many grades in this school? Why not put seventh in the grade school?" asked Jilly.

"Well, as I heard it, the juniors and seniors only are at school half a day. They spend the other half at jobs they're training fer. They switch classes fer different subjects, and they have two lunch schedules, so there's 'nuff room."

A familiar building dominated the next several sections. Dewy described the modern facility that could rival any top-notch hospital around. "The good thang 'bout this one is it's not just for the uppy-ups. It's for the whole town."

The gym, which was only partially open, and the physical therapy section were in an oversized building, wisely positioned next to the hospital. More housing and dining went by before they arrived at waste management. Everyone expected to smell something unpleasant, but it never occurred. It was a high-security building because of the combustible dangers and the science they used. Jilly wondered if any of her dad's work was being incorporated.

They reached the west end. Another walled-off area with windows displayed the chicken and rabbit ranch. They split the space lengthwise with a wire fence between the two species. The animals roamed around, pecking and thumping at each other through the fence line. The ranch on the southwest side had goats. When they got to the engineering building, they wanted to walk the rest of the way. Dewy waved and drove off with the last two passengers.

"Hey, since we're going to lunch, want me to ask Gray if he can join us?" Gabe was baiting Jilly, and Billie jabbed his ribs lightly.

"I imagine he's been really busy trying to get this town up and running at full speed. You saw on the tour how many things are still not ready. Like the bar, Gabe," Jilly teased back.

Gabe, Billie, and Jilly walked the short distance and passed more housing to get to their dining hall. They collected their meals, discussed the tour at length, and talked about visiting some of the sites.

Jilly looked out at the traffic. When she noticed the bicycles, she suddenly remembered, "Hey, where are our bikes?"

"They didn't show?" asked Gabe.

"No," she looked at Gabe. "What do I do?"

"You have to make out a report at security." Gabe watched for her reaction.

Jilly hesitated; surely Gray wouldn't do that to get her to show up, would he? *No,* she thought, *that's not his style.*

Gabe could see she was puzzling over the dilemma when Billie offered, "Don't worry, Gabe will do it for you. Won't you, Gabe?" She was kicking him under the table.

"Sure, Jilly, I'll handle it."

Back in their home, Billie stood looking at Gabe with her hands on her hips. "Why must you torment her?"

"What?" he answered, feigning innocence. Billie's eyes shot sparks of fury.

Gabe looked at her. "Whoa, reel it back, girl. I know I'm poking the bear, but they're both moping around acting so sanctimonious with their 'It's the right thing to do' and 'It wouldn't have worked out'"—he was imitating them in a whiny voice—"I can't stand it. If Jilly were a man, they'd shove each other, throw a few punches, and it would work itself out."

"If Jilly were a man! Seriously? That's a solution? I'm not even going to give you the satisfaction of a response."

"Being in security, I've already reported in. I'm here to tell you, Gray is throwing his bad mood all over the place. All this dancing around and avoiding each other is driving everyone crazy. Just to be fair, we're kind of working him too. I figure he's going to reach a boiling point soon."

"Jesus, Gabe. I hope you know what you're doing. I am going to be pretty pissed if you get fired. That's all I'm going to say."

Jilly was sitting in the yard on a folding chair from the Hold. The temperature felt nice in a thin long-sleeved T-shirt, and she was enjoying being outdoors—well, the new outdoors. Bannon dropped Ari off. He called from the cart that they should have a picnic dinner. Jilly gave him a thumbs up, and the time was set for 6:00. Ari shared with Jilly that Bannon gave her a tour of the town personally. Jilly gave her a sly smile, and Ari tried to hide her own. He came by at six, with three other people in the cart.

"Jilly, this is my sister, Dana, and her husband, Indy Tunner. You probably remember them as Ms. Fuller and Mr. No Name from the initial gathering at Summerhill."

Jilly smiled and shook their hands.

"And this is my daughter, Ellie," Bannon added.

"Hi, Ellie, how old are you?" asked Jilly.

"I'll be six on my birthday," she said shyly.

"When's your birthday?" she asked, looking at Ellie but glancing up at Bannon for an answer.

"She'll be six this coming Friday," he answered.

"Sounds like a party," Ari responded.

They all walked over to the dining hall. The menu was hamburgers, French fries, and a vanilla milkshake. They spread out the blanket at the elementary park. They compared notes from their tours that day. Children were playing on the swings, balance beam, rope climb, and other equipment for older children. Jilly wondered how long it would take before she saw broken arms and other typical childhood traumas. *How fortunate they were to grow up like this. Playing in a yard without worrying about Drangers, disease, and all the other evils we left out there, just gravity.*

As they sat outside, Jilly noticed the lights were becoming dimmer. Bannon explained they set three different kinds of lights on the ceiling, and two more kinds on the walls pointed upward. All had dimming capabilities. Amber and rose lights created an apricot glow for twilight and early morning. The violet and rose lights were for evening and night. Medium lights came on midmorning, and then the sun lights were on for four hours in the middle of the day. They were programmed to dim slowly and blend to imitate a natural day.

"Is there anything you didn't think of?" Jilly was stunned by the attention to detail.

"I'm not sure how to answer that, but if you come up with something, let me know," teased Bannon, and they all laughed. It was just after 7:00 p.m., so Dana and Indy said their goodbyes and offered to take Ellie home and put her to bed.

Jilly wanted to walk in the soft evening light, so she would see herself home. She noticed a beautiful peach glow coming from behind the buildings. It gave the appearance of the sun setting. The late nighttime setting dimmed the glow lights, as they were called, to simulate a streetlight. Jilly decided to wake up early to see the "sunrise" show.

"Just beautiful," she whispered to herself. Her appreciation of the details made her wonder how many people were involved in this design. What had allowed Bannon and Dana to offer this amazing gift to so many?

Now that Ellie was off with her aunt and uncle, Bannon looked at Ari. "I have one more place I'd like to show you. I know that sounds like a line, but it's absolutely beautiful."

"Lead the way," she replied. "Bannon, your daughter is beautiful and sweet."

"She was my inspiration for this, for everything. Gevia, her mother, had wanted a baby so badly, but I didn't think it was a good time, with the worldwide mess and all. She stopped her pregnancy blockers and voilà, we conceived."

"Weren't you mad?"

"Yes and no. There are things you forgive one person, so it won't betray another. Ellie is my whole reason for fighting on."

"What happened to her mother?"

"She was killed along with my parents. Ellie was just four years old. I had lost my whole family except Ellie and Dana."

"So many people bear that pain these days. I was about her age when my mom died. Though I still feel the loss, I barely knew her, but I was devastated when my dad died."

"Dana and I sat up one night about a month after that happened, and we conceived this idea."

Ari knew they had only met a week ago, and initially, it had been a rough introduction. His soft expression warmed her, and her trust in him was growing. She was not trusting by nature, but he demonstrated his trustworthiness and love by saving all these people. He rescued fairness and compassion from ruthlessness and gave them a place to flourish. It changed her opinion of him from disdain to passion.

He led her to the skyroom. She had never been to the briefing, so he knew it would impress her. Stargazing was difficult in the cities because it was risky to go out at night. In the Hold, they weren't allowed outside at all. She looked at the empty round room. "It's nice."

He laughed. "Close your eyes." He opened the skyguard. She heard the mechanism humming. "Okay, you can open them."

She looked up at the view of the sky. "Oh, Bannon. Oh my, it's incredible."

With every word and every expression, he was more spellbound. He wanted to be respectful and take it slow, but if he didn't kiss this woman soon, he'd go crazy. "Would you care to dance?" He held out his arms.

"There's no music." She shyly turned away.

"I disagree. I hear a whole symphony under the stars. And my heart is beating like a drum."

She turned to him, put her hand on his chest, and looked up at him. It was the moment he had waited for. He kissed her gently at first, but her response was eager, and he felt fire light up his insides. She knew a kiss was imminent, and it excited her. She was so attracted to him, both his body and his spirit, but she needed to slow it down. She struggled to regain her resolve. His lips were hot and moist from the kiss. She felt her relentless desire rising. Her sensual side, her primal side, had her spinning. He was the first to break the bond. She stood there still looking up at him, hazy-eyed and lips lightly parted as if they were still linked.

"Definitely music. I wanted to take more time to get to know you, and you me. I guess I got swept away by the 'melody'." He used air quotes to frame the comparison.

"It was a beautiful aria. And just to be fair, you did not go there alone. Slowing the pace seems smart, but I don't want to be a 'wallflower' either." She mimicked his air quotes with her own.

He smiled and brushed a kiss on her cheek. "Don't worry, I see many musical metaphors in our future."

He secured the skyroom and walked her home.

Chapter Eleven

Jilly set her alarm to get up and see the "sunrise" lights. She found the schedule for that and other information about New Haven in a file downloaded to her notebook. She was dressed in slacks and an oversized sweatshirt that belonged to her dad. She expected to see the same scene on the same side as last night, but was enthralled to see it on the other side.

The morning glow lights were shining from the floor behind a short rail on the street side of the tunnel. Jilly assumed the rail was to prevent bikes, carts, and other things that could scuff up the wall, but it also made for a nice sunrise.

"Hey you, trouble sleeping?" Ari came out the door and sat down on the porch step by Jilly.

"Morning Ari. No, I set my alarm to see the sunrise. This place is unbelievable. Just when I think I've seen all its wonders, there's more. I thought living underground would be a sacrifice, and I would feel trapped. Not only is it huge, but it's also beautiful and more real than out there. Did you know we have seasons and weather?"

"What? How?" Ari asked.

"Well, evidently, when it's winter outside, we have summer inside here. The reason is that the tunnel air shafts, which are usually completely open, react to low temperatures outside. They begin to slowly open and close continuously, so they won't freeze up at subzero temperatures. It naturally heats up, and we get warmer days."

"Wow! Not too warm, I hope."

"No, it stays in the sixties at night and reaches up to eighty during the day," said Jilly. "We also have rain at night to keep the dust and grim down. The tunnel naturally seeps water, so it's stored, slightly filtered, and when it reaches a certain level, the ceiling sprinklers spray it out. It would be fun to walk in the rain one night."

"Yeah, we could do that. Well, I learned that because of our high-volume scrubbers, the air pressure and oxygen level in here are high enough to simulate a lower elevation," added Ari.

"I wondered about that when we looked out the hospital window and saw joggers. I meant to ask Dr. Maya, but I forgot."

"This place is a Shangri-La."

"Yeah, it really is. I hope it doesn't end," Jilly said with a touch of melancholy.

"Remember that saying of Mom's that Dad used to say? Don't borrow tomorrow's troubles. It ruins today's blessings."

Jilly nodded. She had heard the saying from her dad, but she had very little memory of her mom. "Sooo Ari, tell me about you and Bannon," Jilly teased.

"I like him, at least what I know of him. We kissed last night under the stars."

"What stars?"

"We went through the corridor between the mini ranches. Up a couple of flights of stairs, there's a round chamber called the sky-room, and the whole ceiling is made of transparent panels. It was intoxicating."

"See what I mean! There's always more. Sounds nice, Ari. I hope I get to go there."

"We agreed to go at a more sensible pace, but I just don't know how to slow down my emotions. They're like a freight train raging down the rails."

Jilly smiled at Ari. "Sounds like a pleasant problem to have."

They sat on their porch step, and a bus drove up with their bikes. The Defender explained the news of their attack at the Hold, and they had put a hold on their delivery and sent them to storage. It was Sunday and the last day off before their workdays began, so they got ready for a ride on the town loop.

Soon after they took off, people began to emerge from their homes. Smiles and waves were abundant, and Ari wondered if she would ever tire of them. They hadn't gone far when they came to the park near the daycare. Ari noticed a woman with two small children playing with squeals of laughter.

Ari and Jilly both smiled and rode on. They peddled past the buildings and houses, noticing the unique designs and styles. Wanting a better look at the fish stream, they peered through the window at the farms. Standing next to the window, she saw trout swaying through the clear water. The farmer was slowly pouring out their morning meal.

They rode to the gym and tried to go inside, but it was the Defenders' workout time and not open to the public for another hour. She had been envious of the first group having more time here, but with so many places closed, she didn't feel like she had missed the novelty and excitement of being there when they opened.

When they got to the mini ranch, they stopped to see the rabbits and chickens greet each other at the fence, though not always nicely. The bunnies and chicks were darling. They liked the goats and watched as the kids leaped and butted each other. They both knew the purpose of the ranches, but they were not conflicted by it. They reached the east end of the tunnel and passed the security building. Dewy was just coming out.

"Well, ladies, nice day fer a bike ride."

Jilly smiled. "Yeah, I could get used to this."

"Would ya'll like to meet me fer lunch later?"

"Sorry, I've got something planned," answered Ari.

"Well, Jilly, whaddya say?"

"Sure, okay. What hall?"

"We'll go to yours. I can sign up at work. See ya then."

Gray watched Dewy sitting at the table with Jilly. He didn't want her to be sad or sulk alone in her house over him, but it would have been validating. Everywhere he turned, he saw her, heard about her, thought of her, and dreamed of her. This town suddenly seemed very tiny, and he knew it would not allow him to avoid her. She'd moved on, and he had to find a way to do the same. Axle and Hannah walked up behind him.

"Gray, we need to discuss something in the conference room."

Jilly read the reader board on the wall of the dining hall, displaying a message about the evening town meeting. "It says, 'everyone attending will receive two credits.' Dewy, are these credits like the ones on the outside? Are there things to buy?"

"I ain't positive, but I think so. It's like, you can do exter stuff round town, or sumthin' like that. Maybe there will be stuff to buy later."

"Is it like barter chips between Dailys?"

"Yeah, maybe, not sure though. I kinda overheard sumthin' 'bout it but not enuff to know."

Jilly enjoyed Dewy's company and hoped they continued to spend time together, but he wasn't enough of a distraction to mend her heart or extinguish the lingering embers of Gray. When Jilly got home, Ari was playing with Ellie while Bannon attended a meeting.

Bannon came in, and Gray closed the briefing room door, while Hannah distributed a notebook to each. Three were briefing tablets that received temporary information sent from a high-security notebook. Gray held his right hand on the screen, opened the device, and sent a file to each member.

Gray began, "Another poison ring was found three days ago. Disturbingly, it was found within the boundaries of New Haven. It took time for us to get it because it sat on the waste management director's desk. He brought it to the lost and found this morning. Hannah and Axle have done all the work on this. I'll let them give you the facts."

Hannah stood next to the New Haven map with a pointer. "It was found in the recycle bin from the north side of the tunnel with the metal detector. All decomposable items collected in the compost toilets go directly to the waste management plant, but the recyclable trash stays in the same bins until it can be sorted. Since residents' trash doesn't contain decomposable items, it can sit for a couple of days. It was from the week before the last group arrived, and though we know definitively the bin is assigned to the northeast, anyone could have added something," Hannah paused before continuing.

"Which is why we can't determine if the perpetrator lived in the northeast area. The first residents were sent all over the place to set up the buildings, and bins were set out to collect packing materials. We checked the cameras, but there is no way to visually identify something that small being disposed of. So, it's possible he, or she, could have lived in the southeast section. However, with this information, we can start by focusing on the first resident group to arrive."

"Good work, Hannah. Ax, what do you have from off-site?"

"On your tablet is a picture of the ring. As you can see, it is a small silver band with tiny pink glass stones encircling a larger clear stone, also made of glass. Although it isn't a punch ring, it does belong to the poison ring family. We discovered faint remnants of a poison that was stored in a tiny pit under the large stone. A bead of poison is snapped in the pit, and as it heats up, it is absorbed through the skin. This poison starts by causing breathing difficulties and flu-like symptoms, and as it progresses, it shuts down organs.

"There was a viral outbreak at the Beta Hold building, and we lost three people, and many others were ill. I checked, and although two were women, none of them died from poison. It was positively identified as a virus. None of them had a ring, but they could have left it with someone before going to the infirmary. The poison degrades after a few weeks, so there'd be no danger from wearing it after that."

"How do you know it was that kind of poison if it degraded?" asked Bannon.

"Dr. Maya could answer that better, but basically, the way it degrades is unique to that chemical. Another problem is that, given enough time, the bead could have degraded without even being worn. There may be no victim at all, but these rings are illegal, so it's still a crime."

"I appreciate the quick research. We'll have to look into those deaths and illnesses, but the question is, do we have any reason to believe it has anything to do with Jilly and Ari?"

"Hard to say," answered Axle. "There are a lot of possible scenarios, but one thing is clear. We have a security breach. I agree the organization of a breach from a conspiracy is worse, but a murderer, that's not the kind of citizen we want around."

"Okay, good info. I'll alert you to our next meeting. Until then, this is top secret. Ax talk to the waste—"

"Yeah, I already did, but he wasn't sure what worker found it. It was left on his desk with a 'to L&F' note. If anyone asks, he said he'll report them to us."

"Okay, on to the outside world," Gray continued. "I have news that the toxbombs have left so many dead bodies lying about that we have a serious disease situation brewing. We should be fine in here, but desperation will bring wanderers. A breach could infect us all. I'm bumping up the out-sites' alert status. Monitoring needs to be a high-priority task. We need to shore up our night duty; it's not homework time. Call me if anything rattles around out there. We're watching animals for illness too. Anything else?"

Everyone looked at each other, but there was no response. Gray cleared all info from the temp tablets and left the room to secure the HS notebook.

Hannah and Axle waited until Gray walked by. "Is it set up?" asked Hannah.

"Yeah, Dewy's going to ask Jilly to sit with him at the town meeting. Gray has been avoiding her, but I bet you, she's back on surveillance, and he's turned on her band."

"What about Ari?" Hannah knew she was enjoying this covert operation more than she ought to, and she was often caught chuckling to herself just thinking about it. *Nothing compares to a little mischief for building bonds and tell-over stories between comrades,* she thought.

"My guess is with all the time she and Bannon are spending together, he's probably watching her," Axle added.

"What about the skyroom? Dewy said she talked about Ari going there."

"You don't think she's got a thing for Dewy, do you?"

"He says no. She slips up, talks about Gray, and gets moody and blue. He can tell she's still pining."

"And she talked to him about seeing the stars in the skyroom! God, she's so naïve, that's a super signal. If you said that to me... You should say that to me," Axle teased Hannah with a sly grin.

She rolled her eyes and gave him a shove. They were as close as two people could be. They had been tight friends through their traumatic childhoods. When Axle went to live with Gray, she lived just a few doors away. They knew each other's secrets, past horrors, and had shared numerous mischievous adventures. They were inseparable, but they both knew the impossibility of a romantic scenario.

"Okay," said Haru. "It's good to be talking with you again. We have a lot to get to, so open the file on your notebooks called 'Town Meeting No. 1.' The video file you see in the bottom right corner explains our constitution and laws. It is mandatory that all citizens above the age of seventeen read and handprint the citizenship agreement.

All students seventeen and older will receive their own tablets tomorrow morning at school. This needs to be accomplished before next Sunday. If you don't get it done, the Defenders will help you find time to complete it. You will not be awarded citizenship until it is completed. And more importantly, you won't be allowed to get any credits until it is received by security."

"We will be electing one senator per tunnel, and one rep per quarter section. There are two main tunnels divided by three middle corridors. They include the southwest, the southeast, the northwest, and the northeast. There are also three corridors. The west, the middle, and the east. If you want to run, you can apply at the security building. Work up a speech, and it will be loaded on the server for your section to watch."

"No promises that break the Constitutional laws will be allowed. Representative candidates may post two signs in the dining hall and one on the food storage buildings in their quarter section. Senatorial candidates may post one in each of the previously mentioned places in their half of the tunnel.

"Debates will be held five days before election day for the primary winners. You may recruit people from your section to make those signs in an up-and-coming craft class. No exchange of goods or credits will be allowed to advance a campaign. A primary will be held, if necessary, to find the top two contenders for each of the positions. Only registered citizens may vote.

"Lastly, we need names for places in our town. All entries must explain a justification for your choice. You may submit name suggestions using this form," he said while holding up the form.

"We will be having Monday meetings until we have taken care of naming places and electing officials for our town."

"When will the bar be opened?" yelled someone from the crowd.

"Wow, I expected that question before I finished. I am impressed with your patience."

Everyone laughed.

"It will have a grand opening the Friday after election day, which is just under four weeks from today. I would like to introduce you to the designers and benefactors of our town, Dana and Bannon Vogel."

People stood up and clapped enthusiastically. Dana and Bannon stood. As Dana sat back down, Bannon walked to the front of the crowd.

"Thank you, thank you very much. I don't want to take too much of your time, but I'd like to explain the reason my sister and I invested everything we owned in this settlement. Yes, we want a safe place for people and their families to live, including my own. We wanted our children to be educated and grow into productive citizens. Those are things worth preserving. They are critical to the health of a community.

"It is precisely that sense of community we are trying to resuscitate and preserve. By teaching these values to our children and living day in and day out in a caring, engaged community, we have learned how powerful hope is. It started as a flicker in the minds of two individuals and grew to hundreds. Together, we looked down the barrel of hell and chose something better.

"Someday, when we go back out into the world, we need to bring hope with us as a weapon against evil and despair. I believe people will come running to be a part of it. If we can spread this message to other neighborhoods, cities, and nations, I know we will become a thriving world again. And that's why we did this."

A round of applause came from the crowd.

"As entrepreneurs, Dana and I believe in the capitalist system of exchange, but we had to create an enclosed system, and true capitalism doesn't thrive in a closet. So we developed the next best thing, Tunitalism."

Laughter arose from the tables.

"Tunitalism works like this:

• Everyone's basic needs are provided in reasonable but limited quantities.

• Credits are our currency, and your CC bands will be used to track your account.

• They can be used to enjoy activities and goods above one's issued needs. Such as the bar, special dinners, coffee, tea, and other items. They may also be used to pay fines and other fees for misdeeds.

• There are several ways to make credits. For instance, you will receive a credit for attending tonight and one for completing your citizenship; other ways are taking extra classes, volunteering, teaching, coaching, and other actions to be formalized and announced.

• Later, we will introduce some entrepreneurial opportunities.

"Thank you for listening. I hope you are adjusting well and enjoying your town. Don't forget to sign up for the legislative positions. They are part-time and pay two credits a week." He waved and walked off the stage to another round of standing applause.

Gray watched Jilly and Dewy sitting at the table during the meeting. He was tired of hearing about them at work. He wondered how far it had gone, and his temper began to flare. He had to talk to her whether he wanted to or not. He had to be honest with her concerning the possible new threat and his responses to it.

"Jilly, Dewy." He tried to hide his disdain. "Sorry to interrupt, but I need to talk with you, Jilly."

"Okay." She knew it must be important for Gray to break his silence and come out of hiding.

"All right, Jilly. Maybe we could meet up later. You wanted to see the skyroom," Dewy winked and gave her his best flirtatious smile.

He could feel Gray's rage boiling over. He couldn't wait to tell Hannah and Axle the bait was set. Gray led Jilly to a more secure area and proceeded to explain the discovery. He admitted he had turned on her surveillance again, but he could turn it over to Axle if she preferred. She told him it was okay and to keep her informed.

Gray paused before he asked, "Are you and Dewy going out officially?"

"No! Why would you think that?"

"Then why would you ask him to take you to the skyroom at night, for crap's sake!" He knew he had to control his temper, but it was difficult. Everything about her felt difficult.

"I didn't ask him to take me. I just said I wanted to see it. And don't get bossy with me; what's it to you?"

He wished he could tell exactly what it meant and did to him to think of her with another. He took a deep breath. "I know we have issues between us, but I still care about you and your safety. Encouraging a grown man, who has been cooped up in security for months, to take you stargazing is misleading at best, dangerous at worst. If you're not interested in him that way, don't lead him on."

"I didn't think of it like that. Maybe he does. I don't know. I'll tell him...something. Are you done?"

She looked so sad.

"Hey, I'm sorry. Look, I'll show you the skyroom, and I won't be weird, no expectations. We don't even have to talk. I'll just let you in. It is quite magnificent and not open to the public yet, so Dewy shouldn't have—"

"Don't punish him."

"I'll think about it. Meet me at the security building at 8:00 p.m."

"Okay, thanks." Then she walked in the direction of her house.

Hannah, Dewy, and Axle approached Bannon humbly. "Sir, excuse me, Mr. Vogel, sir. Excuse my interruption. May we speak to you?" Axle was nominated as the spokesperson.

"Yeah, but please quit calling me, sir," Bannon answered.

They walked a short distance from the dining hall table where he was having lunch with his daughter and Ari.

"So, you know how Gray's been moping around and being a pain—uh, being unhappy, sir?" said Axle.

"Just Bannon will do. And yes, I know all about the Jilly and Gray Greek tragedy."

"Well, we kinda set them up, sort of, and we were hoping to get your help," Hannah added.

Bannon smiled broadly. "Tell me more. This sounds fun."

Gray stood outside the security building. It was five after eight, and he wondered if she would show, but then he saw her walking down the street. She had a flowy skirt topped with a button-up sweater. The kind of sweater with pearl buttons that hugged a woman's figure, and hers was perfectly hugged.

Her slim legs ended in sexy little ankles, while her auburn hair was down around her shoulders. Stray locks fell out from behind her ears. He longed to tuck them back as he had done so many times, but he promised an uncomplicated evening.

"You look nice," he offered.

She noticed he wasn't wearing his uniform. She had never seen him in resident clothes. He wore traditional denim jeans that fit well in the hips but were relaxed down the legs. A crisp white button-up shirt was highlighted by the outline of a white T-shirt. Damn, he looked good. She had dreamed of an evening like this since he gave his first meeting briefing in the infirmary. If this went badly, she'd know it was hopeless.

"Thanks. And thanks for letting me see it."

They walked through the corridor and up the stairs. Gray used his D band to open the room. When he looked in, he was shocked. The sky guard was already down, and in the center of the room was a candlelit table with a bottle of wine on ice and two wine glasses. Soft music was playing from the speakers. He quickly closed the door.

"What's going on, Gray?"

"Jilly, I think we've been set up. This was not my doing, honest. If you don't want to stay, I'll understand. I can bring you back—"

"Gray, calm down. It's okay. I still want to see it. I saw a table and two wine glasses, and I've never had wine before."

He shook his head and opened the door. She had no idea of the thoughts her words put in his head. He walked to the table as she stepped inside with her eyes drawn upward.

"It's so pretty. The night is so clear. I never knew there were so many stars."

He opened the wine and poured her a glass. It was a rosé, a good choice for someone who had never tasted wine before. It made him wonder if her own sister was in on it. Definitely Axle and Hannah, and maybe even Dewy, were guilty. He'd have their asses if this went south. Since no one he knew had wine, more than likely Bannon was in on it too. He poured half a glass for her and a full one for himself.

"Here's my promise." Gray held his glass up. "I will not lie to you, but there will be things I can't tell you. I won't trick you into anything tonight or ever. I promise you will be getting sleep in your own bed tonight."

Jilly smiled warmly at him, and they lightly clinked glasses. She slowly sipped the wine, closing her eyes to fully explore and prolong the experience. "It's not sweet, but I like it."

Gray watched her drink her wine. She had a natural sensuous manner. He needed to stay focused and get her out of there soon. He pointed out the constellations he knew, and Jilly told the story of Orion and the Pleiades. The sisters were pursued by a hunter named Orion, so their father asked Zeus to protect them. He put them into the heavens with Taurus the bull, but Orion still chases them across the sky.

He watched her as she looked at the stars while acting out her animated rendition, but he was distracted by the few buttons on her sweater that were threatening to come undone. Every arm movement was tantalizing. He imagined a slight tug would be all that was needed to release her silky skin and run a trail of kisses down her neck. She finished her story and looked back at him, waiting for a response.

"I can see why your father chose that myth. I struggled with Greek mythology, but I love the way you told it."

Her reaction was hard to interpret. The tension between them was charged with sexual energy, which was doing nothing to calm his incessant need to claim her. He went to busy himself checking out the music selection. She poured herself another glass while Gray was turned away. When Gray went to fill his glass, he noticed how much was gone.

"You know what I want to do?" She was looking up at the sky. "I want to dance with the music and look up at the stars."

"Jilly, how many glasses have you had?" His primal side hoped it was just enough, but he knew how wrong it would be to act on it.

"I don't know, two, and this is three. But they were all little ones." She spun around, watching her skirt float about her. She stumbled, and he caught her before she fell. She put her arms around his neck and looked up at him with yearning eyes. His resolve was unraveling, and all his desires were focused on one outcome.

"Jilly, I promised it wouldn't be this kind of evening."

"I've been thinking a lot about how we used to be," said Jilly. "I miss that. I think I miss that more than I am mad about what happened."

"I think you're a little tipsy."

"Why didn't you ever kiss me? You acted like you wanted to, and I thought you would at the wedding, but you just turned away."

He raised his eyebrow and tried to stay rational. "I felt wedged between my duty and my closeness to you. I knew investigating you was a betrayal. I didn't want to make it worse. I thought it wise to step back until it was resolved."

"You mean when you could stop lying to me?"

"Yes, I lied. It was awful, it felt awful. I can't be any sorrier. I know I betrayed you. But given the same circumstances, I'd do it again. I'm duty-bound to protect you and all the residents."

"I know. I've replayed it in my head over and over. In these times, we purchase our tomorrows with pieces of our humanity. Piece by piece, wrong by wrong, all is sanctioned. We assume we are forgiven because it is the way it must be to survive."

"You're very wise for three glasses in."

"Then why don't you kiss me now? Have your feelings changed so much? I know I'm new at this, but I'm not ignorant."

"There are things you just can't get from books."

"I've read some pretty good books." She gave him her best sexy smile.

"You're dangerous, Jilly." He pulled her close and kissed her. It was a hungry, burning, and long-anticipated kiss. His memory of her scent flashed in his mind, and he drank her in. Brushing the side of her mouth with his thumb, he felt her plump lips willing with desire.

Here in this starlit room, the chaotic world was dissolved; his radar tightened to a circle including only her. He knew he had to slow down; this pace was too fast. He pulled away, moving barely an inch from her lips.

"Don't pull away from me, Gray. I'm not a child to be protected from myself. I'm a nurse, well, almost, I know where this goes."

"You're not thinking straight. I feel like this would be another betrayal. I want to wake up and see you smiling, still wanting me."

"You think I don't know what I want. I've always known. From the first time you held me in your arms at the Hold. I've always known."

She tucked her head into his chest. He smelled of pine boughs and soap, and it was like a memory from her past, like a walk in a forest.

His resistance was breaking down. His mind knew better, but his heart was pounding out an incessant demand to go further and claim his primal right to her. He nudged her chin off his chest with his curled forefinger and looked into her eyes, searching for validation.

He released her and walked over to the edge of the room, where newly installed benches were tucked against the wall. Using his D band, he unlocked the seat and lifted out a couple of blankets. It briefly crossed his mind that he'd need to find a way to hide the evidence from their evening's instigators.

She saw where he was going and joined him in laying out the makeshift bed. He paused and turned to her. "Have you ever been this far?" She shook her head.

"Jilly, I'm not going to abandon you. We can wait. It's not as pleasurable the first time." The reality of the act was finally registering in his head.

"Gray! I know some things too. Like, more wine would help." She tipped her head and gave him a crooked smile while swinging her empty glass to and fro.

"You may not say that tomorrow morning."

He grabbed the almost empty bottle and drained it into her glass. She sipped it, giving him a mischievous glance. He took her in his arms and kissed her ever so gently, and set the glass aside. He wrapped one of the blankets over her shoulders and gently pulled on her sweater, watching the pearl buttons pop one by one through their buttonholes.

He kissed her neck and pulled her down on the blanket, bringing the other blanket around them. He began to work out the rest of the tiny pearl buttons and her sweater off her shoulders. Her pulse quickened, but she threw the sweater aside as a sign to continue.

He held her close and kissed her exposed, delicate skin, soft and sweet to the taste. Simultaneously, he undid her bra and threw it. They both giggled when it ended up dangling from one of the chairs. He took in her perfection and knew he would always hold her close. When he touched her breast and dropped his mouth over the small peak, she moaned and tipped her head, and he moved to repeat the caress to its twin.

Every response had him closer to being over the edge. But he was pretty sure this was her first, and it needed to be an exquisite memory her heart could embellish. He returned to her lips, kissing her, freeing unexplored wild dreams, and she needed more. She wanted to feel every inch of him, to be closer to him, but he continued the gentle tempo.

She moaned, and the need rose and intensified, but he steadied his resolve. Her skirt fell, unzipped and loose, and he slid his hand to the source of her passionate cravings. He felt her body arch, pleading for release. With a continual motion, she felt her body explode, and pleasure surged through her. As the intensity faded, she put his palm on her pounding heart.

Already undressed and teetering on a precipice, he was too ensnared to lament the imminent painful assault. He paused above her and met her eyes, searching for what she was feeling. She nodded and pulled him down and inside her.

He froze at her initial shocked expression. Gathering his resolve, he remained still until she began to move slowly. That was enough to lock him in, and he sought that which he had dreamed of.

He had fantasized about this moment so many times, and he was soon soaring in ecstasy. He would never let go again. Her sweet brand was searing through him, and his through her. He looked down at her, still breathless from the euphoria. She smiled at him, and he kissed her tenderly. Gray rolled over and drew her close. She kissed him and looked up at the night.

He watched her for a time, and they watched the sky, surrounded by tousled blankets and discarded clothing. They were awakened by the sound of the rumble of the sky covers closing and a flashing exit sign near the door. Gray snapped to alertness. His watch showed it was only 9:17. "Something is happening. That's an alarm, and the skylight is going into hide mode."

She looked wide-eyed while holding the blanket in front of her.

"Don't worry, Jilly, it's probably some elk herd or something." It wasn't a lie. Such things had triggered the alarm before.

"We have to go." He held her head up to look at him. "This wasn't just a thing, Jills. It means everything to me. You mean everything to me."

He kissed her and they got ready to leave.

Chapter Twelve

G ray gathered the private evidence and walked Jilly home. He now took the long walk to the security building. He swore if one of them teased him or cheapened the moment, he'd deck 'em. He slowly simmered until he realized he had Jilly, and she had him. And even though it started with a ruse, it ended with the best night of his life and, God willing, the woman of his dreams.

"What's going on?"

He was still in his civilian clothes, and they did a double-take. He seemed to live in his uniform. "We had a breach. Three walkers on the east side near bunker E2. We didn't see any behaviors that suggested they found the bunker, so we just lie low. They just now walked off."

"Okay, good plan. Doesn't seem like they are looking for anything specific. They're just foraging," he decided as he watched the video. "This time of night in the fall does make me question what they were hunting for, and why they didn't heed all the toxic warnings on the outer fence. Okay, up the surveillance two levels, and let me know if they come back. Anything else going on?"

He waited for the smirks and innuendos, but they were focused on the potential threat. "Is this gonna cancel the skyroom openin' to the public next week?" asked Dewy.

"A rumor is exactly what it is, so don't let word of it seep out of here." The skyroom reference was not lost on him, and he gave Dewy an admonishing look." But if there was such a plan, this could be a deciding factor."

"Okay, let's send a stealth drone at 7:00 a.m.," decided Gray.

Axle and Dewy watched him. They smiled at each other.

"Oh yeah, and because it worked out, thanks; if it hadn't, I'd be kicking every one of your asses. Still might."

"Hey, Gray. Welcome back." Axle slapped him on the back and returned to the monitors.

It was Monday morning, the first official workday for all occupations and students. Ari woke up and got in the shower. It was an on/off design. It had a pattern of being on for one minute to get wet and rinse off, off for two minutes to soap and shampoo up, and on for three minutes to rinse off. There was a button labeled "extend" for times when one had not finished, but its use should be infrequent.

Jilly was still asleep when Ari got out. "Jilly, don't mess up your first day!"

"My head hurts. I don't feel good."

Ari laughed. "Hey, just happen to have this pain inhibitor tablet. Dr. Maya gave them to me when we left the hospital, just in case I had pain from our 'attack.' She said I fell pretty hard, but I didn't need it."

Jilly took the tablet and remembered what Gray had said about being set up. She cocked her head and gave Ari a skeptical look as she made her way to the bathroom door and paused. *She never even asked me about getting home late*, Jilly recalled. "Ari, did you know about Gray and me going to the skyroom last night?"

"I might have heard something about that," she replied, curling her lip under her front teeth and smiling.

"Ari! Geez." Jilly thought for a minute. "Well, thanks. It was heavenly."

Jilly's head started to clear as she stepped into the shower. Her body may be out of sorts, but her memory was dancing to a lovely tune. No promises were made out loud, but she believed Gray was hers. She replayed the words he told her. "You mean everything to me," and he also said he wouldn't leave her. Of course, he had lied before, but that was duty. Maybe he needed more information, and this was part of getting it. No, she wouldn't believe that. She had been told he sat by her bed all three times she was unconscious. Saying out loud how many times she had been unconscious gave her a frightening realization, and she quickly redirected her thoughts. That wasn't his duty, was it? The warning light blinked, signaling the water would shut off in ten seconds. She hurried through the rest of her shower and grabbed her towel.

Ari and Jilly flagged down the café cart and got a quick breakfast. Man, she loved this place. Jilly had been assigned to the Rapid Aid Station, which was just a few blocks away. She walked in and saw PA AnnDrea. She remembered she was the crabby nurse from the Hold infirmary. Gray told her that she sat with him and was deeply concerned for her, so she must have a good side.

"Good morning, I was told to report here. I don't know if you remember me, but—"

"Yes, I remember you. You were a patient, twice in the Hold and a third time here in New Haven, as I recall. I trust you are completely recovered, and I hope absenteeism will not become a problem."

Still snarky, Jilly decided. "Yes, thank you. And I am rarely ill. Those were a direct result of attacks. I hope I am safe from that here."

AnnDrea regarded her response with a poker face. She went on to give the day's instructions. Jilly was to put away inventory and familiarize herself with where everything was located. For the first month or two, her job would be to register patients, triage their complaints, take vitals, and settle them in an exam room, or sit them in the waiting room.

She would also be responsible for any transfer paperwork to the hospital. She was hoping to complete her accelerated study plan and finish her degree within six months, and she was happy she could work on it during slow hours.

Ari went to the engineering building. The first day started with a meeting about the mission of the engineering team. They hashed out several versions and decided on: "The engineering team of New Haven commits to the constant improvement and safe continuance of the town with integrity and diligence throughout its habitation."

After a tour of the building, she was introduced to her mentor, Rafferty O'Leary, but he went by Raff. He was in his late forties and a widower. He was always laughing and quick with a joke. His thick Irish accent was charming, and he had a casual demeanor that seemed at odds with his intellect as an experienced and extraordinarily creative engineer. She and Raff would be working on the constant improvement part of the mission.

Their first task was to improve the efficiency of the waste management plant. The current projection showed the incoming waste would overtake available composting capacity within twelve to eighteen months. She was given the specs of the plant to study. The objective was to accelerate the decomposition of the waste in the compost bins with nonthreatening chemicals and/or biological enzymes.

Raff told her to come to his office. She came in, and he secured the door. "I have something we will be using to conduct our research." He turned, held his band up to the wall, and a section of paneling slid to one side. Behind it was a safe, which he also opened with his band. Inside was a well-worn book, and she could tell by the way he handled it, he felt a reverence for it.

"This was your father's notebook." He handed it to Ari, and she opened the cover. She recognized her father's all-caps printing style. She held it, imagining her father pouring his ideas onto the pages. It created an overwhelming feeling of nostalgia, and she held it close.

"When we are researching this information, we will meet here. You can take notes as long as it doesn't compromise the security of these formulas or phases of his work. This is top secret, Ari. You can't even tell your sister."

Ari paused and nodded in agreement, but she regretted that Jilly would miss out on a rare opportunity to reconnect with their father. She handed him the book, and he returned it to his safe. Raff led Ari to her small office, which she shared with another junior engineer working on a different project. She was quiet but seemed nice. They exchanged basic stats about themselves. She was married with two boys, one thirteen, and her oldest, Kendrick, was nineteen. An awkward silence followed the brief exchange, and they both got to work. Ari saw many benefits to having a quiet office mate.

Gray sat in the conference room waiting for Hannah and Axle. He was early, and the unused time quickly filled his mind with thoughts of Jilly. *Should he discuss commitment? No, too soon. But their intimacy presumed that. No, it doesn't. If I do ask for an exclusive relationship, will she feel rushed and trapped? Or if I don't, will she feel used and question the meaning of the night they shared?* His mind started reminiscing when he saw Axle walk in, followed by Hannah.

"You look like a man with a woman on his mind," quipped Axle.

Gray gave him a warning expression. "What's going on with the ring investigation?"

"We've hit a dead end, but we have a plan to leak out that we have it," Axle went on. "So, we let out the news about it being retrieved and watch who scurries about."

"I'm assuming there's more to this plan." Gray lowered his gaze, waiting for more information.

"Yes sir," said Hannah, then she took over the presentation.

Alex Waller looked around the building. Being in a museum was a privilege since the great art sell-off twenty-some years ago. But now he was the curator, the guardian. It was a fantasy until this very moment. He still wasn't sure if it was truly happening and not just a dream.

The museum consisted of eight thirty-five-foot containers, with two sections stacked two high and two wide. Four twenty-five-foot sections were stacked on either side and perpendicular to the longer middle section. The total space was almost 3,000 square feet of interior. He designated the twenty-five-foot side with the lift for storage, his office, and an art maintenance shop. The other side had a restroom and stairs for customers, and it would also hold new items and revolving special collections.

His head buzzed with ideas for monthly displays and local art. The flood of possibilities saturated his every moment with elation. He had a deadline to open that weekend, and there was still so much to do.

"Okay, the display stations and lobby counter are set. Today, I want to arrange the history section downstairs. Fin, that will be your task. Brooke, you'll oversee arranging the recent pieces in the downstairs section, and I will work on the more delicate art pieces upstairs. We are very fortunate that Mr. Bannon preserved these pieces and risked shipping them here. I know I don't have to tell you to be careful and take your time. Use the handcarts and the lift to move items and ask for help with heavy and bulky pieces. We have two Defenders here to assist us. Any questions?"

Alex's band vibrated, indicating he had a call, so he tapped the device to answer and headed to his office near the storage section of the building. "Hello, Gray."

"Hi, Alex, how's setup going? Will we be ready for a Friday opening?"

"Friday! I thought we had until Saturday or Sunday."

"Yeah, that's why I'm calling. I need your help. Can you at least partially open on Friday morning? And do you have a novelty section like mystery stuff? and can you come next door for a few?""

"Sure, just let me check on my assistants. What do you need me to do?"

It was Wednesday, and Jilly was excited when the first patient arrived. It was a woman and her seven-year-old daughter.

"Wow, you can tell you two are related. What is going on today?"

"My daughter is feeling tired all the time. She stumbles and says she's dizzy, and she's had a headache since yesterday."

"Okay, let's get your names and take some vitals. Let's start with you." She knelt to talk to the child.

"I'm Zoey. Is this going to hurt?"

"No," Jilly said with a smile. "Look, I'm going to point this magic wand at your head." Jilly recorded the temperature, which was in the normal range, but definitely on the Upper end of it. "Then you get the superhero cuff hug, and lastly the finger charm. All done."

Zoey shyly smiled at Jilly and then looked at her mom to check for reassurance.

"I need you to fill out this form while I let the PA know you're here." Jilly wondered what horrors the little girl had seen, like most of the children here. She looked scared, and Jilly knew that to Zoey, she was a Dranger. She figured she would be seeing a lot of that. She rang herself through the door and approached Andie, as AnnDrea preferred to be called. She gave her the stats, and Andie studied the chart. "What's your diagnosis, Jilly?"

"I think she's pretty dehydrated. Besides these stats, she said she hadn't had a bowel movement for days. I also noticed chapped lips, dry skin, and she was smacking her mouth."

"Okay, send her in."

Jilly took the clipboard from Marni, her mom, and led them to one of the three exam rooms. A short time later, Andie came out and confirmed her conclusion.

"I will stay with her and make sure she drinks the fluids. I think I'm going to apply for an apprentice receptionist, so you can be in the exam rooms and administer the treatments," Andie stated.

Jilly and Andie had settled into a comfortable relationship. Jilly liked to think she had earned her respect. She had to admit she might be skeptical of a subordinate who had been repeatedly attacked. It made her wonder what others thought about it. The cover stories had been plausible, but at least some suspicion had to be roaming around with her as the victim every time.

"Where do you get an apprentice? I thought all adults were already assigned."

"They're starting a work-study program with the juniors and seniors at the high school as well as the college students."

"What a wonderful idea! I just keep saying it, this place is amazing!"

Marni and Zoey left with directions for hydration recovery and maintenance after Zoey had urinated.

Ari and Jilly met Gray, Bannon, Dana, Indy, and Ellie for dinner. The table was full of chatter about the week so far. Bannon and Dana were lauded as geniuses and philanthropists. Bannon became embarrassed and stopped the praises. He insisted they had a lot of help. Marni and Zoey walked by, and Jilly waved. They cautiously waved back.

"You know," Ari said, "I think that's the woman I saw when we first came to the Hold. I'll never forget the look she gave me, haunting. Do you remember her, Gray? The mother looked so unwell. She looks a little healthier now."

Gray alerted on "the look she gave me" statement, but he couldn't remember noticing her, so he just tucked that info away for later. Jilly couldn't comment on patients, but seeing Marni, Zoey's mother, up close, it was evident she had fallen on hard times. If she had to guess, she'd say it was drug addiction, but Jilly couldn't be sure.

Jilly had agreed to go on a walk with Connor and Libby. It was early in the evening, and they headed east toward the farms. He was so excited to be back in school, and he spilled out words faster than she could listen. It was nice to see him loving his life and all the kids returning to classrooms, learning, and feeling safe. He rambled on about the fourth grade. He liked his teacher and all the subjects except writing.

"And I love lunchtime too because after we eat, we get to play at the park every day! I have a friend named Hayden, and my mom says he can come over this weekend, and we can play with Libby!"

His joy was pouring out of him, and Jilly had to laugh.

"Hey, Jilly, guess what we get to do tomorrow?"

"I don't know what?"

"We get to see the museum. The kids get to be first!"

"Oh wow, that is a treat! I wonder if it will be open this weekend for the rest of us?"

"Hey, I'll ask them."

"Thanks, Connor."

The next morning, grade school students began their walk over to the museum. They were met outside by Mr. Alex Waller. Rows of chairs were set up outside, and Mr. Waller addressed all the students about proper behavior in a museum. While Alex brought the first, second, and third graders in, Fin spoke to the remaining students about some of the pieces they should check out and the history behind them. The first group was led to the history room, that displayed America's beginnings and expansion periods.

"And here is a famous ring," Alex pointed at the small display. "It belonged to a beautiful queen from England. She gave it to Mr. Vogel, and he donated this ring to our museum."

The little pink ring didn't hold the interest of the children, except Zoey. She stared at the ring for a long time. Her new friend Ellie came and pulled her away when the group took off. She put her hand up to Ellie's ear and whispered something. They were led outside, where Fin began his talk with their group, and Alex took the next group through.

In the conference room, Gray, Hannah, Axle, and Bannon reviewed the museum video.

"You know, that's why I love kids. They can't hide anything," said Axle.

"Let's not get ahead of ourselves. There are a thousand reasons she hit on the ring. Tell me what we know about Marni Sanders."

Hannah began. "Twenty-seven-year-old female, never married, worked as a dental receptionist until the office closed six years ago. Her daughter's father appears to be an ex-cop killed five years ago. She's clean and passed the screening. Parents deceased, sister unknown. Same birthdate." Hannah's eyebrow raised. "She has a twin, Merita. I have no info on her."

"Are they identical?" asked Gray.

"Unknown. She could be dead, Gray."

"She could be here, Hannah. Well, I think we need to know what Zoey told Ellie." Gray eyed Bannon. "I prefer we have an experienced interviewer handle this, Bannon. Are you okay with that?"

Bannon let out a long sigh. "She's just a baby, Gray. Could she be in danger?"

"I think we need to find out. Doing nothing can't make her safer. Look, you can watch the interview, and I'll have Hannah do it."

Hannah sat beside Ellie in the interrogation room with a two-way mirror on one side, allowing Bannon and Gray to observe. The longing for a child of her own someday brought out her maternal instincts, and she felt very protective of her. "Hi, Ellie, did you enjoy your tour of the security station?" asked Hannah.

"Yeah, it's a big place, and everyone is nice here."

"So, tell me about your trip to the museum this morning."

"The upstairs wasn't open yet. But we saw a real Native American feather hat from the old Western days!"

"I can't wait to go myself. What did the other kids think of it?"

"They liked it a lot."

"Aren't you friends with Zoey?"

"Yeah."

"Did she like the museum?"

"Yeah."

"What did she like about it?"

Ellie shrugged her shoulders.

"Do you want to see yourself on the museum camera?"

"Yeah!"

Hannah showed Ellie the scene in front of the ring. "Ellie, this is important. What did Zoey say to you?"

"I promised not to tell. She could get in trouble."

"Who would she get in trouble with?"

"I don't know."

"Ellie, I'm worried about Zoey. Do you ever worry about her?"

She nodded her head. "She is sad a lot."

"Ellie, I promise I can help her, but you have to tell me what she said."

"She said the museum man lied. She told me he stole her ring."

"Did she say anything else?"

"No, just that I couldn't tell anyone."

"Ellie, we're going to take good care of Zoey, I promise."

"Okay." Ellie looked down at her fidgeting hands.

Gray, Bannon, Axle, and Dewy watched through the one-way window. He called Hannah to end the interview. "Dewy, Axle, you need to pick up Marni and Zoey Sanders. Make it look routine if you can," he added.

"I need to tell Rand to watch for them on the cameras," Bannon said as he walked down the hall. Axle and Dewy called in, "They're not at their place, Gray."

"I have them on the west-end cameras. They're by the goat ranch," chimed Rand, who was listening in on the radio chatter.

Gray sent more Defenders to secure the tunnel. Axle arrived at the corridor and peeked around the corner. Marni was holding Zoey by the arm, and Zoey was struggling.

"We have to find a way out of here. You shouldn't have told your friend about the ring. Now they want to kill you. Don't you see, Zoey? I'm trying to save you."

"I want my mommy. She gave me that ring, and you stole it." She was crying uncontrollably and struggling to get away.

"Marni," Axle announced as he came around the corner with his weapon drawn. She turned Zoey around and put a stolen dining hall knife to her neck. Axle zoomed in and could see the shaved edge of the once-harmless butter knife.

"Whoa, put down the knife," Axle yelled loudly. "Look. I'm putting my weapon down. You have nowhere to run. Let Zoey go, Marni, or is it Merita?"

"Stay back, I'll cut her. I don't want to, but you're making me."

Zoey was sobbing quietly.

"It's not my fault my sister died. I was only trying to get Zoey here. I promised Marni I would get her here." She was backing up, and Axle could see she was getting more agitated. He put his unarmed hands up.

"Sounds perfectly reasonable. I would have done the same thing. We can get this all sorted out, but you must let her go. Zoey is just a little girl. Zoey is your niece. She even looks like you." He was trying to appeal to the family connection of her hostage by repeating Zoey's name. "Didn't you promise Marni you would take care of her?"

Dewy had run through the mid-corridor and gone down the south side of the tunnel to block any escape. He saw that Axle was backing her right into him. When she reached the corner, she moved her hand away to peer around the corner. It gave Dewy enough room to hit her arm with such a powerful downward motion that she instantly dropped the knife.

Axle rushed forward and seized Zoey, while Dewy grabbed Merita's arms and secured her hands behind her. She cried out from the pain of the injury and his rough handling of her, but Dewy knew better than to give her a chance to break away.

Axle reported in, "We've secured the suspect and the child. She's okay. We're heading back with the child and the perp."

Gray and Bannon could hear Zoey sobbing in the background, and they both took a deep breath and let it out. Hannah was sitting with Ellie, and when Zoey came in. She ran to her friend, sobbing uncontrollably.

"Don't cry, Zoey," soothed Ellie, but she was crying too.

"Gray, do they have to stay here for this right now? Can you talk to her tomorrow?" Bannon was pleading to remove the little ones from this place and the trauma they were feeling.

Gray looked at the terrified children. "Are you taking her home with you?"

"Yeah. She can spend the night with Ellie. I think she could use a break."

Gray looked at the small child heaving in sobbing breaths. "I think she needs watching tonight. She might even be in shock. Just have her checked out first. I don't want anything else to go wrong for her."

"Good idea, Gray. I'll call Haru."

Chapter Thirteen

Ari knocked on Bannon's door. She wasn't sure why he had called, but he sounded tense. When he opened the door, he hugged her. "I'm so glad you're here."

"What's happened?" Ari listened intently as Bannon recalled the evening and its history. "Geez, poor kid. So Haru's with her now?"

"Yeah, in Ellie's room. Ellie's in mine."

"Is this the ring that Gray thought may involve us?"

"The investigation is still ongoing. They're interrogating Merita now."

"It's like a nightmare we keep having over and over. I'm calling Jilly. I just want to know she's okay. She thought Gray was coming over to our place, which explains why he never showed."

"Just don't say anything yet. Gray wanted to tell her."

After letting Jilly know she was staying the night, Ari let it slip that Zoey was having a sleepover with Ellie. Jilly told her she was going to get ahead in her studies because Gray had to work. Before she ended the call, she suggested they make sure Zoey drinks plenty of water.

Zoey slept in Ellie's room and woke up several times, anxious and scared, but the night wasn't as problematic as predicted. Ari and Bannon talked for a while about parenting, children, and how random and precarious the world seems.

"Even here in this highly fortified little paradise, there is no escape from the world's ugly edges," sighed Ari.

Bannon looked at Ari. She was his morning thoughts, his daydreams, and his world. The thought of her in danger made him anxious to keep her close. He wondered how long it would be until the outside world caught wind of their ruse and came after them again. Although her father's work was critical and required protection, he wondered how far he would go when it came to protecting her.

They were reclining on the couch, and he kissed her sweetly on the head. Keeping a vigil on the two traumatized girls meant he was limited to letting Ari fall asleep in his arms. Their relationship had become a commitment, but their work schedules had kept them apart most of the weekdays. They found it difficult to find time to be alone. Something had to change.

Both girls wanted to go to school the next morning, and Bannon told them they couldn't talk about what happened. "Let Gray do his job; don't worry about your aunt. She's in trouble and will be for a long time, but she's okay," assured Bannon. Zoey looked relieved. Haru said he would let the teacher know to call them if Zoey or Ellie seemed troubled.

Ari left Bannon's place excited to get to work. They were performing the first set of experiments at the waste management building. The hydroxyl hybrid radicals were being used to speed up the methane dissipation process. It was a small-scale test to check its volatility. She wished she could share her work with Jilly, or anyone, for that matter. She was so excited to be a part of this discovery. It only iced the cake that she was replicating her dad's experiments.

Gray met Jilly for lunch at Town Hall. Election debates were approaching, and he was reviewing security for voting day. He had lunch delivered, and they sat in the assembly room. Jilly looked around the vaulted room. "Wow, this is cool. The room is round like the White House was, and I love the curved doors on either side. Is this where the legislators meet?"

"Yeah, and it's where the debates are happening Thursday night. Jilly, I want to fill you in regarding the ring." Gray described the scene from the night before. He disclosed the interrogation information he had so far. "So, here's what we got from her. She was approached by someone looking for you two before we staged your deaths."

"It sounds so surreal when it's said out loud."

He raised his eyebrows and nodded. "Merita was a junkie, and they said she could have all the drugs she wanted if she could find you and your sister, but she couldn't. And then when word got out that you were, umm, dead"—he watched her as he spoke the word, but she stayed calm—"even though the hunt was called off, she went to her sister and poisoned her with a poison bead. She wanted to slip into her life for as long as she could carry it off. As Marni got sicker, she told her about New Haven, and she figured she hit the jackpot."

Jilly's eyes widened.

"Yeah, a huge breach. One we would have caught if we had seen them together even once. We kept an eye on the residents to make sure they didn't run into any trouble."

"Yeah, most of us assumed that. So what happened next?"

"Marni wanted Merita to take Zoey to the sanctuary. But I don't think she told anyone about New Haven because she didn't want to mess it up for herself. She wanted to take over Marni's life, especially her job in the dentist's office, where she had access to drugs. She gave Marni the ring as a token of her promise to take care of Zoey and her "love" for her sister."

"Gray, how was she going to get me or Ari to wear that ring?"

"The little bead pops out, and she had two of them, one for each of you. She was going to feed it to you forcibly if you weren't willing to wear it. There are several ways to administer it. I don't even know if she knew all the methods, but we researched it."

"Man, she's a piece of work. She was right next to me in the RAS."

"What?" Gray looked shocked, and his jaw tightened a bit at the thought of Merita near Jilly and his team missing that intel.

"Yeah, she brought Zoey in."

"She was probably scoping the place out for drugs. What was wrong with Zoey?"

"She was dehydrated. Do you think she did that to her?" Jilly was outraged.

"Well, this elevation can cause that, but I wouldn't put it past her. She's a dry drug addict with a homicidal streak," Gray retorted tersely.

"Yikes! So, is there more to the story?"

"She pretends to care for her sick sister, just waiting for her to die. What our evil twin doesn't know is that Marni gave the ring to Zoey a day later, just before she lost consciousness. Thank God, it was too big for her, so she kept it in her drawer under her clothes. It was somehow missed in the scan for rings at the Hold.

When they got here, Merita found it while unpacking Zoey's things. She walked around and saw the bins that had just been collected and tossed it in." Gray continued. "The recycling crew found it and turned it into L&F. The poison had totally degraded by then, so there wasn't any danger. We planted it in the museum, hoping to get a reaction on camera. It was a long shot, but it paid off."

"Why did she confess all of this? She could have just said nothing."

"We already had a lot of evidence against her. And she didn't know the ring was safe when we returned it to her. We pretty much insisted she put it on, so we knew it fit her, and she kinda lost her cool. That and we hinted at a reprieve from her dry spell."

"You didn't!"

"We didn't give her drugs, but she inferred from our...conversations that she might get something to help her sleep if she cooperated."

"Is that legal?"

"The laws are different here, Jilly. We are in what used to be called an emergency lockdown. It's not martial law, but it allows certain precautions for the protection of the whole. It was enacted four or five decades ago."

"What are you going to do with her?"

"Ah, now that's the question. We can have a trial, but then everyone would learn of your dad and his formula. Then what? We have a contingency plan for infractions that includes house arrest and community service, but fraud, murder, kidnapping, and assault with a deadly weapon are beyond those punishments. Do we keep her locked up? We can't let her go. It's definitely in the debate stage."

"Well, I don't envy you," replied Jilly. "I don't know what I think about it. But my lunch hour is almost over, and I have to go. Will you come by tonight?"

"I thought I'd meet you for dinner and take you to my place. You haven't seen it yet."

"Okay, dinner at 6:30 or 7:00?"

"Let's do 7:00. I might get off late." Gray hoped nothing new would come up to ruin their plans.

Jilly walked through Town Hall, passing the receptionist and the framed collage of Jefferson, Madison, Adams, and Washington, encircling Cleisthenes, the Greek founder of democracy. The New Haven Declaration of Independence and the New Haven Constitution were displayed. Next to those were copies of the old Declaration of Independence and the old United States Constitution. She wondered what they would think of the Merita predicament.

Jilly waited for Gray at the southwest kitchen. She walked over to the posters on the street side wall with reminders to submit ideas for the naming of the places and more ways to volunteer. Other posters were for the candidates. After the primaries, eight people were running for the four representative seats and four for the two senate seats.

Bannon was overwhelmingly chosen to keep the mayoral position, at least until the next election. He was one of three people who had a thorough knowledge of the town, and of those three, he was the only one who wanted the job. Candidates couldn't promise more rations or unrealistic freedoms, but they could promise to solve problems and pass legislation to make New Haven better.

The representatives for the west side of the street included Will Benson and Corey Donnelly. Will's platform included a monthly dance and a strict pet policy. Jilly hadn't seen the pets to be a problem, but a dance could be fun. Corey wanted a craft market to sell local hometown items. She was Jilly's favorite.

She couldn't vote in the southeast side election, so she didn't pay much attention to the candidates. One was fighting for freedom from the scrutiny of security. Her son got in trouble, and she felt he was treated unfairly. Jilly knew the case had to do with her son taking a joyride on a cart that ended with a fence being ruined. She didn't know all the details of the case, but it seemed like she wanted protection for her son, not the people.

Her opponent took a poll of the SE's interests and found they didn't want more new programs. Most wanted time to enjoy the town while simply improving on the existing structures and opening up the rest of the buildings. She agreed. There was still so much to explore and so much that was yet to open. Jilly liked his interest in what the people wanted and his thoughtful philosophy, and she hoped the East section voted for him.

The senate race for the south side included Vincent Jeffreys and Carl Casberry. Jilly hadn't decided who to vote for yet. The Senate debate was tomorrow and would be held at the Town Hall Assembly Room. It would be on live feed to everyone's tablet or on the big screens at the dining halls.

She saw Gray coming down the street just after seven.

"Sorry, I'm late."

They discussed the candidates during dinner and found they thought alike, especially about the overprotective mother. Gray was planning on voting for the guy running against her because he'd worked with him and liked his professionalism.

"Can you tell me what happened with that woman, Amber's son? I know he was the one who stole a cart and crashed it into his mother's yard and caused a lot of damage," Jilly asked as they put up their trays and started walking east toward the tunnel center.

"Well, he's a minor, so all I'll say is he was caught, and we assigned community service, but his mom didn't agree because she said it was her property, but it's not hers. It's on loan. They lost their husband and dad to a Neighwah raid eight months ago. She has a serious distrust of Corporates, and she sees Bannon as one of them. She's struggling. It's hard to be a single parent. She's also threatened by her son's relationship with me."

"I can only imagine." Everyone she knew had lost loved ones, and she was among them. "She's worried he will become a Defender." He nodded with a sly little grin. They continued down the tunnel past Town Hall and the daycare.

"It's nice to walk. I enjoy seeing this town evolve. People keep adding special things to their outdoor patios and yards. It keeps it interesting." Jilly was looking around, wondering where he lived. Gray's place was past the southeast dining hall, near the east corridor.

"Who is your roommate?" Jilly asked him.

"I don't have a roommate."

It was neat and clean, but seemed as empty as the day he moved in. "I kind of guessed you didn't make any crafts for your place as we did, but didn't you bring anything from home?"

"Unfortunately, my home was destroyed in a bombing, and I just never found the time or resources to replace any of it. Being a Defender, I was given everything I needed. You're the first person I've brought here, and now you're dissing my home."

"Oh, brother. No, it's very nice. I didn't know they made one-bedroom houses." Jilly wondered what living in a place alone would be like.

"Yeah, there aren't many. They're for newlyweds and the operation directors who are single," said Gray.

Jilly took in the minimalistic, clean look. "You went with the sage and white. We almost picked that. I like it."

"I wish I had some wine," he smiled, "but I did manage to rummage up some carbonated water."

"Ohh, I'd love some." Jilly held the cups while Gray opened the twist-off bottle. "I hope this doesn't give me a headache like the wine did."

"Nope, but it does have disadvantages too. I won't get to see you dance and stumble into my arms."

"We'll see, you never know." Jilly winked and gave him an impish grin. He moved in close and kissed her.

"Jilly, I think we need to clear up some things." Gray looked for her reaction. She was attentive but without a readable expression. "I want to talk about what happened a couple of weekends ago."

Jilly stiffened ever so slightly. "Look, Gray, I know you are more worldly, and I don't want to—"

"Jilly, stop. Let me say what I need to say. I care about you more than anything. I don't want to be with anyone else, and I don't want to share you with anyone else. I want to make you a promise—I'll see only you, and I hope you want to make that promise to me too. Okay, now you can talk."

Jilly was relieved and overjoyed. He told her something like this during their skyroom interlude, but she knew sometimes people say things they don't mean when they are in a passionate moment. "I told you, I have been yours since you held me in your arms in the Hold. I will happily say it; I promise to be only yours."

She put her arms around his neck and kissed him slowly and intentionally. She smelled the forest on him. "Gray, how do you get cologne? It smells so good, like camping when I was little."

"My dad taught me to stuff pine boughs in old socks and put them in my drawers. It started out being a way to hold off showers, which we had a hard time getting regularly. But now I just like it, so when I send Defenders to the outposts, they bring it back for me. They're all doing it now, I guess."

"Hmm, that gives me an idea."

"You give me an idea too." He kissed the palm of her hand, and they climbed the stairs to his bedroom.

The Senate debate was held at 5:00 p.m., and Gabe and Billie sat with them. Billie was six and a half months now, and their little girl was kicking a lot these days. There were a lot of people at the dining hall, but since it was streamed to the notebooks, she knew there were more people at their homes watching. The screen came on, and the moderator introduced the two senatorial candidates. She explained the procedure and gave them each a chance to talk about their qualifications and experiences.

The first question was, "What is one of your favorite aspects of New Haven and how will you protect and enrich it?" Carl went first.

"I love this place! Before I knew about this project, I would hide in my apartment and remember my youth. It was a time when I felt free to enjoy living without fear. But the world unraveled, and we adjusted to the most meager of existences. But now we're back, and I see people walking down the street and stopping to talk. I see children playing and laugh. That's what I love most. And I want to protect it by getting back to the joy of living. There are so many wonderful events and opportunities we can explore. I say we go for those things. You only get one shot at life, let's take ours."

Next, it was Vincent's turn.

"There is a lot in Carl's speech that I agree with. There are so many aspects of New Haven that I appreciate. But I think the blessing I am most thankful for is hope. New Haven has given me hope for the future. I believe this legacy of civility will continue in the hearts of our children. But we have work to do. They are behind in understanding the essence of civility, which involves trust. They play today, but they remember their terrifying yesterdays.

They are behind in education. They are back at school now, but according to the teachers, their scores are lagging, and their under-developed study habits compound the problem. To protect what we are building, we must have a vision beyond today.

To enrich our environment, in this experiment, I would introduce a mentor program into the schools. Students from Upper grades would help those from lower grades. Teaching is the highest level of learning, and citizens reaching out to others is the highest level of civility."

The debate went on, but Jilly already knew whom she would vote for. Vincent, or Vince, had the best understanding of what it meant to serve. Carl seemed to be more about self-indulgence. The speech went on, and Gray put his arm around Jilly and gently rubbed the back of her neck with his thumb. It was a sweet gesture, and she wondered if he was aware of its effect. Billie was becoming uncomfortable sitting for so long, and she felt relieved when it ended.

"I know who I'm voting for," stated Billie as she went to stand behind Gabe's chair.

"I do, too," shared Jilly. "Are we thinking the same way? Do you want to share?"

"Vincent talked about kids and moving at a steady, boring pace. I want more fun. Half of the fun things to do aren't open yet. I'm voting for Carl."

"Most places are opening this weekend after Friday's Naming Ceremony. I am worried about the children. I see what Vince is talking about when I see kids come into the RAS. Even Connor is behind in some studies, and his grandfather worked harder than most to homeschool him. I'm voting for Vince."

Gray saw where this was going and immediately changed the subject. "Hey, I put in a couple of names for places. I love my name for the bar, *Shangri-La*."

"I put in the name *Brycen* for the park near the daycare," Gabe chimed in, seeing what Gray was doing and wanting to keep the new conversation going. "Brycen was a two-year-old killed by a speeding Dranger vehicle the day before his transport date. Whenever I walk by, I want to imagine him playing there. Did any of you submit names?"

"That's very thoughtful, Gabe. I like the bar name too," replied Ari. "I submitted *Janet Bonnema* as the name for the engineering building. She was hired as an engineer to work on this tunnel, but they misread her name and thought she was a man. They tried to get rid of her, and the other men threatened to walk off the job if she didn't leave. So, she dressed like a man, snuck in the tunnel, and did her job."

"I love that story, Ari," praised Bannon. "I think all of your suggestions are a shoo-in for winning. I didn't put in any names because I want people to feel ownership of this town. There are still a lot of people who see this as mine, and they act like my guests."

"I thought the hospital name should be *Asilo*. It means a safe place to shelter," added Jilly. "I think we should all win. Our names are thoughtful and reflect the spirit of the buildings they represent."

Less than a week later, the Naming Ceremony happened at the high school park. It was like a carnival. There were games and sweet refreshments. All the names the friends submitted won, and they each got awarded three credits, one for the entry and two for winning. A couple holding the hand of a little boy, around five, came up to Gabe and tearfully thanked him for naming the park after their little angel. Gabe was proud and watched them walk away, hoping he never had to experience that kind of loss.

Other names included Madison High School, Treagan Park (by the high school), Sojourner Daycare, Wally's Recreation Room, and Mandalay Bay for the southwest diner. All the names had interesting backstories because it was part of the criteria. Edith Wilson Elementary School honored Woodrow Wilson's wife, who became acting president when her husband died in office, making her the first female to hold the role of United States president. Samsara is a Hindu reference to the cycle of death and rebirth. Its symbolic meaning made it perfect for the museum and its art pieces, which were saved and reborn. Billie and Jilly loved the little girl from daycare who named the rabbit and chicken farm Blue Rabbit Farm because one of the rabbit breeds was called an American Blue.

Ari looked at Bannon. "This brought the town together on so many levels. They've put their stamp on it and see it as theirs now. I couldn't be prouder of you."

Dana and Indy walked over to Bannon. "So, I know we have been discussing adopting Zoey. We want to talk to her about it before it's official. Can the girls come over for a while? I thought we could let them both know because Zoey and she are so close; they're like sisters."

Bannon smiled and happily gave his consent.

"Ellie, Zoey," Dana called them from the park next to the Mandalay Diner. "Would you like to go to my place for a little while?"

"Yay!" they answered in unison.

"Perfect. I think Haru will accelerate the process. It was his advice that suggested Zoey and Ellie need each other, but they also should have their own space to grow and develop as individuals. Telling them together is a good plan."

Bannon was thinking of some plans of his own with a couple of hours alone with Ari. She had his heart fully tangled in hers, and Ellie had become close to her too. They gave him stability and a foundation he wanted to build upon. They had an agreement to see each other exclusively, but their jobs kept them apart. He wanted her to live with him, so they could have nights and mornings in each other's arms. He had held back his notions of making the bond permanent, but maybe today, he could get a sense of how she felt.

Ari walked slowly from her office to meet Bannon. She and Raff made an alarming discovery today. They exposed a whole dead rabbit to their newly enhanced air dispersal system for the hydroxyl hybrid compound. She knew it would be corrosive, but she understood the full impact of its powerful potential when the meat fizzled and even bounced slightly as it completely disintegrated in less than a minute. Almost nothing was left but an unrecognizable sludge and skeletal bone fragments, which when examined, were pocked and still reacting to the compound. The idea of a living being undergoing such a gruesome death sickened her.

They also did experiments with air pollutants. The hybrid radical particles do not behave according to the ideal gas laws. It demonstrated, to the best of their understanding, that the hybrid compound was attracted to other gas particles without heat or pressure. That shouldn't happen, but it appears to be the reason for the accelerated cleaning effect.

She and Raff both understood the ramifications of this being used as a weapon, as well as the unknown possibilities of such an unstable compound. They wondered if they would be required to be a part of using it in that way. When Ari walked outside, Bannon was waiting for her. She knew she couldn't even tell him about her day, but he knew better than to ask those kinds of questions.

Ari and Bannon walked hand in hand, passing the buildings that would display the new signs tomorrow. They called out the buildings' new names as they went by each one. Bannon lived on the southeast side of town, which he called Big Ed's side. Ed Johnson was the legislator who pushed the tunnel bill through Congress. He called the southwest side of the town Johnson's side. All the new names added flavor and depth to the town's cohesiveness.

She walked into his three-bedroom house. It was larger than most, but not in a pretentious way. Bannon was afforded an office and a larger living space to conduct meetings before the other buildings were completed. He and Zoey were some of the first residents. His home was decorated with gorgeous art pieces that were his favorites, but not of museum quality. Curtains hung in front of the vaulted windows, which reached the full height of the two-story living room. A plush rug with a fleur de lis design complemented the perfectly aged mahogany furniture. The club-footed table was matched with six chairs.

She wondered if others were envious of him bringing his personal furniture. She asked him about that, and he told her there was a place on the inventory form that allowed for the transportation of professionally maintained antiquities. Some went to the museum, some to storage, and other pieces, people have in their homes.

He poured her a glass of vodka and cranberry juice. "Wow," she said, "this must be a special occasion to break out real juice."

"Well, it's reconstituted, but every occasion with you is a special one. Be careful, it's not just juice. It has vodka in it." He led her to the plush, luxurious, pearl-colored, rolled-arm sofa with silky black stripes.

"I've never had that." She took a sip. "It's got a slight burn." She sipped again. "I could get used to it. Do I need to keep quiet about having it?" He knew she was fishing for his justification for being able to have things others weren't allowed to have.

"No secret needed. The Shangri-La Bar will be open tomorrow, and those with credits can get a drink. We'll be working instead of enjoying ourselves, so I confiscated a couple of shots for us."

"There'll be a big crowd tomorrow. We'll be working our butts off."

"Yeah, I'm sure we will." Bannon was trying to steer the conversation in another direction. "Ari, I want to talk to you about how much I enjoy being with you. I'm not good at small talk when I know what I want to say, so here goes." He smiled at her and raised his glass. "I want to know what you think about us living together."

She had thought about this, but she didn't expect it to be discussed so soon. "I am not necessarily opposed to that. I'm wondering what would happen to Jilly. Would she keep our place? Would I have access to both places? Would I be registered here or there? And most importantly, what would that look like to Ellie? I guess what I mean is what would it mean to us?"

"Whoa, I'm not talking about a temporary situation. What I'm saying is, I love you, Ari. Will you marry me?" He pulled out an elegant diamond ring with blue sapphires embedded around the sides. He poised it in front of her finger.

"Oh my, I'm not saying no. I'm just...wow. It's beautiful. The answer is absolutely yes." Her words were muddled, and she felt disoriented. "I think we should have an engagement time. I probably said that wrong. What I meant is I love you, but we've only known each other for a couple of months."

"You make perfect sense. Just to be fair, I've known you for years. But I fell in love with you in the hospital that first time, while you held your arms crossed and glared at me defiantly." He gave her his teasing grin. "But yes, an engagement would be sensible. We don't even have to set a date right now. Can we announce it at the bar opening?"

"That would be perfect, but first, we should talk to Ellie."

She closed the distance between them and let the ring slip onto her finger. The kiss was deliciously slow, and the drinks were soon set down on a side table.

Chapter Fourteen

The Shangri-La opened up at 5:00 p.m. to a line forming several blocks down the street. The structure was big, with four forty-five-foot containers stacked two high and two thick. Four twenty-five-foot containers were stacked and turned perpendicular on each end of the building. The section protruded out ten feet more than the rest of the building creating a sound barrier for the houses down the street. It had brick siding on the lower level with the same color painted on the Upper level. Contrasting white accents trimmed the darkened windows. The name Shangri-La was painted on the Upper level, in a stylish italicized font, with white letters outlined in black.

A white fence delicately entwined with meandering ivy ran across the front of the outdoor area enclosing the peach-colored tables with black wooden chairs. Three palm trees stood sentinel on the corners, and a gap lined with two flower boxes created the entrance to the outdoor area and access to the inside. The indoor décor was dominated by rich wood paneling and vintage tavern furnishings. The service bar was at the east end, and long counters lined both sides of the room, providing ample seating. Downstairs, the music played while upstairs, two wide-screen monitors played sporting events from another time.

Gray, Axle, Dewy, Ari, Jilly, and Bannon were inside, getting ready to check in customers. They were volunteer bartenders, servers, and, if necessary, bouncers. The bar would be open every Friday and Saturday from 5:00 to 12:00. There was a three-drink limit due to the difficulty of acquiring alcohol. In the last two weeks, there were volunteers for every possible task around town. Everyone wanted to earn credits for the bar. Outside the tunnel, bars were extremely dangerous places, so the appeal of this venue was great. People's bands were scanned as they walked through the turnstile into the establishment. Some sat in the beer and wine garden outdoors, while others headed inside.

Gray and Bannon were already pouring orders. Ari and Axle served drinks downstairs, and Dewy and Jilly worked upstairs. There was a dumb waiter system between the floors, so they didn't have to travel up and down. It was getting rather crowded, but it was such a cheerful, grateful crowd that there wasn't any trouble. Plus, everyone knew getting kicked out of the bar was permanent until one attended a hearing to reinstate bar privileges. Soon, the center tables were moved to the side, and people started dancing to the music. Axle saw Hannah walk in with a friend, so he went to take their order.

"Good evening, ladies," he spoke loudly over the music. "Welcome to the Shangri-La. What can I get you?"

"Do you have something called a gin and tonic?" asked Hannah.

"Yep, and for you?"

"It's Tanya, and I'll have the same."

Hannah smiled at Tanya. "How great is this?" Hannah felt very blessed to have Tanya in her life, but she didn't know where the relationship was going. She was just floating along, enjoying the ride, but she knew Tanya would be all the way down the aisle if she had her way.

Several minutes later, their drinks arrived, and Axle scanned their CC bands. They sat laughing and telling stories. They gestured for another round, and soon, Axle brought it. A slow song came on, and Tanya pulled Hannah onto the dance floor. They danced and talked intimately close to each other, and Hannah rested her head on Tanya's shoulder.

"Hey, Ax." Gray smiled and pointed out the two. "Your woman's gone rogue, dude."

Axle rolled his eyes. Hannah was his closest friend, and he'd known for a long time she was gay. Gray knew too, but it didn't stop him from getting in his jabs at his brother.

"Well, I hope Dewy isn't hittin' on your woman upstairs. You know he's sweet on her."

Gray flicked water from the glass washer at him, and Axle walked away laughing.

Bannon turned off the music and spoke into the microphone. "Can I have your attention? I have an announcement." He gestured at Ari to join him.

"We're engaged!" He pulled her in for a kiss while cheers thundered through the bar and into the street.

"So, one free drink for everyone here!" More shouts and cheers rang out. Friends and residents congratulated them, and high spirits permeated the crowd.

The bar finally closed at 1:30 a.m. A cleaning crew was scheduled for 7:00 a.m. the next morning, so after securing the scanners and alcohol, only minimal cleaning was completed. Another crew would work tomorrow, and the friends planned on coming as patrons then. As workers, they were not allowed to drink, and as customers, they could only come to the bar once a week. Supplies were limited and hard to get, but there was still a good storage room full for now.

It was Monday morning, and Gray let himself into the highly restricted security area. He leaned on the wall and peered through the one-way window at the prisoner. She was a paradox of the most lethal kind. Her crimes were numerous and grim, and the evidence irrefutable. She killed someone, falsified documents, breached the security of the tunnel, threatened a child with a weapon, and took a hostage.

It was a slam dunk case. *Yet how can we put her on trial?* Gray thought. *It would reveal information so sensitive that it would be detrimental to the survival of the town and probably millions more on the outside,* and more importantly to him, *it would threaten Jilly.*

Bannon walked in and solemnly nodded at Gray. No words were required to share the irony of her crimes versus the ones they must choose. He put the prisoner's sedative injections on the counter in front of the window. It was five more cc's than usual, and Gray fixated on the syringe.

"You know, Gray, I never told you this, but there was a young man who discovered Tyson's identity. Everyone was looking for him then."

"Who's Tyson?" He looked over at Bannon.

"Ari and Jilly's dad."

"Shit, I thought it was Leland."

"My dad erased Tyson Connor thoroughly along with his daughters' names, which even I don't know."

"Who was this young man?"

"He was a boyfriend of Ari's. He wanted to join the Neighwah. He saw a wanted poster of Tyson, but it was before he had been physically altered. My dad and Tyson assumed the poster included Jilly and Ari as children, and he recognized them. He confronted Tyson because he wanted to know why they wanted him. Tyson told him he was a scientist, but it wouldn't have mattered what he told him. His cover was blown, and Tyson was his ticket into the Neighwah."

"What did they do?"

"They detained him illegally and agonized over and over how they could ever let him go. He was innocent and barely twenty years old. They designed elaborate options of detainment, even recruitment was discussed, but none of the solutions were sustainable because they would have to last for decades, perhaps more."

"What happened to him?"

"Long story short, they killed him and disposed of the body, so he'd never be found. Ari brought him up to me briefly once. She thinks he joined the Neighwah and got transferred away or killed."

Bannon stared through the glass woefully.

Gray turned to face him. "Fuck, Bannon! Are you suggesting something?"

Bannon looked at him, his expression grim. "I just think we're having the same discussion they did. She is not even innocent. But if this is discovered, or we let the legislators get wind of it, we're all screwed. Whatever we do, it has to be done before the election. Those women, our women, and the whole town are at serious risk."

"I've gone round and round. I don't want to be this person." Gray rubbed his forehead.

Bannon put his head in his hand while leaning on the glass with the other. "It's an impossible scenario; there is no win. It's a matter of how much we lose."

"If it must be done, it must be done by us, together. We cannot assign this to anyone else." Gray felt the full weight of shame now.

Bannon nodded, remembering a similar pact had been made before.

"What if they ask about Merita? What if Zoey does?"

"We'll say she's being held at an off-site prison. If they press it, we'll say the site was hit."

"We're thick in the weeds now, my friend. Blood brothers from spilling *her* blood."

The two men stared through the glass for a few more moments. This scene of her alive in the cell would haunt them forever. The glass stood as a temporary barrier between this moment and all their moments to follow. The more they thought about it, the more culpable they became. They looked at each other and walked into the cell.

Gray told Jilly he needed to visit the out-site bunkers at the edge of the barrier, and he'd be gone for a week. The road to them was completely underground using a series of buried containers. There were four sites spread out in a fan, a quarter of a mile away from each side of the camouflaged tunnel entrances. The seven-foot-wide passage intersected an underground, horseshoe-shaped road connecting each site manned by three Defend on a revolving schedule. He was bringing supplies to the Defenders at both the eastern and western sites. This job was usually done by lower-ranked Defenders, but he needed to get away.

Gray tossed his luggage and the supplies into the cart trailer. He packed personal gear and surveillance equipment for scouting beyond the barrier. The drive wasn't nearly long enough, and he longed for the days when he would ride his motorcycle down the highways for lengthy trips into the wild lands. He wondered if he would ever get to do that again. He reached the middle of the horseshoe and turned left to reach the far northeast site.

Using his band, he let himself in. "Whoa," a startled Defender quipped. "Sir, what brings you out here? Everything all right?" The young soldier took a quick check around to make sure his station was in order.

The bunkers were painted off-white paint and were well lit. They consisted of two thirty-foot containers side by side and one twenty-foot container turned sideways, all buried underground. Each had a full bathroom, a limited kitchen for heating food and cleaning up, a living area with a large monitor for recreation, a bunk room with lockers enough for three Defenders, and an observation room. The observation room displayed intel from the cameras, drones, and sensory equipment set up outside. It was constantly monitored day and night.

Gray gave an easy smile. "Relax, Defender. I just thought it was time I got out and checked on you guys. I also want to do some recon outside. Any action lately?"

"No," he said. "We've seen some movement, but it doesn't look like the human kind. This time of year, it's probably wolves or elk."

Gray looked over the screens and locator displays and checked the logbook. "Okay, I'll unload your supplies. I brought you something, and I'd better hear that you shared." He smiled, thinking about the boxes of cookies he packed for each site. He unpacked the new supplies and gathered the trash, compost bin, and laundry. Similar exchanges happened at the rest of the sites. Every month, a new crew of two to three Defenders came out with just over a week's worth of supplies. Every week, a Defender would drive the next week's supplies. Drinking water was especially important because the collected water at the sites wasn't potable. Gray planned to spend a couple of nights in the commander's bunkrooms located at both ends of the tunnel. He needed to work out his crime before he faced Jilly and her inquisitive nature.

When he finished checking each site, he headed to the outside access. He knew the snow was deep, and the temperatures were dangerous, so he put on his camo snow gear. The access to the outside was shaped like a rock pinnacle. It was too tall and steep to hold the snow. He cleared it with the observation crew at the middle site and opened the hatch.

It was good to be outside and feel the wind whipping at his gear. The sky was filled with dark, low clouds, and the blowing snow faded one's visibility. Positioning the binoculars, he scanned the horizon as far as the weather would allow. With snowshoes on, he headed toward a crop of trees barely detectable in the swirling snow. By the time he got there, he had lost sight of the rock access, but the scanner still registered the marker. He leaned against a tree to take in the solitude and the cruel conditions.

The act played unwillingly on repeat in his head. Merita was curled up in a restless ball, asleep on the cot, the sedative from the last dose still lingering but not enough to satisfy her cravings or dull the pain from her injured arm. They contemplated injecting her while she slept, which seemed more merciful, but they decided to face her while they delivered the verdict. She was surprisingly calm, and she said she knew it was coming. She didn't even beg for a reprieve, but she eyed the syringe more with hunger than fear.

They all prayed and asked for forgiveness. She asked to inject herself, and they removed her inflatable cast. Gray took out his sidearm and aimed it at her in case she tried something desperate. He wished she would because then it would have been a defensive move. But she willingly took the needle, as if she had a choice, and injected herself. They quietly loaded her body into the incinerator late that night.

Gray pushed away the memory and took in the openness of the outdoors. Finally, he was free and out under the sky, even though the windchill was brutal. The stinging pain helped him struggle with all the secrets and choices he had made that he kept from the others. He remembered he promised Jilly he'd bring her some pine boughs, so he began to gather as much as he could carry in his pack.

Just then, he caught something moving out on the edge of his sight. He tucked behind a tree. Staying very quiet, he waited for his quarry. Using a gun could get unwanted attention as well as possibly cause an avalanche. He was not the best knife thrower, but he could hit a small target most of the time. It was only silence and wind when the snow crunched ever so slightly.

He peeked around. It was a mountain lion. She had caught a rabbit. He watched her from a distance. She was a magnificent predator, a master at the ruthless tasks of survival. No guilt, just raw power, a taker of whatever sustenance dared to be available. Several minutes passed before she walked off, leaving the pristine snow stained in violent red.

He stayed for a moment, considering her. He tried to connect her survival story to his, searching for validation. But he came full circle to the ironic purpose of the project, to save civility. But if civility had been followed, Merita would have been able to tell her story. Then, when a guilty verdict came, for he believed that was certain, real justice could have been served. Would she have been put to death by a jury of her peers? Unknown. If only that were possible. It was evident that the laws needed tweaking to be finite and fair, and the plan was to allow the legislature the job of pounding out the resident rights.

But even if the best laws were on the books and followed with fidelity, the amount of trust required from each resident to protect this information was unrealistic. These circumstances could not abide a public path, not then, not now, or ever. Bannon and he shouldered that burden to save the innocence of their residents. He supposed all through history, people have made awful choices despite their honest hearts. Were they heroes, or self-appointed jurors and executioners? Not even history is allowed to judge. They were as invisible as their deeds.

He gathered up the boughs and headed in the direction of the marker arrow illuminated on his wrist scanner. He passed the bloody scene and crunched forward. He could see the rock perfectly now, but some snow-covered shape was near it. Alert and cautious, he tried to decide if it could be the lion. When she stood, he knew. It was the lion.

He could see her well now, and he realized he was paused out in the open between her and the scraps of her kill. He was still. She was still. They were fully aware of each other. Eyes locked as each calculated the other. He relaxed just a bit, hoping she would follow his lead, but she stayed poised, her gaze lowered and steady. His respect for her was growing. He envied her. She did not have civil laws beating around her head. She knew her purpose with complete clarity, and it gave her confidence. He lifted his helmet visor carefully and spoke to her.

"You need to go and be free. Stay away from this world. Live where you rule, where you fight to survive, and claim your prey with honor, not regret. That's your magic; it makes you strong, makes you feel alive. I wish I could be like you. But there is no bridge between our worlds. Go before my weapon ends your life too."

She regarded him for a time and finally turned and left. He liked to think they understood one another, but he knew it was the human voice that signaled her to leave. "I wish I could go with you," he whispered and headed to the access rock. In the distance, he heard her growl, and he accepted her claim on the territory.

Chapter Fifteen

Jilly was giddy to see him, and he was fully distracted by her welcome home. She was his reason to regain faith in himself as a good man. He liked to think he had gathered some perspective on his quest, but he knew it was only the beginning of his journey.

Gray was of a muddled heritage, as were most people of the time. Like all Defenders, he was DNA-coded, so false identification was difficult. So, he explored many of his genetic links and gathered their cultural insights. In times of division by skin color, people were categorized by standards that were unrelated to qualifications.

Although categorizing was still very prevalent, no one cared about skin color or culture; it was power, territory, resources, and weapons that gave one status. Maybe it was always about that. It seemed little had changed, like the term Daily. It was just the latest word for the people lost in the low levels, at the mercy of the current political tide.

His mother's heritage reflected centuries of the American melting pot. His father was a mixture of Native American tribes, and he taught Axle and Gray what his father taught him. Gray found his connection to the land and the masculine challenges fit his character, so he tended to identify himself with his father's culture.

His father spoke of quests taken to gain perspective and challenge one's physical body. Though it was considered an antiquated tradition, both Gray and Axle made a vision quest when they turned seventeen, to seek wisdom and earn their manhood.

In late summer, seventeen-and-a-half-year-old Gray took his motorcycle and headed into the thick Sawtooth Mountain wilderness in central Idaho. It was before the border roads became heavily manned with armed soldiers. He slept under the stars, hunted for food, and built a shelter.

For three weeks, he was gone without contact with another person, and he felt freer than he had ever been. He thought he had nailed this challenge thing until two Drangers stormed into his camp. He had just returned with a deer, and he offered some to them. But they wanted his bike and his rifle. That, he could not allow.

He didn't see any weapons on them, but he was cursing himself for not reloading his rifle and having it ready. They charged him, and he whipped out his knife quickly, defeating the first, and the second ran off. His father trained his charges to respect all life but to hunt and fight hard for survival. It was the first human life he had taken, and he was sickened. He buried the body and moved his camp. He spent two more weeks seeking peace.

His definitive moment came when he was glassing a ridge on the other side of a ravine. Two male bears were fighting for breeding rights. It wasn't over food or self-survival. It was for the species' survival. They fought with powerful blows and locked each other in deadly holds. Each determined to claim the female as their own.

The champion stood and roared as the lesser bear ran off to lick his wounds. He took that in, and the correlations revealed his philosophy. Let live when possible, fight like hell when it's not, and don't lose. He packed up and rode back to the burial site. He blessed the grave as his father taught him when his mother died, and he rode back home with a winter's worth of dried meat for his family.

Gray reflected on his first quest and found his answers were still valid. Only one outcome could prevail. Merita fought for her survival at the expense of her family. She lost, gave up, and ultimately chose death. She didn't even try to argue or struggle. She had a weakness that ate away at her dignity. She judged herself and found she was guilty. They gave her the venue, but not the ultimate verdict. That was her own.

Since Corey had won the SW senate election, plans were made to open a craft market. The other sections wanted to join the effort, and a large monthly market was scheduled to open in the middle of a very busy December. That was only weeks away. Bannon allowed residents to purchase some of the nonessential goods with credits.

As a shipping magnate, he had collected a vast supply of items as payments from failing businesses. These items were stored in the horseshoe barrier made from shipping containers, forming a large area in front of both entrances.

The east tunnel entrance area extended 300 feet out, but the west entrance to the end of the barrier was 1,000 feet. The inner circle of containers held essentials, and a staggered arrangement provided access to the less essential goods stored on the outer rim of reinforced containers. At the top of the wall was a line of razor wire with break-away barbs, demonstrating its primary function. Winter access would have been difficult, but the buried tunnel leading to the out-sites made it easy.

Bannon extended many residents a one-to-one ratio of their existing credit to allow them to begin their businesses. Although the residents were happy to purchase the goods, they were unaware of the vast amount of commodities Bannon had accumulated through scrupulous and unscrupulous means. Winter Solstice Day was approaching, and the market was eagerly anticipated.

Treagan Park, near the high school, was covered in tables and people shopping for goods. The complete section of the tunnel was closed and barricaded. Each side had three openings: one entrance and two checkout lines. CC bands were used to transfer credits and sales.

Defenders provided security as greeters and cashiers. Jilly had taken the pine boughs Gray brought her and crushed them to infuse them in soap. She made thirty-two credits more than she spent on the soap mixture.

Ari and Jilly purchased some baby outfits for Billie's baby, due in just over a month. The baby shower was the next weekend, and Winter Solstice was the week after that. Jilly learned from Axle that Gray used to play guitar, but he lost it when his home was destroyed. He seemed overly reflective these days, and she thought music would be a good gift.

Bannon had encouraged the residents to learn to play a musical instrument for future concerts, so he was willing to lend credits for purchasing or renting them. Jilly had to borrow nineteen since she didn't make quite enough of a profit from her soaps.

The sister's new family gathered together to open presents. The eight of them sat among a series of boxes decorated with markers and tied with string. The children went first. They got coloring books and crayons from Jilly and Gray.

Ari got a new jacket from Bannon, and she gave him a picture of them together at the bar opening in a crafted frame. Dana and Indy used their credits to get approved for a bunk bed and bedding delivery, so the girls could have sleepovers at their house. Then Bannon and Indy left the room.

They returned with two nine-week-old kittens, one for each girl. Their noisy joy frightened the small felines, and the girls quickly changed their demeanor. Several months ago, a cat was found in one of the storage containers that came from the Hold. After a month in quarantine, it was discovered she was pregnant. She had a litter of four black-and-white kittens. Zoey named hers Nonnie, and Ellie named hers Nikka.

Jilly was extremely excited about her gift for Gray. She hoped there wasn't a reason besides its loss that caused him to give up his musical interests. Gray looked at the large box with bewilderment. He had no idea what it could be and worried about her investment in it. He opened the guitar, and he looked as though he had just been reunited with a long-lost friend.

"How did you know? Axle, no doubt. Jilly, honey, this is so perfect. What did it cost you?"

"I owe a little bit, but most of it I got from selling my soaps."

Before he could reciprocate, Jilly gave Ari a small box. She was overcome with nostalgia at the two pictures. One of the two sisters was taken a couple of years ago. The other one was with all four of them before their dad was cosmetically altered. She passed them around, and Gray and Bannon gave each other concerning glances.

"Wow, that's only a few years old, but this one is decades old. I thought all those things were destroyed," said Gray, looking over at Bannon.

"It was stuck at the back of Dad's desk. I found it when we were packing for the Hold, and I saved it for this day."

Bannon and Gray gave each other understanding nods. Gray came over to Jilly and took a small box out of his pocket. He stood her up and took her hand. "Jilly, I love you so much. I cannot see my life without you in it. Will you marry me?" The ring was a medium gold band holding a single modestly sized diamond.

Jilly's eyes welled up as he slipped the ring on her finger. "It was my grandmother's."

Jilly looked at it on her finger. It fit her perfectly, and it shone and sparkled with even the tiniest light. "It shines so beautifully."

"So does that mean yes, or..."

"It means positively yes! I love you so much," and she kissed him.

"It isn't large, but it is a white diamond and has been handed down in my family through several generations," Gray told her with pride. Jilly was mesmerized until her sister jumped up.

"Oh, Jilly, we should have a double wedding!" The sisters hugged, and Gray shook hands and accepted congratulations, and jabs about Jilly's debt being his own now.

Before the busy month ended, Billie had her baby shower, which supplied her with numerous outfits and toys. The New Haven Town Hall sent over an ample supply of cloth with Velcro diapers, as well as the thin disposable liners that could go in the compost toilet. As the baby grew, they would exchange them for the next size. Winter Solstice arrived soon after. Jilly gave out her soaps to the households of friends.

Gray was routinely called into work, regardless of the holiday, due to an increase in petty crime. Now that people were settling in, the more impulsive residents were testing the rules and the responses. He had anticipated civil lessons would be required to educate reckless youths, and three had been caught trying to steal goods. The legislators had already approved his plan for community service and a couple of civic classes.

Unfortunately, one of them was Amber's son. She was the angry mother who had run for representative and lost. No matter how fair the system was, it could not help Amber acknowledge her son's shortcomings. Gray called Haru to be present for the meeting. He hoped it wouldn't escalate into a juvenile hearing, which would leave a permanent record in her son's file.

January arrived, revealing a new attraction: the Season Room. The large mid-section room was finally opening and would offer several activities. From January to June, when the temperatures were warmer in the tunnel, a swimming pool would be available.

The actual pool area was 37' x 18'. It would be kept between 75°F and 78°F. A schedule of swim activities would be available for sign-up in one's notebook. The pool season would conclude in the spring with competitions. Rumor had it, the next activity was a simulated beach scene.

Jilly and Ari signed themselves and their guys up for the adult-only time. Three weeks later, the four of them slipped into the cool, clear water under the heat of the solar lamps. Jilly could not remember ever swimming, but she had waded and dipped into a few creeks. Gray was swimming up and down the length of the pool in the thin lap section. She decided she wanted to learn to swim.

Bannon was an excellent swimmer. He had pools as a child and young man. They discussed it and decided they would volunteer to teach swimming not only to their wives but to others. Jilly couldn't believe how tired being in the pool made her. She had planned to work on her dress, but she went to bed early instead. She slept more soundly than usual and woke up equally refreshed. *Swimming is my new favorite thing*, she thought.

Billie and Gabe's little girl was born on February 20 at 3:00 a.m. She was 6.5 pounds and healthy. They named her Katie Bliss Houser. Jilly and Ari visited them in the hospital and readied their house for the homecoming. The sisters wondered as they held the tiny infant if they would ever have children of their own.

They were safe for now because they were considered dead, but as soon as the word was out, they would be hunted again. Even in New Haven, life was threatened by the eventual breach. They couldn't hide here forever.

With a casual suggestion from Gray, the legislators passed a new bill requiring New Haven emergency drills to be practiced once a week for the first month, then once a month. Some residents questioned the timing and wondered if a breach was expected. But most wondered what had taken so long.

They had weekly drills at the Hold, so it was logical to have them here. The explanation was that the Hold residents were under the security team's jurisdiction, but the town was under the government's, and they had only been in office a couple of months.

There were three different scenarios. One was called the disaster drill and required evacuation to an environmentally safe part of the tunnel. The second was the crime drill, which involved a violent event or intruder. And the last was the quarantine drill. The first drill day involved a disaster in the southeast tunnel.

It did not go well because the residents tried to save their belongings, and the time it took could cause fatalities. Gray was confident the efficiency goals would be met with practice.

Haru put a mini-sermon on the feed explaining the approaching Easter season. He showed pictures of the past and the traditions to demonstrate ways to celebrate the Ascension of Christ.

"It is the most hopeful of all holidays, and it should be revitalized," he asserted. He encouraged the resident entrepreneurs to create items for the market. He also invited everyone to come to the newly opened church. Sermons wouldn't be held in the dining halls anymore; they would be in a large area off the middle corridor.

Each corridor had two rooms, one on each side, that had been dug out. They had been used for storing household items during the early stages of the town's construction. Since all the houses were furnished, the rooms were mostly empty.

The New Haven Nondenominational Church of Worship would hold three services, two on Sunday and one on Wednesday evening. A schedule of religious study classes would be posted soon. Jilly and Ari attended the second service with their extended families on its opening day. Jilly noticed the colorful glass windows that were lit up from behind.

The wooden lectern looked antique with beautifully carved designs. The ten rows of pews were made of richly stained wood and varnished to a shine. The Bibles and hymnals were new with tight bindings waiting to be softened. Each pew row, one on each side of the middle aisle, could easily fit eight to ten people.

They sang songs, and Gray even played guitar with the small musical ensemble, accompanied by a beautifully tuned piano. Jilly liked singing, and she had a nice voice. Haru preached about taking time to get to know each other and not rushing into commitments.

"Here, we have time to walk and talk to each other. We can reflect in places by ourselves without the worry of attack. Allow God's plan for you to unfold. Pay attention to what is going on inside of you. Take care of that scared child as well as the guard dog at the ready."

As they walked back home, Jilly turned to Gray. "Do you think we are moving too fast?"

Gray answered, "We can move as slow or as fast as you want as long as we're together." He kissed her head, and they walked hand in hand down the street.

It was a Saturday in late April when Gray, Bannon, Hannah, and Axle were called to the conference room. Rand, the resident tech genius, had a dismal report.

"I've been having trouble getting intel from the off sites. The signal drops and spikes like the signal range is riddled with dark spots. I checked our equipment, but I couldn't find any problems. So, I've been careful—very careful"—he contended as he looked up at Gray—"as I monitored public radio and personal signal traffic. It's not our equipment. The newest front in the war of wars is in space."

"A NO-Techy faction hacked into fifty or more strategically positioned satellites with laser capabilities. Blaming technology for the world's plight, their goal is to eliminate as many electronics as possible. A couple of years ago, they began hitting small satellites. At first, it was undetectable because they chose targets that were obsolete or had a very minor user base.

"They have been very covert about it, but they tactically set into motion something called the Kessler Effect, and it has been catastrophic. As each satellite is hit, shrapnel is sent hurtling off to eventually hit another, and the action repeats itself exponentially. The word is out because it has reached a critical point. Even our stealth satellites are vulnerable to this kind of attack. We have all but lost touch with the off-sites and their away teams."

"Do they know what you know?" asked Gray. "Can we get any kind of message through?"

"I think they received my last one this morning. I haven't been able to reach them since," answered Rand.

"We need to pull them in," ordered Bannon.

"Okay, let's plan a retrieval." Gray set his team on gathering supplies, Defenders, a single meeting zone, and a route. Rand needed to create a secure com-line and relay the plan in code. One hour later, they came back to the conference room.

"As far as we know, the Hold is still silent," offered Hannah. "I suggest we use the Alpha building because the Defenders we're taking are more familiar with it."

"The off-siters have mini-transports, but we need them to know to meet there and when," interjected Axle.

"They can destroy the equipment they can't easily pack. It's too risky to leave and let it fall into enemy hands," Bannon sanctioned.

"Let's set our deadline for tomorrow morning, and as soon as we can get confirmation from the out sites, we'll set a hard meet time for the mission. If we can't get through, we'll arrive early and wait on the edge of the Hold. Rand, I need that line."

Rand and Deed worked into the night and established a signal via old telephone lines. He sent a message in Morse code, and although the message itself was encrypted and untraceable, it was detectable. When the confirmation was received, a timeline was set. The plan was to travel there at dusk, load the off-siters, and return in the afternoon.

If the site was compromised, one team would take the east-to-north route and the other the east-to-south route. Both would drop off two Defenders for flank-and-charge maneuvers. It was a K6-all order: kill in a combat situation, and eliminate all combatants. The departure area was on the west side. Of course, all orders are sanctioned as "monitor and adjust" as the situation calls for it.

Eight Defenders, including Hannah, Gabe, and Dewy, boarded the multi-terrain transport with snow tracks, named the Brute. The road was still deep in snow. A stop on the way at a hidden bunker held two faster warrior transports. Both were loaded with weaponry and seating for six, which wasn't enough to transport everyone.

The hope was they would also have the mini-trans for transport back to New Haven. The mission was to reach the outer area of the Hold, recon the area, move into Alpha, retrieve the twelve off-siters, and return undetected. A second team of four followed to hide the vehicle tracks using various methods.

Twenty-four Defenders, almost a third of his entire force, were designated in various capacities to this mission, and it weighed heavily on Gray that if it went wrong, their defenses would be compromised, not to mention the loss of good soldiers and friends. The snow was receding, and the Drangers were no doubt moving up the mountain. At least the playing field was level because everyone was blind without reliable satellite access.

Driving the Brute to the bunker went off without incident. When they reached the staging area, a drone was sent up to recon the Hold. "I've got two trucks already there. There are fifteen heat signatures on the north side animal hold. That's not right. We're only expecting twelve Defenders total, and only two of the four vans are here. I hope they didn't rescue any Dailys. We'll have to leave them here," Hannah reported.

"Here comes another transport. Two Defenders are coming out; wait, I can't get a DNA scan. It's just not registering as anything." Hannah tried to adjust the drone's sensors. They all got up to watch as the three Defenders surrounded the van and took the off-siters hostage. "Shit, they're hostiles!"

Dewy was driving team A in one transport with Hannah and two more Defenders. Gabe was driving team B with three more. They headed to Alpha Hold.

"Okay, then," said Dewy, "so much fer a neat extraction. Let's recap the hostile plan: hit the east side, split toward the poles, drop off boots, reclaim our fuckin' real estate, K6all, and extract the hostages.

One D drives, and the rest man the turrets until two get dropped off. We've gotta shit storm here. Drangers are suited up as Defenders, so we don't know who's who out there. But if they act hostile, drill 'em. No uncoded chatter, and our peripheral clock has just gone alphabetical, so refresh that. Another minitrans is due. Lots goin' on. Watch out fer each other."

They approached the east side and split up Gabe went south, and Dewy went north. Dewy stopped at the medical entrance on the east side of the building and dropped off A team's two Defenders. While Gabe went to the storage area and dropped his two from the B team, Dewy and Hannah drove west across the parking lot area in front of the animal hold.

Hannah stood ready at the turret. Suddenly, from the animal Hold a combatant opened the door and threw a sticky bomb just as Hannah took him out. The bomb hit the driver's side and exploded, leaving a gaping hole in the door. Dewy slumped at the wheel, and Hannah rushed to take over. She got around the corner, stopped, and helped Dewy's unconscious body to the floor.

"Hang in there, Dewy. You're going to be okay. I'll get you home, buddy." He looked pretty bad, and she prayed he'd be all right. She continued to the rendezvous point at the kitchen's loading platform on the west side. Inside the Hold, the A team Defenders that were dropped off at the med door made their way to the Defenders' office. They made it before five of the Drangers, dressed as such, were heading behind the long shelf bordering the mess hall.

The B team Defender called to his partner. "Beta 3 to Beta 4: red shirt and ripped brown coat friendlies. I repeat red and ripped friendlies," to report he recognized them. Using the shield at the base of the fence, they aimed at the other three carrying weapons across the yard. One went down, and another ran with a limp behind the borrowing shelf on the mess hall side. They yelled threats regarding the two hostages, but the B team was approaching a kill position. Each enemy held a hostage in front of them and slipped out the west door in the mess hall area.

Hannah saw them come out with the hostages, and she leveled her weapon on the window of the dangling door. She had a shot at the wounded Dranger, so she fired, and one Dranger dropped. But the hole in the door was like a target, and the other Dranger shot back. They were using drill-mos, and her suit did not protect her. Grabbing her abdomen, she cried out. As her consciousness tumbled downward, it was Axle's name that slipped out in a slurred mumble. She went down and didn't get up. The two hostages overpowered the last Dranger as he took aim and tried to run, but they took him down.

Dewy couldn't move his legs, but he dragged himself over to check Hannah. She was moaning, and Dewy tried to hold his hands over her abdomen, but the bleeding was profuse. "Hang on, girl, you owe me a dance and a beer as I recall." She was unresponsive. "Just keep fighting; I'll get you home. I promise I'll get you home." His last words faded as he fell unconscious again. His hands fell away, and the bleeding continued. Gabe heard Dewy on his com and sent Beta 2, the medic, to assist.

On the helmet com, team A was making their way to the animal hold, and team B ran to assist. Alpha 3 motioned for the B team to secure the outer door. They obeyed, running past the utility room next door and out the exit. Beta 4 positioned herself to take out any runners. Beta 3 edged over to breach the outside door when signaled.

Team A finally gained access to the existing cameras by plugging into the network directly. They located the hostages on the west side of the room. The two Drangers were conveniently stationed away from them, guarding the door.

"Hostages to the left, two hostiles located on either side of the door." Alpha 3 said to 4 on a one-to-one com-line. He made a counting motion with his fingers, and on three, they shot through the walls on both sides of the door. Together, they kicked in the door and rolled to the sides as the gunfire erupted from the opening. Beta 3 shot open the outside door when she heard shots being fired. She took out one, and the other was already on the floor, wounded, and as he went to raise his weapon, he was taken down.

"Area secure, threat eliminated," Alpha 3 reported on the com-line. Gabe was in charge now, and he ordered A team to go straight to base with the four wounded. Two off-site Defenders died in the animal hold. So, along with the Drangers, there were eight bodies to deal with. B team would stay to purge the Hold and dispose of the bodies. And he needed to find the four missing Defenders. They were either locked up somewhere, dead, or they hadn't made it to the rendezvous yet.

Chapter Sixteen

The med team was working on Hannah en route. She was bleeding from her abdomen, and the internal wound foam wasn't stopping it. An IV was pumping plasma into her, but not as fast as her heart was pumping it out.

"How's she doing?" asked Jax Nakano, a rescued offsite Defender.

"I'm losing her. I can't stop the bleeding; she has a hole in her liver. Her organs are failing, and I can't stop the cascade effect," the only med-aid they had answered. She momentarily looked at Jax in her T-shirt and underwear. They had stripped her of her uniform, but luckily, they were too busy for anything else. She had a serious knife wound to her left side, but she had foamed it herself, and the bleeding was under control.

"Who's hurt?" Dewy gasped in a weak, barely awake voice.

"You are, Dewy. Welcome back, but do not move! You have a serious injury," but when he started to struggle, the medic called out the order, "Put him back under, Jax."

"No, no wait, I wanna...I wan...kno..." He was fading, back down, deep into the inky black pool. They arrived at the outer bunker and loaded the patients onto the cart. The medical team was ready with the ambulance trailer. They loaded Dewy and sent him off in haste. They could wait for the next one. Hannah was gone.

Gray was talking to Dr. Maya. He sat down dazed by the news that Hannah had died. The better news was that Dewy was expected to recover, but his recovery would take many months, possibly the better part of a year. More than three hours passed before Gabe returned to New Haven. He was greeted by Gray's exasperated somber expression.

"Seven Defenders dead! Four were injured, two seriously. What the hell happened out there?"

"The best we can figure out, Drangers stumbled on the Hold by drone or pure luck. The only other possibility is that we were betrayed somehow. They paid no attention to the quarantine warnings. It must have been in the last day or so because our recon had the Hold silent and no heat signatures. Without satellites, our surveillance depends on short-range drones, which have to go back to their base to download data and footage.

"I think the hostiles were considering taking it for a base. It's possible they detected our message, and maybe, but this is a stretch, they deciphered it. In any case, when the first off-siters showed up, they didn't know they were there until they were ambushed. We found their bodies dragged off into the brush, and a truck hidden.

"Why didn't their cross scanners work on the stolen gear?" asked Gray.

"They were all turned off by the Defenders days ago. One of them told me that in the last day or so, someone had been accessing that program. It made them a blipping target. They couldn't contact us to let us know. The first group of Defenders arrived hours early. They abandoned their off-site because two Drangers were snooping around, so they bugged out quickly in the early morning. In haste, they destroyed all their equipment, even the stuff they were supposed to have on them, so they had few recon abilities. When they got to the Hold, their truck was attacked and riddled with bullets. One of the hostiles was using drill-mos. They went right through the vehicle, whoever got in the way, and then drilled right out the other side. We lost two more Defenders that way, including Hannah."

"Then the Drangers put on Defender gear. It gave them protection, but they couldn't use any of the technology. Yet it allowed them to capture the next two groups."

"Is it just me, or is something not right? These are trained Defenders!, So, why can't they follow procedures, and more importantly, why can't they fight?" Gray was yelling now, so he took a breath and regained his self-control.

"To be fair, their specialty is technology, not combat. They've had no formal physical training or combat drills in four months, and we weren't able to brief them before they left." Gabe answered.

Gray shook his head. "Well, that's going to change. We're tripling our combat drills and reinstating procedure classes for everyone who can't pass the tests! We *will* be combat-ready. Okay, keep going."

"Using these live hostages, they opened the door to secure the area. But then, here comes the last group, and they repeat the process. This is the group we witnessed."

"Did they all come early? We should have been there first." Gray couldn't believe how badly it had gone down.

"We got there before the go-time by fifteen minutes. The transports were slow going through those boggy, snow-covered roads, but I think they felt unsafe in their locations after the transmission. They bugged out early. Again, no contact was available." Gabe knew the mission was a mess, and he felt like he'd let Gray down.

"So, we should have accounted for heavy snow and poor road conditions in our plan. But damn it, they should have waited somewhere and arrived at the scheduled time. Man, oh man, we need to shore up. This whole mission sucked. You and I know we will be located eventually, and we'd better be ready." Gray gave Gabe that look that meant serious business.

"Yes sir, I fully agree. To continue, the ambushes happened so quickly they had no time to react." Gabe was trying to stick up for his fellow Defenders, but he knew a grueling schedule was already cooking in Gray's head. "The rest you got from the drones and our helmet cams. I don't know how much the enemy knew before they got there, but it worries me what they know now."

"Have you debriefed them at all?"

"No sir."

"Okay, let's set that up immediately. I want you to conduct the interviews while I'm on the observer side." Gray watched him leave. This would have been Hannah's job. He missed her already, but he couldn't grieve now. The battle was ongoing until he knew what they were up against.

Gray went to the hospital and upstairs to Dewey's room. Bannon was already there with him. Dewy was sleeping, and Gray quietly briefed Bannon on the mission. Dr. Maya came in and checked his chart.

"Fill me in, Maya. First, tell me about Hannah," asked Gray.

"Well, she was DOA, but I doubt I would have been able to do much even if it had happened right here. That drilling bullet ripped a large hole in her liver. That kind of bleeding is hard to stop. I'm sorry, Gray."

"Has anyone told Tanya?"

"No, I wanted to talk to you first. Is there some covert way we need to spin this?"

"No, I think the residents need to know the threat is real, but I don't want to evoke any crazy reactions, just caution and respect. Tell me about Dewy."

"He has a bad spinal bruise, a cracked vertebra, T11 to be exact, and he also has some cord damage. He must have turned away from the door just as the bomb went off. There is damage here and here." She pointed to the image on the screen.

"The good news is we have a regenerator, and it works well on this type of injury. It takes time, though. He'll begin a treatment schedule in a couple of weeks. It should be fully repaired in about six months. But it's slow, so he'll be in a wheelchair for some time."

"We'll help him through it. He can be stubborn, but I'll make sure he complies with your treatment. I'll talk to Tanya. Man, she's going to take this pretty rough. I think they were planning a wedding." He was recalling the way Axle fell apart as he watched the feed.

"Should we send Haru with you?"

"No, I'll suggest she speak with him, but it's her decision. Right now, I want to touch base with the other wounded Defenders."

Maya pointed to the curtains across the hall. Only two, Dewy and Jax, were still in the hospital. The rest had been released. Gray visited Jax first since she was awake. She told him she had fought with the Drangers, who were taking her gear, but they overpowered her. She had forty-three stitches from a long knife wound to her left side, but it didn't go deep enough to hit any organs. She would be kept overnight as a precaution and released the next morning.

Gray held Tanya as she sobbed. "I can't do this, Gray. I'm alone. She was everything worth living for. I, I can't." No words existed to soothe such moments, so he offered none. He called Haru and stayed until he showed up at Tanya's residence. As he left Haru to console her, he heard him tell her in his soothing buttery voice, "She rests in a world of goodness and light. She is at peace, and I know she would wish it for you." Gray couldn't imagine losing Jilly, and no words existed to relieve that kind of pain for a while to come.

Gray told Jilly to meet him in the conference room for lunch. When she got there, she saw he was upset. His eyes were red, and something was very wrong. When he gave her the news about Hannah, her tears welled up. She held Gray close and spoke quietly in his ear.

"I liked her, respected her, and I know you were close to her as well as holding her in high regard. I'm so sorry, Gray. How's Axle?"

Gray just shook his head. He let down his guard, and they cried together. He hadn't even gotten to Dewy yet.

Jilly contacted Andie, asking for extra time at lunch to visit a friend admitted to the hospital. Andie okayed her request, having heard about Dewy's injuries. Jilly went to Dewy's room. Axle was there, and Dewy was groggy but waking up.

"What is goin' on? Hannah, okay?" Dewy slurred.

"Calm down, Dewy. You're hurt pretty bad. Please stay still, and I'll tell you whatever you want to know," Axle spoke as Jilly held Dewy's hand.

"Okay, just tell me she made it."

"She had a severe hole in her liver, Dewy. She didn't make it. It's sad, I know. We're all torn up about her. But we are worried about you too. You need to focus on your own injuries. You have a battle yet to fight," cautioned Axle. "Please fight, Dewy. I need you back. I can't lose you both."

Dewy broke down, and they did their best to be there for him and each other. Dr. Maya came in a little while later and wanted to talk to Dewy. They got up to leave.

"We'll be back, Dewy. You'll be sick of our company, we'll be here so much," consoled Jilly, and she kissed his forehead.

Two beautiful services were planned for the seven young Defenders at the new church. Haru had to add two more to accommodate all the people who wanted to come. The legislators designated a memorial wall for the lost Defenders and one for all New Haven's lost citizens, including those who were chosen but did not make it to the town. Dewy had to watch it on a screen because he couldn't be moved yet.

Billie and Jilly sat in their yard at the table they had jointly purchased at Christmas with their credits. The legislators sold such items for only a few credits to help dress up the town. Their little yard was now edged with a low white fence and a gate in the middle. A vine of realistic ivy wove its way between the posts, and a few wispy vines draped down here and there.

Two faux trees sat toward the back of the yard, which was covered in soft carpet grass. All the plants were manmade reproductions, but their realistic appearance gave a tranquil place to sit and relax. They came with replaceable branches with fall colors and spring flowers, providing a seasonal ambiance throughout the town.

Billie and Jilly took turns playing with Katie. She was growing so fast. They sat telling stories about their memories with Hannah. They had done lots of walks and trips to the market with her. After she met Tanya, she naturally spent less time with them, but they still went to the market every month together. She will be missed was all they could say. They talked about Dewy too. They needed to help him fight through his physical therapy because it would not be easy. The monthly regeneration treatments would set him back because he would need a week off from PT. The road back was feasible, but it required a lot of stamina and determination.

Jilly held Katie while Billie went inside for a minute. She was so beautiful. She had curly golden-brown hair and big brown eyes like her mom. When Katie smiled, which was often, it made Jilly smile too. With Gabe's little dimples, she could melt an iceberg, as Dewy would say. Gray and Jilly had babysat several times, and Jilly was surprised at how good Gray was with babies. He told her he had his niece and two nephews living at his dad's house for almost a year. They moved somewhere in Wyoming, and he hadn't heard from them since. Jilly had mixed feelings about having a child, at least for now. She and Gray said they both wanted kids someday, but they never discussed a time frame for it.

Friday night arrived, and Axle, Gabe, and Gray needed a night out. The Shangri-La was their ticket to numb their grief. They met at Bannon's place and had some smooth, aged whiskey to begin the night. Bannon went along as a designated sane person. The new dartboard occupied much of their time. One resident started to question them regarding the casualty count of the recent mission, but Bannon ran him out before a brawl happened.

It would have been just what the guys were gunning for, but it wouldn't work out after the dust settled. Bannon figured the guy was being more stupid than critical, but a big bar brawl was not an option. But this crew was amped up now, so Bannon grabbed a bottle of whiskey and walked them down to the gym. It was after hours, but he opened it up.

He set them up in protective boxing gear, and they beat the daylights out of each other on the sparring mat. When they began sobering up, he got them home. *They'd feel and look good in the morning,* he thought, shaking his head. *They'll be primed for the increased drill schedule, but the physical pain will serve as a tonic for the real pain.*

Jilly, Billie, and Ari tried not to be shocked at the condition of the men, but their swollen faces and newly scabbed, still bloody lips and eyes were hard to ignore. Billie was the first to talk. "Did you work it out then?" They just glared, but when they looked at each other, they grinned, but not so much that it would split their lips back open.

Six new Defenders needed housing. Eleven houses were still empty, and five had two bedrooms. This took up three, and the last two were needed for new adults moving out of their parents' houses. Four marriages were coming up, and three more women had positive pregnancy tests. A housing shift was needed soon.

Dewy had been released, and his home was installed with a stair lift. Axle traded houses with Dewy's roommate to be there to assist him. He was gaining strength every week, but the new growth was fragile, and he needed to be patient. He was quickly running out of that, but he knew the price was too high to be reckless.

Bannon called Gabe, Axle, Gray, and Dewy to the briefing room to watch something. They expected it to be about some world or local news. They dreaded the expected Dranger infiltration, but they hoped it wasn't that yet; they weren't ready. They came in and sat down. Bannon wasn't there yet, and they all turned to Gray.

"Don't ask me." He threw his hands up in uncertainty. Minutes later, Bannon came in with a cooler and a bowl of popcorn.

"I thought we'd watch a boxing match," he stated. He turned on the video, and there was the New Haven Gym, and the opponents looked very familiar.

"Excellent," said Dewy. "Only a beer could make this better."

At that moment, Bannon opened the cooler and passed out a beer to each. "This is because you paid for those beers, and I dragged your butts out of there before you could drink them."

After they enjoyed the show with expletives and laughter, Axle raised his beer to gesture a toast. They all held up what was left of their beers while Axle offered a heartfelt salute to their dear friend. "To Hannah, we miss you and wish you peace and love for all eternity, and all the women you want in heaven."

They all responded with "Here, here."

May was halfway to June, and everyone was excited about the two new activity centers opening. One was the beach scene. The pool in the gym was switched out to resemble a beach with palm trees, sand-like flooring, a wave pool, and several sky and breeze programs. The day program offered a sunny sky with drifting clouds. Six different evening programs were available, each one running for an hour. There were three different sunsets. Two were varying degrees of storms, and the last one was a star-filled night with a full moon.

The Harold Seger Observatory was the other grand opening, named after the astronomer who predicted the meteorite strikes twenty-four years ago. He explained the time to prepare was now, but there had been little interest in extensive preparations for a possible scenario. It was the breaking point that exposed a long series of catastrophic decisions. The realization came too late, and the irrevocable cascade of declining nations was initiated.

During its naming ceremony, the public opening on June 1 was announced. By late May, sign-ups for the show were filling up. A walk-through viewing was free and open to all, but the enhanced show cost credits. The astronomer/meteorologist would be giving a short lecture and be followed by a dramatic video on the ceiling panels of powerful storms or cosmic events to enhance the experience.

The natural sky was mostly clear with only wispy clouds to contrast the brilliant blue. She forgot how much she missed the sky. It was the hardest thing she had to live without. Jilly wondered what the video would be like up on the ceiling, displaying storms and cosmic events with impressive realism, like they were actually happening. She and Gray had used all their credits to pay off the guitar and items for the wedding, so it would have to wait for another time.

The multi-wedding celebrations were planned for the first week of July, hopefully on a sunny Saturday. The exciting news was that it would be outside the tunnel. Without surveillance satellites, they were safe from discovery, but determining the weather was back to old-school instruments. Unless something within the atmosphere flew over, which they could detect, there was little threat.

Jilly and Ari had spent time moving most of their things over to their new homes. Their two-bedroom, single-person dwelling was in high demand, so the sooner they were out, the sooner the new Defenders and twenty-one-year-olds would be independent and on their own.

The outdoor area was encircled by containers, two high and two thick. It formed a horseshoe area outside the tunnel entrance on the west side. The east entrance was similar but much smaller. The weather had been the deciding factor for the date, but it was cooperating so far. The four grooms stood waiting for their brides, dressed in various nice garments. Bannon had an Italian suit from his days of traveling for business. Gray wore his officer dress black uniform with a white button-up shirt. He looked at the other grooms and thought about Hannah and Tanya. They should have been up here too.

The crowd had been chatting until the music began to play. The first bride came out and stood by her groom, then Ari came out second. She had a sleeveless white dress that fit her curves nicely. It was an elegant classic style accented with a single diamond pendant necklace. Jilly was the last bride to walk out of the tunnel. She wore a white dress that came to her knees in the front and went to the floor in the back. The sleeveless bodice was fitted and flared to an A-line skirt below a thin black belt. The material was light and flowy. A delicate row of black lace lined the inside of the high-low hemline, creating a striking contrast where it was exposed at the back of the skirt.

The ceremonies were presided over by Haru, who spoke of love, wisdom, and lasting relationships. Jilly's favorite words were, "Hard times are inevitable, so become good navigators, and be each other's loyal crew in stormy weather." She and Gray had already been through some difficult times, but they seemed to get closer because they trusted each other, forgave each other, and helped each other. She believed they could weather whatever came next as long as they were together.

The BBQ elk was compliments of Gray, Axle, and Gabe. A group of four musicians played music, and it sounded like heaven to hear live instruments. Everyone was dancing and having a blast. Gray got up and played a song to Jilly with the help of the band. She was overcome with love for this man and enjoyed hearing him play. He toasted a congratulations to her on graduating and receiving her nursing degree. They had been overwhelmed with the loss of their friend, helping Dewy, the wedding tasks, and her finals. They attended the graduation and had a quick drink at the Shangri-La. They both agreed it was important, but they just couldn't spend more credits on celebrating.

A glass of champagne was given to each adult, and several toasts were offered to the couples. The town had got together and purchased an hour alone for each couple at the beach scene. Normally, fifteen to twenty people could enjoy the beach, so the gift was greatly appreciated.

Tanya approached Axle and asked him to dance. "I've been mean-ing to talk to you." He could see that Tanya felt awkward about what she was about to say.

"Yeah, I've been busy with our increased drills, but I think it will let up now. How have you been doing?" he asked sincerely.

"I miss her, especially today. We would have been up there too."

"I know. I'm so sorry."

"Hannah and I talked a lot about having a baby."

"I didn't know that."

"We were going to ask you to donate." He stopped dancing and stiffened his stance. "Ax, you were her best friend."

"Is that why you wanted to talk to me? Are you asking this now, without Hannah here?"

"It's what she wanted, what we wanted. It would honor her."

"It's a terrible idea. I don't think us getting together would honor her."

"Just think about it. It doesn't have to be weird. It would be a simple medical procedure."

"That I know isn't true. No non-married persons are allowed to purposefully get pregnant. And there's nothing simple to me about having a child."

"I need something to fill the emptiness, Ax. I'm dying here."

"I don't take creating children lightly, Tanya. It's a big deal to me. You can't expect an innocent child to end your grief. I hope you find peace. You should talk to Haru. I wish you well, I do, but I can't do that. I'm sorry, I can't." He ended their dance and walked away. He knew he had been too terse with her, and he felt horrible about her loss. But he lost Hannah too. How dare she ask him to betray her? Engaging in a tryst to create a child, and then burdening that child with the task of healing her. It was abhorrent. He was seething mad, and he wished he could climb over the barrier and be free. Drangers be damned, living in the tunnel now would feel like a trap.

Gray noticed the tension between them. He would find time to talk to him later. Today was for Jilly and him. It was a treat to be outside in the fresh air and sunlight. When it started to lightly rain, no one wanted to go in. The crowd was giddy, looking skyward with their palms up to feel and enjoy every raindrop. Though a periodic midnight rain was part of the tunnel's simulations, they missed the breeze and the immense sky it came from. But they also knew surveillance was compromised by inclement weather, so they headed inside as the reception ended.

Axle stood at the edge of the barrier when the call to go in was given. Jax, one of the off-site Defenders, was working security during the wedding. It was her first official duty since coming to NH. She noticed him. She knew he outranked her, but he was not moving toward the door. She made a slow walk toward him, hoping he would begin to head in. Maybe he was on off-duty duty, like so many dedicated Ds. He looked at her, and she could see him contemplating her approach. She stopped but kept her eyes on him, trying not to enjoy the contest. He jerked his jacket in place as if it irritated him. The nonverbal warning was proof of an already raw mood. She challenged him right back by continuing her approach. *Why was he so pissed at his brother's wedding?* He broke the posturing game and headed in, not making eye contact with her as he walked by.

A week later, an off-site mission was planned to improve surveillance capabilities due to the people spotted near the tunnel. They were probably Fringers. Fringers were tribes of deserting soldiers and escaped Dailys who lived on the fringes of the territories. They were blamed for all sorts of crimes, but little was actually known about them.

They were routinely seen making their way up the mountain in summer to gather food and escape the mayhem of territorial disputes. So far, very few climbed this far up. Staying at this altitude was tough in the summer months and brutal in the winter months, which lasted most of the year. Without satellites, it was impossible to cover enough ground with short-range stealth drones to establish their whereabouts. It was time to improve their surveillance capabilities.

Two teams were required, and Axle was one of the first to volunteer. Gray still didn't know what transpired between Tanya and him. He worried she might have criticized him somehow for the Defenders' part in Hannah's death, or something along those lines. But Axle wasn't talking, and he respected his right to work it out himself. They were alike in that regard.

Gray decided to send one team east and the other one west. Axle showed up the next morning, packed and ready. Two other Defenders were already partnered together for the east mission. Axle was relieved that Gray took him up on his solo trek request. But he was surprised when he saw Jax walk in with a pack in hand. They engaged each other glare for glare, then he turned the same look toward Gray.

Gray cleared his throat and began the briefing. "You each have maps of your assigned zones. The terrain is treacherous, the predators are out, and the weather is unpredictable, so work together and don't split up." Gray looked directly at Axle.

"The mission is to set up surveillance drone stations at the designated locations. We have altered two of the minitrans to be more all-terrain. The engineers called them mini Brutes." They all chuckled. "Name them if you want to."

"Stage one: Use a mini Brute to reach a suitable central location where you will assemble your first base camp. Camo and booby-trap the shit out of it; it's where your home base and storage will be, and it cannot be found.

Stage two: go to one site a day, set up the surveillance station, send the signal to engage, and return to base. If location changes are required due to terrain or whatever, grab the geolocation of the new site. Use the old stations and beacons to triangulate. Changed locations will not be activated until you return. Once you send the engage signal, we will activate it. If you need to contact NH due to an emergency, you will have to return to one of the activated stations and resend the "engage" signal. It won't tell us where your base is, so designate a meet site using our new offsite codes.

Stage three: disassemble your base, restore the area, and repeat stages 1–3 at your next location. Stage four: After you have secured all twenty stations, return home. Questions?"

Axle started to grab his gear, and Gray motioned him over. "Are you okay to take this mission? You can keep your shit to yourself, but I can't have you going emotional on me."

"What makes you think she's ready? She's an off-siter. They were anything but prepared out there."

"So, you blame her for Hannah? Hannah was a good soldier. It sucks she's gone. She did her duty; don't cheapen her sacrifice with shit you know would piss her off. As for Jax, I vetted her myself. I've retrained her. She's ready. It's you I'm wondering about. Can you follow orders? Or should I pull your ass right now?"

"If you trust her," he sighed, "I trust her."

"Pull it together, Ax. I know you're still working out losing her. You've been taking care of Dewy, and though he still has a long way to go, he's going to be okay. You've had a lot on your plate, and I've tried to give you your space, but I need you to be here completely. You're my brother; I know you. The outdoors is like medicine to us. Go, figure this out. I want you back. And Ax, don't take your shitty mood out on Jax."

Jax was already settled in the driver's side of the mini-Brute when Axle came to the garage. He looked at her, and she defiantly looked back. "You know I outrank you and can drive if I want to," he snapped.

"I figured you could stew in your mood better if you didn't have to think about driving," she snapped back.

This is going to be a long month, he thought. While she drove, he took the opportunity to decide on the first home base location. The silence was heaven to Axle, but it was irritating to Jax.

"So, we're supposed to name our trans here. What do you think of Raven? They're smart," she asked.

"I don't know. I think the best first spot is here on this ridge. We can hit five stations if you can keep up to get to these two."

"I agree on the base location, but I'm thinking I'll be helping you keep up."

Axle tried not to smile. He couldn't let her see that, but he liked her spunk. "Wolverine."

"What?"

"I like Wolverine. They're smaller than some animals in size but fierce."

"How about a combination like Rolverine? She can be smart and fierce. But since you outrank me," she mocked with a lippy voice, "you can decide."

"Good, wake me up when you figure out how to get there. And don't roll me or drive me over a cliff."

Jax tried to decipher what he meant. Was it Wolverine or Rolverine? Every little thing was a chess move, but he would soon find out she was good at chess too. "Rolverine it is," and she made the entry, so the vehicle would respond to its name. A smile came over her face. Check, she thought in her head.

Jilly checked the results again. "This can't be," she worried. She called Andie over. "This is the third positive pregnancy test this week, and we had two last week, too. None of these are sanctioned, and all the women are still on their blockers. I checked. Are these tests giving false positives?"

"At least this one isn't false. She's over four months along," Andie said, looking at Jilly. "We need to call Maya."

Andie knew a population boom could cripple the town, so she quickly alerted Maya. Maya discovered that the improved health and diet of the residents caused their hormones to overcome the low blocker dose. The word went out that the blocker dosage needed to be increased. A population boom could put a lot of stress on the town. All in all, there were seven new pregnancies before the mini-boom was under control.

One of them was Ari, and she had known for just over a month. The blockers messed with her cycle, so she didn't know until a month ago. Now she was beginning her fifth month. "Have you told Bannon yet?" asked Jilly.

"I'm working up to it. We barely talked about kids because we have Ellie. He told me that Ellie's mother got pregnant on purpose after he told her it wasn't the right time."

"Well, you didn't trick him. It just happened. As mayor, he has been well-informed on this issue, so he can't blame you. The longer you wait, the more problems it will cause."

"I know, I know. I'm going to tell him tonight. I just have to be direct."

"Maybe, this issue requires a little more finesse. Ask Dana to take Ellie. Make it romantic," said Jilly.

Dana was happy to take Ellie, so Ari went through her plan. Bannon came through the door and collapsed on the couch.

"Man, what a day. We have seven unsanctioned babies on the way. We spent the day hashing out a new family guidance plan. Housing is going to be a tangle of trading spaces. I'm sure some will pitch a fit over it, but what are we to do? We can only house and feed so many people. I can't be happier that it's Friday."

Ari took a breath and brought him a cup of water from the dispenser. "Well, it sounds like you had a long but productive day. Ellie is over at Dana's, so I thought we'd go to dinner later tonight."

"That sounds excellent," he smiled at her. "How was your day?"

"It was...great," she said, pausing between each word.

"Everything okay?"

"Oh yeah, yeah. I was just wondering if after dinner we could pick up Dewy and go to the Shangri-La. Axle is on offsite duty, so he's on his own." She thought to herself, *There is no way this is a good time to announce this dilemma.* Dewy said he would meet them at the bar at eight. When they showed up, Gray and Jilly were with him.

"I guess we had the same idea," Gray smiled, giving Bannon a friendly slap on the shoulder. Jilly made eye contact with Ari and soon figured out she had not told Bannon yet. She made a gesture to follow her to the bathroom.

"Okay, what happened? And why are you at the bar? How are you going to pull off not having a drink?"

"He came home complaining about the number of pregnancies and the new law that he had to work on today. I didn't think about the drink thing. What should I do?" Ari had a panicked look in her eyes.

"Okay, I'll talk to Gabe; he's bartending. I'll make sure he makes you a virgin drink. It's going to work out, Ari, I promise. Bannon is a good man."

Jilly ran to Gabe and explained the issue. He gave her a wink. "I think I know a little bit about this kind of situation."

The night went on with everyone talking and enjoying themselves. Bannon talked a little about the baby issue, and Ari bristled. Jilly and Dewy caught it, but no one else seemed to notice. On the walk home, Bannon and Gray were talking, and the rest of them trailed behind. Dewy was starting to walk now, but it was limited to short distances, so he was in a chair tonight. Jilly was pushing Dewy, and Ari was walking next to him.

"Ari," he questioned, "you okay?"

"Oh yeah," she answered quickly. "Fine."

"Girl, what's goin' on? You're lousy at lyin'. Tell me ta mind my own business, but we're too close fer lyin'."

Ari started sniffling, and Jilly slowed down. "I'm one of those women everyone is talking about," cried Ari.

"One of what women? Wait, you're... That's awesome! Oh, you afraid ta tell the mayor? I guarantee you he'd be excited."

"Excited about what?" asked Bannon. Noticing them falling behind, they paused and listened to their discussion. "Ari," he asked, "are you crying? Honey, what's going on?"

"Gray, let's go." Jilly tucked her arm in Gray's while pushing Dewy with the other.

"What is going on?" Gray asked, grabbing the wheelchair from Jilly.

"Gray, it's time ta get, trust me," said Dewy. They walked off while Gray was still trying to get answers.

"Just tell me, Ari. Everything's going to be okay."

"I'm one of those women, Bannon."

"One of what women?"

"The pregnant ones." She started sobbing. "I didn't trick you. I swear. It just happened."

"A baby? You're carrying our baby?" He took it in for a second. "That's wonderful!"

"But you said it was a problem for the town, and Gevia tricked you..."

"Shhhh," he kissed her forehead. "This is splendid news. Forget what I said as the mayor. I'm overjoyed, Ari. Our own little person." They kissed and headed home with his arm around her.

The new legislation stated that permits for pregnancy had to be applied for, and blockers were mandatory for all adult males and females. Only a certain number of babies could be born each year. First-time parents would get up to 75 percent of the permits.

Several protesters were marching with signs in front of the Town Hall. Bannon was not threatened by the fact that citizens were involved and interested in their government. It was proof of their belief in freedom, and it was safe to disagree. And although outdoor events were held about once a week during the warmer months, he fully expected the younger members to demand more freedom. They had not signed a concealment waiver to remain in the town, and he was not sure how that would be resolved.

Chapter Seventeen

Axle woke up suddenly when the vehicle came to a stop. He didn't mean to fall asleep. He just wanted to tune out her yammering. He checked the navigation beacons, confirming they had arrived at the base camp location. The beacons were set out this spring to substitute for the destroyed GPS satellites.

They were turned on by a coded frequency, but they were not very secure. They were undetected so far, but the new, more secure stations would replace those and be able to launch drones from over fifty miles away.

They exited the vehicle and got to work setting up the base camp. They found a well-secluded place under the tall pines. It had good cover but was still dappled in sunlight. A nearby cliff would serve as a good launching area for the scout drone. Rolverine was not as small as the term mini implied. It had a large area for storing their supplies, stations, and shelter.

The flex-up shelter had sturdy walls, a ceiling, and a floor. The whole structure was then covered with a camo stealth blanket, which prevented thermal and material scans. The menu consisted of field rations, but a quick heat unit made them more palatable; besides, Axle didn't plan on eating that crap every meal. He planned to hunt for some fresh food. After setting up the cots and stowing their gear, they decided to hit the closest station site.

They stashed Rolverine, covering it with another stealth blanket. It was still quite full of stations, so the hyper-lock with self-defense capabilities was activated. They gathered the needed supplies and headed out through the steep wooded area. The site was only one and a half miles away, but the terrain was challenging. They were in fierce competition the whole way.

Axle saw Jax's foot slip off a ledge, and he offered her his hand. She scowled and fought her way back to the foothold. When Axle grabbed a weak tree root while climbing up a ridge, she just smiled and offered her help. There is no way he would accept it either. At the site, he unpacked the drone and prepared it to carry the station up a tall tree to secure it to the trunk.

"When you secure the area, I can fly it up to you," Jax asserted. "I'm a pretty good pilot."

"I can manage," quipped Axle. He wondered if everything was going to be a battle with her. He climbed the tree with all the gear and the complete drone station on his back. He had a hard time trimming the branches with the burden of it, but he had to provide the drone with clear landing access. He should have left the heavy drone below and let her fly it up to him, but he didn't want her help. He didn't trust her.

He held the box in place while he deployed the attachment bands. The two round flex bands dug into the tree, holding the station secure. Because they didn't encircle the trunk and the material was flexible, it allowed the tree to grow without damaging the station or the tree. He tested the drone and was satisfied with the installation. The first job was done despite their unimpressive teamwork.

"I'm going for a quiet walk. I'll see you back at the base." Axle thought that if Gray witnessed their lack of cooperation, he would have punished them severely, and that only fueled his resentment.

"Good, see you then. Don't fall or anything. I don't want to have to come find you," snapped Jax.

"Ya know, you might want to address your senior officer differently from now on." He gave her a serious look. He was getting tired of the fray.

"Yes sir," she snapped and gave him a salute. He disappeared over the hill. *Finally*, he thought, *peace and quiet.*

She was grating on his already shredded nerves. He took a minute to listen to the sound of the creaking pines and the wind quivering through the forest. It had a soothing effect, and it began to relax him. He found a wild strawberry patch, and the tart treat tasted so good, not like the bio-cloned food at the tunnel.

Gathering a couple of handfuls, he moved on and stumbled on some wild onions and harvested them. Fireweed gave a peppery flavor to food, and he collected some of that too. But he was especially thrilled when he caught the white hue of ghost pipe. It was a waxy-looking plant that, when gently cooked, tasted like asparagus. As he made his way back to base, he couldn't make up his mind whether he'd share or not.

When he arrived, Jax was sitting on a log watching over a silver box with an oversized reflective lid. The lid sat several inches above and was attached with a funnel-shaped support system. "What are you doing?" asked Axle.

"It's this stealth oven that Ari wanted me to try out. There is a heat source inside, but the cover absorbs the heat that escapes and directs it back into the oven through this funnel made of heat-conducting metal. It conserves the heat so well, it's not detectable by thermoscans, so it's safe to cook outside."

"Huh," he had to admit, the idea intrigued him. "What are you cooking?"

"A rabbit," she answered, taking a peek at the meal inside. "I'm happy to share." She had thought about their turbulent interactions. They might need each other, and they were acting unprofessionally.

He thought about which direction he wanted to go here, and he decided to be respectful back. "That's nice, thank you. I have some sides. Can we add these wild onions and fireweed to your rabbit?" It felt wrong to be so nice. But he peeled the outer layer off the onions and ripped up the fireweed, then he handed them to her.

She opened her oven and added them to the small pan inside. "What does fireweed taste like?" She wondered if he was rendering her meal inedible.

"It's got a light peppery flavor; not hot, though."

"Cool." *This is going better than expected*, she thought. "Thanks."

"I'll go in and cook the ghost pipe."

"Ghost pipe?"

"It's like wild asparagus. I have dessert too," he said, more to one-up her than be generous. He showed her the berries.

"Wow, we're going to eat like kings!"

He watched her fuss over the new contraption and wondered when and how she met Ari. Jax had been offsite for almost a year, and before that, she was in recruitment training. She'd never been to the tunnel before her rescue. He knew very little about her, and he should have reviewed the off-site Defenders' records before this mission.

Since he thought he'd be on his own, he decided to put it off until he returned. The real reason was that he felt too angry at their sloppy execution during the extraction mission to read anything objectively. Gray had debriefed the team, but he missed that meeting. Gray gave him some room to grieve. He needed it, but now he didn't know who his partner was or what her skill sets were.

Yet, this woman seemed extremely competent. She was fit and strong. She had no problem completing a task, but her attitude toward authority, or at least his, stunk. There were twelve NH Defenders and twelve off-siters involved. It should have been more than enough to overtake seven Drangers. He couldn't understand what caused the plan to get so dicked up. Seven dead Defenders. Hannah was gone, Tanya was left in tatters, and Dewy was crippled up for half a year, maybe more. His anger toward her started simmering again.

They worked professionally during the rest of the installations from their first base camp. Their interactions were all business, and the cold silence was awkward to Jax, but to Axle, it was more tolerable than pissy engagements. They followed the protocols for leaving their camp, and Axle made sure he was in the driver's seat as she loaded the last of the gear. He saw her bristle at the move, and it gave him an ugly satisfaction.

Jax sat in the passenger seat, thinking deeply. She knew he blamed her for the death of his friend and the six others who had died. And then there was Dewy. The more she thought about it, she couldn't blame him. Someone or something had tipped the Drangers off that day. It was the only explanation.

If it were a person, she was sure it was one of the off-siters, but she wasn't sure if it was one of the ones that died, or if there was a traitor in the town. She told Gray everything she knew. He said he'd look into it, but she didn't know him well enough to believe him. Maybe he blamed her and her crew too. She was the lead officer, and whether she was to blame or not, she was responsible.

Axle watched her looking out the window for over an hour, pondering something. He assumed it was about that day. He caught her often in such a state, and he figured she was reliving it, changing actions, weighing each decision. He wanted to ask her about it, but he knew it would just start another sparring match.

He felt ashamed of his behavior on this mission and that he hadn't gone on the extraction team. Why had Gray held him back? He explained it should be routine, and the younger Defenders needed real mission experience, but he, too, was shocked at the results. Axle vowed that before they returned, he'd have some answers from her.

Gray sat across from Dewy as he told him about Tanya. She had approached him about being a surrogate father, and he told her no. He felt bad that she had lost Hannah, and he understood her fear of being alone for the rest of her life. She was only twenty-two years old, and she felt the likelihood of finding a gay woman she could love in such a small town was highly unlikely. But Dewy didn't want to ruin his status as a Defender by breaking a law, and he didn't think a baby would solve anything.

Tanya was prescribed a mild sedative to help her sleep, and she gave Dewy a triple dose. He woke up to her undoing his pants. It was a struggle with the drugs and his injuries to remove her, but he threw her on the floor, and she crumpled into a crying heap.

Dewy tried to make light of the scene. "Yeah, I'm constantly throwin' these girls off o' me," he smiled. His tone got more serious as he asked about this person, whom he used to call his friend. "Whadya gonna do to 'er?"

"Dewy, I know you're trying to shrug this off, but this isn't a joke. She tried to rape you, that's not funny, no matter who you are. She's a mess. What if she had succeeded in getting pregnant? We'd have to take the child from her, then what? You'd have a child to raise who came from that situation. She needs help. That's what I'm going to aim for, but it's in the legislators' hands now."

When Gray came home, he wrapped Jilly in his arms. He didn't know what he'd do if someone tried to hurt her. He needed to protect her. Protect her from violence, but also from the horrible things that come with his responsibility. She knew about Dewy because he told her first. He went to the RAS to make sure he hadn't re-injured his spine. She said he had to tell Gray. He would get in trouble if it came out later, and he hadn't reported it to his superior officer.

"I know you had a rough day with Tanya and Dewy. Is there anything I can do to help?" Jilly asked Gray.

"I wish it were Friday. I need a couple of days to work this out in my head."

"I know this dilemma still lingers from the Merita situation, but..."

"Jilly, please don't go there," he warned.

"I don't want to know what happened to her, but I don't believe she's at an offsite. We pulled them. You don't have to carry this alone, Gray. It was an impossible scenario. If there is blame, I'm as much involved in it as anyone."

"It's complicated. Please stop." He saw the concerned look in her eyes. "Jilly. Look, I faced that demon, and I fought back, back to you. I formed a perspective I can live with. I don't need to discuss it." Gray gave her a stern but hurtful look, and she decided to drop it. She sat him down on the couch and went behind him to rub his shoulders.

When the news came out about Tanya's trial and its charges, the activists came out in droves. Some wanted her to be in counseling, some wanted her jailed, and some wanted both. A couple of extremists wanted her executed. Gray wondered if they had the stomach to carry out such a sentence themselves. He hoped not. A jury was chosen, and a date was set for Thursday.

This was to be the first big criminal trial case for New Haven. Since trials had not been performed for decades, both the prosecution and the defense lawyers were in uncharted territory. They had settled a few minor disputes and infractions, but this trial held many firsts, including what to do with a convicted criminal.

Axle and Jax were at their last base. The first two installations had gone relatively well, and they were ahead of schedule. They had a total of six at this site, but one was going to be particularly difficult. It was on a rocky cliff, and it had to be done by hand. The station had to be set inside a small crack in the rock and secured with anchors.

They were unable to access the inside of the gap to set the anchor bolts. Axle wanted to climb down the rock face, but Jax pointed out that he was much better suited for the job of pulling her out.

Axle was a very experienced rock climber, and Jax was still learning. She was probably capable, he thought, but he could handle it without incident. It was true, he could pull her out much easier than she could pull him, and no doubt the experience would improve her skills. But he wanted to do it himself without any accidents. They had both held their tempers down to embers, but they were both ready to flash.

"Fine, you go. I'll be there to save your ass. God knows you couldn't save mine," snapped Axle.

Jax whirled around and hit him square in the jaw. He had not expected that. She stood in a fighting stance while he was rubbing out the blow. "You want to have this out right now? I know you blame me for the deaths of the Defenders at the Hold. Well, I am responsible, so let's just finish this bullshit." She gave him a steady glare, burning a hole right through him.

"Hey, just calm down," Axle said, knowing he had pushed her too far.

"Never tell a woman to calm down!" she yelled as she charged him again. She tried to sweep his legs out from under him, but he countered with a spin and block move. She jabbed his ribs and swept him again. This time, he went down. She pinned him, but he rolled her under him and gained control. He outsized her by almost a foot, and though her fighting skills were excellent, his were too.

He held her hands above her on the ground while straddling her. They were close now. He could see her dark honey-brown eyes spitting fire at him. They were perfectly almond-shaped and exotic. She had full lips against caramel-colored skin. He was seeing her for the first time, and she was quite beautiful in a cornered animal sort of way.

"I don't want to blame you or anyone, but it was a disaster. I can't see someone with your skills overseeing that. Why don't you just tell me what happened?"

"You read the report," she grumbled.

"Well, that's my mistake. I was too pissed to look at it," he admitted.

"Let me up first." She gave him a defiant look.

"I'm fairly sure I know how that will go. Just start talking."

"I was the lead on this mission, but I wasn't to take charge until we arrived. My team was scheduled to arrive first, but we were third to hit the Hold. I didn't know then why the first two didn't follow the ETA plan, but the takeover was already in play.

"They killed the first crew before they ever made it to the parking lot. I don't know why the second crew was captured. They say they were caught off guard. I guess it's possible. A lot of those crews didn't maintain any kind of training schedules, and they got lazy. But when we arrived, the second crew greeted us, and then three Drangers came out dressed as Defenders."

"Do you think they were tipped off?"

"I don't know. Can I get up now?"

"In a minute. What happened with the scanners being turned off?"

"They were being accessed whenever we would leave the bunker. The scanner would come on without us activating it, and soon, we would detect unknowns approaching. We disabled them, and it stopped happening."

"What happened when you were taken hostage?" asked Axle.

"We could only see the faces of the second crew. They acted like all was well, no hostile signals, then suddenly the Drangers in D gear put weapons on us and the Defenders without helmets. We were disarmed."

"I wonder what the report says about not throwing signals to alert you to the hostiles. That's suspicious."

"Gray said he'd look into it. I told him everything."

"How many from the second crew survived?"

"Two, now let me up."

He loosened his hold and stood up, offering her a hand.

She swatted it away and leaped up. Grabbing her daypack, she took off. Axle debated following her, but she needed to blow off some steam. He thought about the possibility of a traitor inside NH. He sat down, deciding not to attempt the installation alone. He needed to think. About ten minutes went by, and he heard a shot. It was loud, so it wasn't hers.

He grabbed his weapon, took off, and sent up a drone in the direction she headed. He was efficient at search patterns, and he flew the drone methodically. He had a sense of urgency, knowing every moment could be her last, but sloppy work could mean losing her too.

Finally, he spotted her. She was in the company of three Drangers. She was crumpled on the ground and not moving. He made his way to a ledge above them. Suddenly, she popped up and grabbed a Dranger that got too close. She held a knife to his throat. It stunned the other two, but it didn't appear they were concerned about their comrade. They were grabbing weapons, and Axle took both out. The one in her grip tried to grab her knife; it was the wrong move, and Jax sliced his jugular.

Axle made his way down to her and retrieved the drone. "Are you okay?" He saw the bullet burn on her arm, her ripped shirt, and her swollen cheek. He quickly went to grab the weapons and noticed they amounted to a couple of slingshots, three good-sized knives, and one rusty revolver. Her weapon would have been a prize for them.

"Fine. I'm fine," Jax spoke weakly.

Axle saw the fading look in her eyes, and he sat her down. It was then that he noticed the blood spot on the back of her head. She had taken a blow to the back of her head, and it was bleeding down her neck, beneath her short black hair, and down her bare shoulder.

"Can you walk?" Axle asked as he grabbed her gear.

"Yeah." She went about a quarter of a mile and grabbed onto a tree for support. "I just need a minute."

But Axle hid their gear, grabbed her, and put her over his shoulder. She was yelling and struggling weakly, but it wasn't long before he felt her go limp and stop fighting. He treated her wounds with the medkit. Her injuries were no doubt painful, but less severe than he first thought. He used some of the herbs he had been gathering and made her some tea to ease her nausea.

"What happened?" he asked.

"They hit me from behind with a slingshot. I dove behind a tree and turned and shot, but I couldn't locate them because my vision was blurred. They shot back and winged my arm. Then they am-bushed me. I got some good jabs in, but there were too many, so I played dead. I was waiting for my chance to take out at least one of them. And I must admit, I was hoping you heard their shot."

"You'll have a hell of a headache, but it's not too bad." He looked at her ripped clothing and contemplated the Drangers' plan for her. The thought made him roil inside. He touched her chin with his pointer finger and turned it slightly to see the bruise on her cheek. "Did they hit you?"

"Yeah, but I was hitting them too. I'm not a damsel in distress here. If you pin me with some victim bullshit, I will kick your ass." Her look was full of rage and warning.

Axle smiled. He was beginning to like this woman.

"Seriously, though, what can you tell me about them? Are they wanderers, or do you think there is a camp of them somewhere?"

"They're low-funded for sure. Their weapons were old-school garbage. I didn't hear any chatter about reporting me to anyone or bringing me to a base. That being said, they weren't camped there. I didn't see any gear."

"Yeah, I noticed that too. Do you think they knew you were coming, or did they just get a lucky break?" He thought about how close the encounter was.

"It's close enough to our camp that they might have discovered it. We should probably move."

"Yeah, I'm afraid you're right. I'll start packing up."

"I'll work on the stuff in here."

"No, you're going to take it easy, so you don't break the chem-sutures and start bleeding again. That pain blocker is giving you courage, but it's the stupid kind. I'm going to recover the gear I hid and start packing up."

She knew he was right, but his snitty remarks sent her back into battle mode. The moment he walked out of the shelter, she began packing it up.

When Axle came back, the interior packing was completed. She sat on the one foldout stool left. He sighed and walked around to get a look at her head. She was fine, and he thought he probably would have done the same. He had been babying her, but not because she was a woman as much as he was still hashing out the incompetence of the Hold mission.

They packed the items, collapsed the shelter, and collected their camp security devices. He drove while she flew the drone on recon to find the Dranger base.

"Got it," she exclaimed. "It's 1.3 clicks northeast. It's not much of one. Wait, I see a heat sig. It's faint. Whoever it is, isn't doing well."

"Great, we've been exposed. Okay, let's stash Rolverine and check it out. Full gear. And by the way, I overrode your name entry and changed it to Rolver. It's easier to say." He smiled and made a "one point for me" gesture, which she forced herself to ignore.

When they reached the site, they discovered a collection of items that would normally be abandoned as useless. In a ragged shelter, they found two bound women. One was dead from serious injuries, and the other, much younger, had a leg injury and appeared malnourished. But as far as their equipment could detect, she was not ill from disease. She tried to fight them at first, but Jax calmed her down and began to treat her.

Outside the shelter, Jax approached Axle with what she had learned. "They're traffickers and not particularly good ones. They offed one of their hostages. The survivor's name is Aniya Peters, and she has a bad break she got while being dragged around on a leash. She's malnourished from being on a hunger strike, but it's not critical.

She's from Lakewood, but she said it was burned in a lightning strike. She and her mom were captured from their Fringer group while they were traveling to find another campsite. Her mother died trying to protect her. She didn't say anything, but it's doubtful she wasn't raped. She's a month from nineteen."

"Well, shit! We cannot drive her to a settlement if what she says is true. And I guess we can't leave her here, either." This scenario had been discussed many times. The protocol was to eliminate Drangers and provide refugees with supplies and leave. If possible, deliver them to the closest settlement. But bringing them in was not sanctioned.

"I say we take her to our next camp until we finish our work. Then we see where she is health-wise. Maybe we'll find a camp to take her," suggested Jax.

"Well, since the two of you are injured, you're staying with her. We can't trust her alone at our camp."

Jax fumed. His logic was sound, but she knew it was a win for him in their little war. She couldn't let him know she saw it that way. "I agree," she answered calmly. "But first, we need to bury her mom. Then I suggest you hold off on that cliff installation. It needs two people, and we'll have to figure out a plan when we get there."

"We'll see. We have to be careful what we say. She can't hear any of our info. She can't know what we're doing."

Jax nodded, and Axle wondered why she was being so agreeable.

Axle found finishing the three installs on his own was easy and enjoyable work for the next three days. Jax would cook, clean, and take care of Aniya, and he could feel her rage about the domesticated arrangement. He often laughed out loud just thinking about it, but not in front of her.

The final cliff install day had come. They had to decide how to play it with Aniya. Her health was improved enough for her to hobble around with the field cast, but not enough to set her free and on her own. The installation should take about four hours. They decided to pack the site up and secure her to a small area with water, a bucket, a power bar, and a distress beacon.

They also set a camera on her, so they could check on her. They arrived at the site quicker than expected. Jax was healed up well enough that he agreed to belay her down to complete the install.

They bickered over every step, and by the time Jax finished and he pulled her up, they were both ready for a fight. She came at Axle with a sidekick to the ribs. Axle grabbed her leg and easily spun her around before putting her on the ground and sitting over her.

"And here we are again. Me on top," he smiled. She was enraged and tried to move her knee upward toward his crotch, but failed. "Jax, I teach this stuff, and I outsize you by, well, a lot. Just stop. We have to work this out." He looked into her furious gaze, and with all her movement, he was becoming aroused. She was all challenge and desire, and he was burning with male heat. He needed to kiss her. He wanted it so badly his breath became heavy as his eyes looked directly into hers.

"I don't know about you, but all this physical tension is killing me. I don't know if I like you or hate you, but man, I want to kiss you. I want to do that pretty badly." He checked her gaze for any signs of rejection or disagreement. But she had a sly smile forming on her lips and fire in her smoldering eyes. He leaned in slowly, knowing it could be a trick.

The first touch of their lips was electric, and he heard her soft moan. He raised his head slightly and saw that her eyes were closed, and he returned to her lips, trailing kisses down her neck. She struggled to free her arms pinned above her, but he smiled and shook his head. A stubborn part of her wanted to break free to reclaim her control, but that part lost out to the need welling up inside her.

She could feel his arousal, and it only increased her own. He carefully freed her hands, and he pulled her on top of him. He was ready to react if she was bluffing, but she started ripping off her gear, so he followed suit.

She was down to panties and bra, and he expertly unfastened her bra with a single-handed move while pulling it off in front with the other. He noticed the significant scar running down her left side. It was long and angry, stretching from under her left arm and curving toward her belly button. She grabbed his chin and redirected his gaze to her eyes. He pulled her down toward him and kissed her side with the scarred trauma slowly making his way to her breast. He took the firm flesh into his mouth with wild urgency. Then she pinned his hands and began her assault on him. She moved rhythmically with complete self-indulgence.

He watched her face rise to the sky and then look back down at him with a primal, possessive stare. She was driving him mad with sexual cravings. He countered her by grabbing her thin thong panties with two hands, ripping them in half, and tossing them aside. Their most sensitive places were skin-to-skin now, and the initial shock of the shift in power froze her in place.

She considered him for a few seconds, but then she began to slide back and forth. He waited for his moment when she would be in the perfect position, and then he maneuvered inside of her. The many weeks of tense anticipation broke free, feeding their frenzied union. They were like wild beasts in heat, seizing their own pleasure, which only surged the fever between them. At last, the climax roared through them both. Axle heard her cry out, tipping him over the edge, and he let out a guttural groan of pleasure.

Panting and sweaty, she looked down at him. He was breathing hard, and his eyes were closed. He looked sated. He opened his eyes and pulled her down for more kissing. He thought words might ruin the moment, so he wouldn't allow any. Maybe he would come up with something to say, but the more they kissed and explored each other, the greater the need grew again.

Five hours after their departure time, they arrived back at the base. Jax slept on the way back, postponing the awkward conversation. Aniya was fine but hungry, so they ate some rations and headed toward NH. Axle spied a herd of elk and stopped.

The two hunted in silence together, with perfect synergy. They took down two elk. One was a big bull, and the other was an injured cow. They skinned and gutted their kills, packing the meat in the station boxes they saved, and they headed to the town. Maybe fresh meat would help the shitstorm of a mood Gray would be in when they showed up with Aniya.

Chapter Eighteen

Bannon and Gray looked from the mayor's second-story office at the high schoolers protesting outside Town Hall. On the other side of them were the parents demanding legal custody of their teens and the protection of the town.

"We knew this was coming, Ban. They didn't sign up for this. When they reach the age of consent, we'll be keeping them here against their will." Gray stood at the large one-way window, marveling at the demonstration of free speech while at the same moment worrying about its trajectory.

"But that's why we had all children over eighteen sign a waiver. The age of consent in New Haven is twenty-one. We have another year and a half." Bannon walked over and sat at his desk, staring at the golden hammer plaque from the New Haven ground-breaking ceremony. He reflected on his hopes for the project while the shouts of heated tempers tolling below threatened his dream. "Why do they rally against me? I gave up everything to create this sanctuary for all of us. Don't they remember what it was like on the outside? Can't they be just a little grateful?"

"It isn't personal, Bannon. You should be proud. This is exactly how democracy works. It's true to a core set of principles, not a person, and they finally feel safe enough to flex their constitutional rights. A constitution sets up the framework to level the field between leader and citizen. It provides civilization with the ability to evaluate and align laws to grow with the changes of time. Change is coming, and we need to accept that." Gray peered through the tinted office window. He was focusing on Amber. She was a wounded soul who leveraged her misdirected rage to incite the crowd. She was effective. He had to give her that, but this crowd was dancing on the edge. "We both know their signatures were forced by their parents. I think we have to offer them something. It can't be freedom to leave the tunnel. They have to know that, but this conflict must be dealt with before someone takes it too far."

"I know, I was stunned by your security report. Petty crimes are up twenty percent, and physical altercations went from a total of four since we moved into the tunnel to two this week alone. I get both sides, though, I do. Just like the parents below, I must allow New Haven to grow up and evolve. These parents are afraid of the very freedoms essential for young adults to mature. I also feel the dread of letting go, knowing the incalculable risks and things that can go wrong. It's a painful transition requiring a perilous trust in one's inexperienced offspring, but I agree."

He exhaled a long, breathy sigh while propping up his head. He grabbed a couple of downer tabs and threw them back before continuing with his committed response. "I know liberty hates confinement, and though our liberty is confined within walls and locked gates, it has the most crucial components, the freedom of speech on the street and at the polls. When that is provided, liberty will always struggle against its borders. Liberty, in any form, has always been messy because it isn't satisfied to reside within the ease of its center."

"Well," stated Gray, "I have some evolutionary suggestions. They want to be treated like adults, and I think that's a good idea. I met with the senior high school and the underage college students at Madison High School. They gave me some ideas. They want voting rights for those over eighteen. I say we let them elect their own representative, who attends some legislative meetings and presents their issues. They wouldn't have voting power, but they would be heard, and we could see how that tracks.

There are some bills up for a vote in November, and they could participate in that. This system of governing is new to everyone. We are all learning how to navigate within it. We could establish social awareness clubs that teach and encourage civic responsibility. They also complained that they wanted a place like the Shangri-La. We could empty the east storage area in the corridor. It's by the security building, so we can keep an eye on them." Gray waited for Bannon's response. He knew this project was his baby, but his baby was taking those first wobbly steps, and falls were inevitable.

"I like those suggestions. I say we get the social studies teacher to help them write up a bill for the legislation. They should present it too. It was always my understanding that the citizens would be involved in the running of this town. It's just so hard to know where the line is between liberty and survival."

Bannon contacted the social studies teacher, who was excited to give them a real-life assignment. The legislators opened the floor to new bills twice a month. He believed they would be ready for the meeting after next, and Bannon got approval for the students to attend.

The first group of Defender trainees prepared for their initial round of survival school. They were excited because tonight they would be issued their gear. Dewy was walking with a cane now and was the training instructor. The Brad Anderson Middle School classrooms were used for evening training sessions. He looked at them and wondered if he was ever that green.

He joined the Defenders at seventeen. His family had died a year ago, and he was a Daily on his way to being a Dranger. It was the only real way to survive without a family or clan. That's when he was recruited by Rud. Rud was employed by Vogel as a guard at one of their buildings. When Banner died, Rud was called back to Colorado, where his son, Bannon, was consolidating his resources. Rud brought his crew and Dewy with him. Rud was killed during a Dranger battle at one of those sites, but Banner kept Dewy on, though his training was incomplete. That was five years ago, but it seemed like a lot more.

Summer was quickly waning, and the fall chill was taking over more each day. New Haven had just celebrated its first year in the tunnel. Though there were rocky starts, turbulent incidents, and dreadful responsibilities, success was evident on the faces of the residents. The learning curve was steep and still in play, but everyone agreed freedom was worth fighting for.

Axle and Jax arrived back at the tunnel and contacted Gray from out-site W3. He relieved the current on-duty Defenders, telling them to go back to town. He knew they had to hold up here for contagion clearance. He asked to talk to Gray.

"Hey, Ax, welcome back. How did the installs go? Any trouble?"

"All accomplished. We ran into a couple of Drangers. They tried to beat on Jax, but it didn't work out for them."

"So, that's why you're hanging at the out-site. Is she okay?"

"Yeah, she's good," Axle and Jax were trying not to smile.

Gray caught the subtle innuendo and sighed. He kind of figured there was more than animosity between them, and was rethinking putting them on the same team. "So, I guess you didn't kill each other. Anything else?" asked Gray.

"The good news is we got some elk meat. Two nice ones."

"Okay, good. Something tells me I'm going to be more interested in the bad news."

"We have an outsider."

"With you!"

"Yeah, she's young, Gray, and injured and abandoned."

"Shit, Axle! Damn it! No doubt she's a Fringer with all manner of diseases. You know the protocol. You'd better spill it before I drive out there and spend the next four weeks retraining you two myself."

Axle and Jax both gave their reports. When they finished, there was a painful silence. Gray rubbed his forehead and had to admit he couldn't think of anything he would have done differently. "Okay, I'll have to tell Bannon, and then I'm sending a medic to assess Aniya and Jax. Gray out." His abrupt disconnect let them know he was irritated. Ax knew the legislators had talked and talked this situation out, and no acceptable solution that preserved their sovereignty could be found. Gray had a rough bout of arguments in store.

The medic came in a bio-suit and cleared Jax's injuries, but he determined Aniya needed to go to the hospital. The fracture was not healing properly, and there were signs of infection. He loaded her into the secure trailer and drove away, leaving Axle and Jax alone at the site.

"So, should we talk about this?" he said as he made a gesture between them.

"Oh, honey, that's so cute. Are you a talk-about-your-feelings-af-ter-sex kind of dude?" Jax was mocking him with a condescending demeanor.

Axle felt his ire rising again. "Ya know, you don't have to be such a bitch. You could just say you want me." He smiled and opened his arms.

She laughed. "Ya know what? You're kind of growing on me," she replied and straddled him in the chair.

"Oh yeah," he sighed. "I can vouch for that," and he planted a greedy kiss on her lips.

Aniya stared through the plastic carrier she was caged in. They explained the reasons, but she was feeling very vulnerable. Her leg was in a constant state of pain, and she didn't want them to touch it.

"Hi, Aniya. I'm Dr. Maya. I hear you hurt your leg. We're going to take an internal scan. Have you ever had one?" She shook her head no. "It doesn't hurt, but it will show us your leg bone." Aniya just stared at her.

They moved the machine into place, and Aniya closed her eyes. "Look, Aniya, here is your bone that's broken. See that jagged line right there? The bone won't heal correctly unless we line up the two sides."

"I don't feel the machine going inside me." Aniya had a surprised look on her face. "Those are my bones? Can you fix the broken one?"

"Absolutely, we'll need to reset it, but you'll be asleep, so it won't hurt. Did you get any other injuries while you were held by the Drangers?"

Aniya shook her head. Dr. Maya ordered the anesthesia. When she was under, she ordered a rape kit too. The bone was set, and the rape kit was negative. She was still a virgin. Many girls stayed virgins due to the dangerous times. Disguising them as males, dressing them in unflattering attire, and arranging marriages were some of the antiquated solutions that had come back in style. Her value was higher if she was intact, which is why they abused her mother instead. She made a call to Haru and advised him of the situation. Aniya's presence was still highly classified, so only authorized persons could visit.

On the first day of Tanya's trial, opening statements were made, and Dewy was called as a witness. He hated being any part of hurting Tanya, but she had put him in an impossible situation. When the defense cross-examined him, they asked him about Hannah.

"She was a very good friend. She saved my life, so yeah, I do feel I owe her."

"Yes or no, is lying about her girlfriend how you return her loyalty?"

"She would want—"

"Your Honor, please instruct the witness to answer yes or no," the defense lawyer insisted. The judge told Dewy to comply.

"Yes, I am being loyal to her."

It was only the first day, and Dewy was spent. He decided to call Axle at the out-site. He must be going crazy, stuck in that small bunker with his nemesis. He dialed up the off-site phone, and when the camera came on, Axle and Jax were leaning up against the wall lip lip-locked and unaware they were being watched. Dewy let out a couple of expletives while snickering at the irony.

"So campers, glad ta see we're gettin' along. And here I thought I'd be breakin' up a fight or sumthin. Ya'll better be more careful in front of them cameras, or there's gonna be a briefin' 'bout your debriefin'." He was laughing out loud now.

"Shit, Dewy, what the hell? I didn't hear the phone buzz."

"Ya, I believe that. Maybe I should call back later."

"No, is something happening?" asked Axle.

"No, I'm just pissed off about this trial thang."

"What trial?" asked Axle.

"Tanya's. You didn't hear?" Dewy explained the events that led up to the trial. "I feel like an asshole. What do you think Hannah would think of it?"

"Wow, shit. You know, she asked me the same thing at the wedding." Axle shared.

"No shit!" Dewy was stunned.

"I got pissed. Nothing about it sounded sane to me. There is no way Hannah would have agreed to that. And I'll be damned if I would let her raise my kid. Shit, she's lost it and gone full-on crazy bitch. You know, I think she was way more into Hannah than Hannah was into her. Hannah said they had some issues to work out before they vowed up."

"But her lawyer said they were engaged," Dewy questioned.

"Not really, but the news was bandied around by Tanya, and Hannah just didn't want to humiliate her. At least, that's how I understood it. But I did think they would get married with the rest of them. I didn't know her issues included being a controlling psycho asshole."

"I think she's genuinely sorry. She just went kinda berserk when she lost her. I just want it to be over. I want to lose this cane and..." Dewy trailed off, not wanting to complain.

"Dewy, you're gonna recover. Hell, you're almost there. You only have two and a half more months of re-gen treatments, and then you can go balls-to-the-wall and work out to your heart's content. When you are cleared for running, we'll start jogging in the mornings again, and when I get back, let's sneak into the farm and go fishing."

"That would be awesome, Ax! Hey, I gotta go. You kin get on back to whatever that was you were doin' out there. Just do something about the camera, dude, seriously."

Jax stared at Axle. "Whoa, some news. No wonder you were so pissed at the wedding. She must have lost her mind to try and rape a drugged guy when he's disabled? Damn! Would that even work?"

"I think we should conduct some research. I'll pretend I'm drugged and incapacitated, and you try to arouse me, for scientific purposes." Axle smiled, sticking out his tongue in an exaggerated expression.

Gabe was in charge of the off-site drill. He gave the three Defender trainees a briefing before their first off-site training mission. "Your goals on this mission are to build a shelter, effectively utilize the gear provided, survey the area, hunt for small game, create a system of stealth trail markers, light a fire, and, most importantly, work together. You have prepared for this mission, and your combat skills are why you're in the first group. However, be careful and take precautions when encountering wildlife out here. Mountain lions, wolves, and grizzlies are serious threats, and you're not weapon-trained yet."

A hand shot up from Easton. "I thought there weren't any grizzlies in Colorado."

"Yeah, that was true for a long time, but several decades ago, a wildlife preservation group transplanted a couple of dozen in this area. It was assumed they moved on or died out, but we've been spotting them. Their brown coloring and a large hump on their shoulders are distinctive characteristics. They're here, trust me, and you don't have tech weapon clearance yet, so be smart. Use your head. It's better than any weapon you'll ever carry."

Gabe discussed a few more topics and fielded a couple of questions before he took the newbie Defenders outside the container wall. It was their first time outside of the barrier in a year, and most had never been in the woods. They were the first three trainees ready for this level of instruction.

Easton Mundy, Kendrick Henry, and Lana Sheldon worked well together to set up the camp in the designated area. Following their lessons, they built their shelter out of downed limbs and covered it with pine boughs. They covered the ground with the small tarp they were issued and used binoculars to survey the area.

"It feels so open out here," Lana remarked. "It's kind of weird after being in the Hold and then the tunnel for so long."

"I know, there are so many trees, but these trees are real with real critters in them. Who knows what's hiding in them?" Easton speculated as he looked up at the treetops and around the mountainside.

"I think we're ready. I'm nervous, too, but I really want to nail this test," stated Kendrick.

They all agreed and began discussing the hunting technique to use. They decided each would build a snare trap. It would be a competition to see who got an animal first. They would send a signal on their Defender wristbands that would let the others know to return. They each went their separate ways, agreeing not to go further than a mile. By piling the plentiful granite rocks in patterns denoting the direction to the next tree, and the use of the compass on their bands, they could make it back to camp.

Three hours later, Kendrick came back to camp with a marmot he trapped using part of his one power bar. He sent his signal, and about twenty minutes later, Lana came back. They waited for Easton for almost an hour, but he didn't show. They decided to follow his markers and find him. The day would be ending soon, and the markers had stopped. They called out, and they heard a faint voice. Kendrick walked over to a ledge and found Easton stuck on an outcrop.

"How did you get there?" asked Lana.

"There's a bear. I jumped down here when he charged me. Be careful," answered Easton, "he might still be around."

Lana unwrapped the rope on her belt and sent it down to Easton while Kendrick glassed the area. Easton did his best to climb up, but he hurt his ankle jumping down to the ledge, making the ascent painful and difficult. Kendrick spotted the bear on the other side of the small ravine, and he motioned for them to get going down the trail. They held Easton between them, and he was hopping and limping along. A hundred yards down the trail, Kendrick had an idea. They should lead the bear on a false scent trail. They each had one power bar in case they didn't catch any food. Lana and Easton continued at a slower pace back to the shelter.

Kendrick took the bars and ran off to find his marked trail. He started the trail of bait at the oddly shaped tree he remembered from his hike. It was pretty far from their camp, and he felt the bear would eat the food and move on. He tossed the candy down the trail away from camp and quickly ran back to meet them. They cooked the marmot over the fire they started with dried moss and pine needles. It was surprisingly good. They decided one person would keep watch for a few hours, and then they'd switch.

"What do we do if the bear comes here?" asked Lana.

"Let's sharpen some sticks. I mean, it's better than nothing," said Easton.

After creating two spears each, Lana and Easton settled down. Kendrick said he would take the first watch. He heard every creaking bough and insect sound like the forest volume was amplified on high. He held his spear at the ready, and he was going over the moves he had been taught. The gibbous moon gave off enough light that he saw its outline in the distance. Its bulky size and distinguished hump told him it was a grizzly, and probably the same one that threatened Easton. It was a formidable foe for their first battle.

He watched the male grizzly lumbering toward him. He didn't think he was aware of him yet, but no doubt he had caught the lingering scent of their marmot dinner. He quietly woke the others up, and they all took a stance, spears in hand. As the bear came closer, Kendrick was struck by his size. He seemed heftier than his assessment of him across the ravine.

"Get outa here, asshole! You're fucking with Defenders!" They had learned that shouting in deep voices frightened most wildlife to flee, as well as increased their courage and that of their team. Shouts of agreement from his comrades solidified their bond.

But the bear ferociously swatted the ground, sending needles and sticks flying. He reared up, roaring, accepting their challenge. Their hearts were pounding, and they fought the terror building inside.

"Warriors!" bellowed Easton, leaning heavily on his one good leg. Before they could act, several shots were fired from behind them, and the bear took off. Stunned and worried about who was behind them with real weapons, they turned around.

"Officer Gabe!" Lana shrieked with surprise. "What are you doing here?"

"This is only survival class one. It's the only class where you don't get weapons, so we keep an eye on you. The goal is to teach you to work together and learn to improvise, not fight grizzlies in hand-to-hand combat."

"We had this," Easton stated, with a bit of irritation in his voice.

"Maybe," Gabe offered, even though he knew exactly how badly that challenge would have gone.

"Do we still pass?" asked Kendrick.

"I think so, yeah," Gabe laughed. "I believe I'll camp out here with you tonight."

"It's my turn to take watch," said Easton, and stood leaning on his spear.

"Okay, Easton, I'll just stoke this fire." Gabe began blowing the embers back into a fire and added some of the stacked sticks they had gathered.

"How were you watching us?" Easton asked, staring into the fire.

"Drones, and we told you to camp here because of the cameras we planted in this area. We have lots of them near the tunnel entrances, and there is a team in one of the out-sites monitoring those feeds. Hey, you guys were awesome. You accomplished every task, and your bravery and teamwork were extraordinary."

"Did you see the bear chase me over the ledge?" Easton asked, wondering why that wasn't Officer Gabe's moment to jump in and save him.

"No, but we located you on the ledge, and the bear was leaving. You had a solid area to stand on, and your team was on its way. We watched your rescue, which is when we discovered you had injured your ankle. When you got back to camp, it was easier to maintain our surveillance. I was only fifty yards away, so I knew I could respond in time if that old boar came around. He was a brute. I was impressed when you started sharpening spears. But honestly, Easton, that bear would have knocked those spears right out of your hands with one swat. The rest would have been pretty ugly, and your mom would have had my ass."

"If we had taken that bear, maybe my mom would get off my back. She hovers over me and treats me like a kid. I understand why she worries since losing my dad, but I can't live with her for another year and a half. I want to be on my own." Easton dug at the ground with a stick. His mom was Amber Mundy, the angry parent who lost her run for office and caused a lot of dissent around town.

"Yeah, that age twenty-one thing is brutal. But we just don't have enough places."

"Why can't we make some of the houses into bunkhouses? We could sleep two or even four in each bedroom."

Gabe nodded. It was a good idea and worth consideration. Hard to make warriors out of kids living with worried parents, and Defender bunkhouses might be the answer. When the class got back the next afternoon, Gabe approached Gray with Easton's idea. Gray said he'd look into the housing situation and see what he could do. They had already been discussing the difficulty of training Defenders while they lived with their parents.

The legislators passed the bill for the dance hall and the teen representative. The dance hall was moved to the middle corridor storage area because a Defender barracks was to be housed in the east corridor storage room. It would house all single Defenders under twenty-one or waiting for housing. It would allow the Defender regiment to maintain discipline and encourage personal responsibility.

The dance hall was named Derechos. A *derecho* is a wide, long-lasting group of thunderstorms with violent winds. It opened three weeks after being approved. On Fridays and Saturdays, it played music and offered refreshments. People sixteen to twenty years old were allowed, and it was chaperoned by volunteers. Two credits bought access and two non-alcoholic drinks. The barracks took a bit longer, and several parents were trying to cancel it.

"We were told the age of consent was twenty-one. Now, you are taking our children away at nineteen," Amber yelled at the legislature. "My son was almost killed during the survival class. He shouldn't be able to attend dangerous activities without my permission!"

"She has a point," acknowledged Corey, the representative from the southwest side of the tunnel. "I think we need to sort out the age of consent thing at the legislative level. The age was set at twenty-one to prevent our youth who came here as children from breaking the residency creed, but now their rights and occupational responsibilities are in question."

"I think we need to review the bylaws and return in one week for debate," Bannon decided.

"I second that," said Vince, senator from the south tunnel.

A town debate schedule was set up for the four dining halls. There was a high interest in the bill, which changed the age of consent from twenty-one to nineteen. The details included legal independence from parental custody, legal accountability, setting up a dorm for single residents over nineteen, full voting privileges, and mandated signing of the Resident Creed. Drinking alcohol, getting married, and being eligible for housing were maintained as rights reserved for those twenty-one and over.

The arguments for the bill centered around the need for nineteen-year-olds to begin taking on full occupational responsibilities. Like most, their college education would be conducted in night classes. Defenders especially needed to be out of parental custody to fulfill their training.

Arguments against the bill included that they lacked the maturity to vote responsibly, and that they would cause trouble around the town without parental guidance. It seemed to split the town in half, so Bannon offered a suggestion. "How about we have a six-month transition to the bill?" But it didn't seem to turn the tide.

"How about we make the age of consent nineteen and a half?" offered Gray.

"What difference does that make?" yelled Amber from the crowd.

"Well, the difference is the town already approved barracks for Defender trainees over nineteen and a half. This would keep them home for another six months. But I have to warn you, if the law isn't the same for all the nineteen-year-olds, they will all sign up for Defender school."

Chatter ensued among the crowd. Amber tried to speak, but Easton stood up and spoke first.

"It's true, kids can be rowdy sometimes, but we need responsibilities and a purpose. This is our town too, and that means something to us. We've outgrown being kids at home. How will we ever learn if we don't get to try? Do you think maturity is a birthday gift we automatically get on our twenty-first birthday? No, we have to try it, mess up a bit, learn it, and then we can earn it."

Gray and Gabe looked at Easton. He had come a long way from the whiny kid that his mother had protected from everything.

"He will be an excellent Defender," said Gabe. Gray nodded in agreement.

Before the bill was voted on, Amber tried to start a work strike. The residents were reminded of the law they agreed to in the Town Creed. *Those refusing to work will be fined credits. If the debt reaches more than one month of possible credits, the violator will be assigned community service or sent to the holding cell to be tried for breaking the New Haven Creed.*

Only six people were willing to go through with it, and when they saw the low turnout, even Amber gave up. It would go to a vote, and the people would decide. The bill passed with a 67 percent majority. The party at Derechos was chaperoned by Gray, Gabe, and Dewy. The crowd was hopping, but relatively manageable.

"They should have a feisty night," said Gray. "They just won their independence. They can't access alcohol or drugs, so it should be easy to keep too many stupid ideas from being realized."

Tanya was convicted of second-degree sexual assault and second-degree kidnapping, and assault with a drug with the intent to rape. She was sentenced to two years in a holding cell. She would be allowed to do community service tasks during the day with supervision to work on decreasing her sentence. She was assigned counseling five days a week for the first month and twice a week for the rest of the first year. At the one-year point, she would go before a review board to determine how the rest of her sentence would proceed. It was a bittersweet day for all. This was the biggest trial in the town so far, and most agreed the trial and sentence were fair. The justice system prevailed, but like every prosecution of justice, the lives of those involved would be changed forever.

Axle and Jax returned after a month at the out-site. They took many opportunities to do outdoor reconnaissance. Axle could feel Drangers looming too close for comfort. Now and then, he would see smoke from a campfire. And once he thought he heard gunfire. Old weapons made loud noises, but the last Drangers they encountered used those weapons. He sent out drones every day but never located any wandering Drangers. He did identify abandoned camps, and sometimes, dead bodies from skirmishes.

He and Gray discussed increased drills in the outside east arena. It was time to prepare. He also assured Jax that all the Ds from the Hold had gear inspections. The two Defenders that survived the second transport had been under investigation for a month, and so far, nothing seemed out of order. It was possible that if they had been compromised by one of their own. Maybe the traitor was one of the five off-siters who died.

Along with Axle and Jax returning from isolation, Aniya needed to be introduced to the town. The news of her arrival was given on the nightly news feed to everyone's tablet two weeks after her arrival. The first reactions were fear and curiosity, but soon enough time went by, while she was still in quarantine, that the hype died down. Many believed more outsiders should be saved, but the reality of supplies, housing, location security, and infection ended those conversations.

Dewy was walking without a cane now, but his back tired easily. He was chosen to drive Aniya around for a tour of the town. He took her on the full loop, and when they reached the hospital again, he stopped.

"Wow, I can't believe how many cool things there are to do here. It's sad my mom couldn't have seen this," Aniya sighed. "Where will I live?"

"Well, you're gonna live in the dorm with the other single people under twenty-one. Your occupation tests said you'd be workin' on the farm. Do ya wanna go check that out?

"Yeah."

They drove to the west end with the Blue Rabbit and the Gruff Goat Ranches. He parked, and they were let in by Billie.

"Hi, Aniya. I'm Billie. Welcome to the Gruff Ranch. Watch your step and especially your backside; the goats will shove you around if you don't."

Billie showed her the pens and how they alternated which goats could be in the yard to play and feed, while their pens were cleaned, then they'd trade for a new group. The bedding was a soft, reusable material that was rinsed and cleaned in a large, round, spinning vat. Then they visited the Blue Rabbit Ranch. It was divided by a fence that separated the chickens and the rabbits.

"I took care of chickens at one place I lived when I was little. I remember getting eggs in the morning. I like working with animals. I think I'll like this job."

"Well, as long as you know this is where we raise our food. We take good care of the animals, but they aren't pets. They're livestock," warned Billie.

"I know. My dad used to tell me that too, when he was alive. I won't have a problem doing my job, Billie."

Dewy took Aniya to the New Haven College Dorm for Women. She had been given some work clothes and a tote from the town donation bins. Bannon issued new items from the town storage: two pairs of shoes, a week's worth of undergarments, two casual outfits, a nice outfit, a swimsuit, a light jacket, and a warm one for outside days. Dewy packed that bag into the dorm lobby and introduced her to the dorm manager. He was feeling stronger these days, but he knew climbing stairs and carrying luggage would send him to Maya for hydrotherapy.

Dewy was excited about a new girl being in town. She was nice-looking too, but that's why the Drangers were trafficking her. She seemed naïve, but how could she be, living on the outside? He had just turned twenty-two and wondered if it would be weird not being able to go to the same club. Maybe he'd have to volunteer at Derechos on a regular basis. He could take her to the beach and the skyroom. He had credits, and lots of them, because volunteering gave him a purpose while his body felt useless and weak. He suddenly felt anxious at the thought of every single guy in town having the same thoughts. He knew he had to say something.

"So, Aniya, I feel bad just dropping ya off alone. Here's how ta reach me if ya need anythin', I mean anythin'. I know ya don't know anyone. I have tons a' credits, and I'd be happy ta show ya the club, the beach, and the skyroom if ya'd like. And I promise ta be respectful. I'm a Defender, and if I'm not, Gray would toast me over. Please watch out fer these guys in here. They're going to be all over the new girl. If ya need any of them set straight, let me know."

"Thank you, Dewy. Is that your real name?" She was curious about him.

"Well, it's a bit of a story, so I'll have ta tell ya later."

"Like, later tonight?" she invited herself.

"Just like that. How about I bring ya to the dinin' hall in two hours?"

"It's a date." She felt safe with him. And she needed to feel safe. This town had too many people. They were out walking and hanging around on the street, but she felt trapped inside this huge prison with no place to run.

Dewy pondered this new girl. She was raw. She had never undergone the training to live here, so he wondered how she would deal with it. Her paperwork reported her to be barely nineteen. Haru had her on a counseling schedule during her hospital stay, but she wasn't allowed to interact with anyone face-to-face. And everyone around her wore a plastic barrier that diminished their connection with her and her with them. Haru set up a video call with her peers, but it was only for one hour a day.

Though she had lived in a Fringer camp, no one but other Fringers knew much about that lifestyle. But it was pretty clear that anyone living on the outside would be in constant fear of Drangers and Neighwah soldiers. The whole purpose of the intensive training at the Hold was to let go of fear and learn to be a community. He wondered how best to help her adjust, and he realized locking her up next to him was not what she needed. What she needed was a big brother, and for now, he felt better about that role.

Chapter Nineteen

The great housing switch looked like a tangled mess to everyone but Dewy, Deed, and Rand. They played the logistical strings of resettling like an orchestra. Three two-bedroom houses were converted into three bedrooms. That gave nine spots for singles over twenty-one still in the dorms waiting on housing. Gray moved into Jilly's place because it was a bit bigger, and she was happy to stay near her best friend. His house became available to couples whose children had moved out. All in all, thirteen residents switched to bigger or smaller dwellings.

Summer was winding up, and the town looked forward to being outside. The residents were blissfully unaware of the turmoil in the outside world until a couple of college journalists began giving town reports on the notebook feed, causing curiosity about the world's state of affairs to stir. Rand and Deed had little to offer, and as far as they knew, no one could access or launch satellites due to the Kessler effect's shattered debris encircling Earth. Radio broadcasts from old-fashioned AM and FM broadcasts were rather opinionated, and little was verifiable. The territories had ramped up their factories to generate more weaponry, but the quality and technology were inferior to previous models due to a lack of computer chips.

China was dominating for a time by collecting and hoarding military weapons, causing other countries to feel threatened. Old allies of once-democratic nations were able to join forces and connect with the wife of the next in line for China's General Secretary. The current leader was dying, and her husband would be in charge soon. She knew he was planning to kill her and their three daughters to spend his life with his mistress and the two sons they had together. She and her children were extracted from China, and she disclosed the locations of most of their strategic strongholds. Most of the targets were hit in a sudden seventeen-minute raid with short-range toxbombs and nukes. Without satellite guidance, the long-range attempts caused extensive damage, but it was not debilitating. She did it to save her children from assassination, but she and her daughters were murdered anyway.

China was able to retaliate with some short-range missiles of its own. But the surprise was the number of ships they had off the east and west coasts of the former United States. The destruction of the two coastlines was complete enough to earn their new nickname: the Toastlands. The retaliatory propaganda rhetoric set on repeat was the only broadcast coming from China since the attack.

Most of the radio chatter lately was centered around locating a certain person or some group, but it was not newsworthy, and more than likely, they were coded messages from various groups to others. The good news was that the tunnel was a difficult location to reach without gear and supplies, which were getting harder to find. The bad news was that supplies were getting harder to find, and the protection of winter was almost a month away. Though they easily had a year and a half's worth of supplies in storage, they needed a way to manufacture more for the future or find trading allies off-site. And they must be able to defend their home.

Ari went to Gray and Bannon with a defense proposal. "I have two new defensive weapons to propose. The first is a deoxy compound.

It is absorbed through the skin and can permeate most gear, and increases one's need for oxygen. This will cause the intruders to retreat down the mountain to catch their breath. If they are exposed repeatedly, they will not be able to be at this elevation without an oxygen supply. We also have an antidote for Defenders who might get exposed. They can carry this melting tablet and be unaffected.

"The other weapon is a high-frequency device that gives off a painful hum. Again, it goes through most gear and causes the intruders to retreat. We developed special ear protection that reduces the effect on our Defenders, but we couldn't eliminate the noise completely, or they would be unable to communicate with each other. The pros of the deoxy compound are that it is invisible and helps maintain the confidentiality of our location. The con is that it's expensive to distribute in large enough quantities. The sound device is super cheap, but it discloses the site to intruders and doesn't prevent them from returning."

"Cool, good work. I like it. Work up an exact cost analysis of the deoxy. Seems like the weapon of choice until the word of our location is out. We will inevitably be found, and maybe we have already been discovered. But this location is difficult to reach and attack. I think most don't have a clue what's up here, or they think it's more trouble than it's worth. But if word gets out about our supplies, all bets are off."

The deoxy was used a couple of times, but the formula dissipated in the wind, making it difficult to use effectively. But the sound device became a staple to ward off the occasional wandering band of raggedy Drangers.

It was late one summer afternoon, that the citizens were shocked with pulsing lights and the intruder alarm ringing soundly throughout the tunnel city. In the security building, the Defenders were well into their busy protocols.

"Gray, we got another pack coming up the east ridge." Gabe was on out-site duty, and the Drangers had been trickling up the mountain in small groups for a week now. "Dispatch another drone and transmit the audio wave." Gray was monitoring the drone footage.

It had taken most of the summer, but one by one, the station drones had been flown back and equipped with sound amplifiers that could target an area hundreds of yards away. He presumed they had been located, and life in the tunnel would soon experience a dramatic change. He was happy the barometer was plummeting, meaning a monster of a snowstorm was on its way. Though it was early in the fall for such a blizzard, once the mountain was covered with deep snow, it was doubtful it would get warm enough to melt. Then it would be difficult and illogical for the Drangers to reach them. He watched the monitor as Drangers grabbed their heads, trying to block the ringing pulsing through their cheap headgear. They immediately headed back down.

"It's unfortunate we were discovered so soon, but it's done. Deep winter is still several weeks away, and though the approaching storm may save us, it could be tomorrow or several days before it hits. And there is always the possibility that it doesn't hit us hard enough to secure the tunnel. We need to be prepared. I want to initiate plan 4R instead of the Fortify plan."

Gray and Bannon had gone around on this issue. Plan 4R included expanded Reconnaissance, Reclaiming the Hold, Recruiting new Defenders, and establishing a large Resistance movement with allies. Bannon argued the cost of life would be high because sending so many Defenders to the Hold would leave the town with less protection.

"True the Hold was attacked, but it's not safe here either. The time for hiding is over. It's time to defend what's ours." Before Bannon could respond, Dewy's call came in from his out-site position on the west gate.

"Gray, I've got a real situation here! I got sixty to seventy Drangers movin' up the west side, and the audio wave is not workin'. I repeat, no effect. They are about four klicks out and charging. Please advise."

"Ax, all hands now!"

Gray and Axle initiated Strongpoint defense strategies. All available Defenders started moving the mobile barriers from the storage containers into formation across the west yard. They knew the drill backward and forward. The perimeter and inner yard were set up in under fifteen minutes, and they got into their assigned positions.

Bannon oversaw securing the residents according to the attack drill. All hospital staff were to report to the hospital or the RAS, all occupational buildings were secured, and residents reported to their assigned lockdown locations. Within minutes, the lights were dimmed to a pulsing red glow, the streets were cleared, and the large outer door locks were in battle mode with most of the Defenders ready in the yards. They were locked outside, except for one heavily guarded entrance that allowed the wounded to be transported to the hospital. A team of four trainees was positioned at each end in case of a breach.

The waiting was unbearable. Their old, dreadful existence they thought they had left behind wasn't gone after all. It rapidly returned with a vengeance, erasing all the impressions of being protected and sheltered from harm. They took the chance to build friendships and real relationships, and now the darkness of the real world was back attacking everything good. The hum of stunned thoughts rang in everyone's minds. *Was it all an illusion, a short intermission to reality? After coming so far, was the curtain closing?*

Of the sixty-one total Defenders, forty were positioned on the west gate where the enemy squads were approaching. No movement had been seen on the east gate, but if enemies began moving up there too, they'd have to send more Defenders to the east.

The Defenders in the yard heard the first sounds of battle from the distant drones controlled from the out-site bunkers. Their only off-site weaponry was drones for close range and a few missile launchers for vehicle targets. Each bunker unit was completely sealed with only two ways to enter the tunnel on each end of the out-site bunkers. There were two small access doors at each end of the tunnel through hidden entrances beyond the container wall at the E1 and W4 bunkers. They were hard to find without access to the signal marker, and it required headquarters to undo the remote padlock and a cleared Defender band to open it.

On the west side, Drangers were weaving in and out of trees and rocks. Some began climbing the container wall while others tried to take out the armed drones. Eight Defenders were lying behind turrets on the container wall, ready to fire on anyone reaching the top and breaching the razor wire. A Dranger's head popped over and was reduced to a bloody stump as it tumbled down the ladder. Soon contorted Dranger bodies were littering the top of the container wall when the order was given to retreat to the mid-barrier. Two wounded Defenders were carried over shoulders down the ladders. Other Defenders quickly slid down on the rails, but as quickly as they dropped, passing the eerie mixture of Dranger and Defender blood as it dripped down the inner wall. Medics quickly drove the shielded cart over to load the two Defenders and take them in.

Like spiders on the march, they came, one, two, three at a time, completely breaching the wall. Soon, too many came at once. An angry cloud of bullets flew in every direction, attacking like a swarm of fearsome Asian wasps. The enemy invaded the yard in alarming numbers. This time, the Drangers had formidable armor, and it took several hits to take them out. Two crashed into Jax's barrier station. She tried to smash the one who fell on top of her with the stock of her weapon, but his helmet held strong. The other Dranger smashed her face shield with a poison punch located on the butt of his gun, and she heard the dreadful crack.

Axle ran over and gave her an assist, charging the Dranger and stabbing through his already breached suit. But another Dranger shot him, and he could feel the vibrating bullet searing through him, tearing through his insides, and the warm liquid filling his suit. He turned and fired his automatic weapon point-blank, punching a hole into the bastard's gear. Axle felt lightheaded and collapsed, his strength fading into a world of hazy shadows and then darkness. Another Defender took aim and punched numerous holes in the two Drangers, heading to finish Jax off. Brave and meagerly armed medics loaded both Defenders into the bullet-banged cart.

Dewy yelled over the com, "Gray, you're not gonna believe this. I think we got an assist."

"What do you mean?"

"There's Drangers out here shootin' the ones chargin' our perimeter. They all seem ta have the same green headbands. What's goin' on?"

"I don't know, but for now, they're off the target list." Gray sent word to every helmeted Defender on the west side, "All Ds be advised: green headbands are off the target list. Assist authorized. I repeat, assist authorized."

It was a bloodbath for the attacking Drangers, and their bodies were strewn across the yard in grotesque death poses. None were left alive. With no more Drangers coming over the wall, the Defenders headed up to the wall positions. The drones could be heard chasing the runners, but when they reached the top of the platforms, they couldn't believe their eyes. Forty or more Drangers with green headbands stood with hands up in surrender.

The whole battle lasted eighteen minutes, but it marked the end of their peaceful world. Gray had no idea what the surrender game was, but he had read many books on warfare, and he knew feigning surrender was a legitimate combat strategy. All the Greenbanders, as the Ds were calling them, were in drone custody, so he was confused by the move.

"Gray, come in. Can you answer? Is everything secure at the west gate? Respond," Gabe reported anxiously.

"Yeah, we're on recon, but the west is secure," Gray answered, preoccupied with the dilemma before him.

"Gray, you're not going to believe this."

"Let me guess, you have Drangers with green headbands surrendering at the east gate."

"Well, that was an amazing guess. Does that mean it's on the west too?" Gabe couldn't presume what was happening. But he hoped Gray knew.

"Yeah, don't ask. I'm as confused as everyone. Do you have them secured?"

"Yeah."

"Okay, stand by."

"Gray," Dewy called back. "I have a guy with a white flag asking to speak to the person in charge."

"Have a drone send him a com box. The obsolete version."

Bannon looked at Gray. "This is still a military situation, so you should be the one to talk with him, but don't promise anything." Gray nodded, and the Greenbander leader spoke.

"I am William of the Guard, and I am a friend of the sanctuary tunnel." The Greenbander stood proudly while he talked. Gray sized up the tall, muscular, dark-skinned man on the camera feed. His arm was oozing blood through a ragged white bandage, contrasting his powerful dark coloring. He wore leather britches and a vest with elbow guards. He had a rifle on one shoulder and a compound bow on the other, and he was holding a large blade. His leather armor was covered in blood, and Gray had no doubt most of it did not belong to him.

"How did you find out about us?" Gray didn't trust him, but he couldn't understand what possible advantage this man thought he had attained. There was no way he was letting them in.

"I've been running the Guard underground, and I learned about the attack on your offsite facility. The Neighwah know you are here. I don't know where they got their intel, but you are on the grid, and they are interested in taking you down. This was just a recon mission."

"I don't know if what you say is true, but we do seem to be in your debt. Is this all of you? Are there more of your underground Guard?"

"I, too, am hesitant to give away information, but if you refer to Guards on the east side, those are ours. We sent reinforcements when we heard about a small faction moving up there."

Gray considered him for a moment, pausing to bait him for more information or some sign of nervous weakness, but it did not come. He was a confident and seasoned warrior. "Are any of your soldiers wounded? Do you need medical supplies?"

"Yes, that would be appreciated," William replied.

"Give a list to my medic, and we'll send what you need over the wall." The medic took down the supply list and hurried off to the hospital. Gray, not wanting to engage in small talk banter, got straight to the point. "William, leader of the Guard, what do you want?"

"I want to be allies, to join forces. I believe your people are honorable, but we are strangers. How do we make a pact with this thick wall between us?"

"Dewy, send a rope ladder and bring him over the wall and into the yard. I'm coming down."

Gray put on his gear to protect himself and the town from any viral exposure or unexpected moves from this bad-ass renegade. Gray approached the giant man who dwarfed his own six-foot-one stature. Knowing every move was assessed and noted, he decided to remove his helmet to signify strength and sincerity. He held out his bare hand, and the two men shook hands, demonstrating their confidence and resolve. In the backdrop of dead Drangers being loaded onto trailers, the two men talked for forty minutes, with Bannon and legislators listening in.

William explained he had taken over the Hold soon after it had been attacked last year. He admitted he had more soldiers there, and he wanted the supplies to secure it. Fencing; cameras; and electronic access; a power source for winter; medical supplies; food, and more. They needed to leave by morning to avoid the storm.

"Gray, it's Maya. You need to come to the hospital."

"William, I need to check on my soldiers. I'll present your proposal immediately to the officials. We'll set you up for the night." Gray turned to the com-line attached to his vest and barked off his orders. "Gather supplies to make a tent city outside the wall, and send food. Do the same for those on the east side. Maintain lockdown and absolute security." They shook hands eye to eye with competing grips, and Gray turned and left.

He arrived at the door and considered the viral exposure issue, but decided the time of hiding was done, and he walked through. No one said a word.

"Gray, there are some Defenders in bad shape. Ax is one of them. I've got him stabilized, but it's touch-and-go." Maya led him to Axle's curtain and left him to sit with his brother.

Jax was listening behind the curtain as Maya described Axle's condition. She was in and out due to the detox meds running through her. She faded out again when Gray went to see how the other soldiers were doing. Six Defenders in total were wounded. Two were discharged, and four were in the hospital. There was one Defender who died in the yard. Most were saved by their gear, but a few Drangers had weapons that could penetrate the Defender suits. Gray walked down to see Kendrick. Easton and Kendrick's mother were sitting with him.

"How are you doing, Kendrick?"

"It's my leg, sir. They say I'll heal thanks to Easton. He got me and carried me to the medics. He crossed the yard with me over his shoulder, sir. He saved me."

"Good work, E." Gray patted him on the back. He had given him that nickname back when he was a rowdy troublemaker. "You're a credit. I'm glad you're on our side." Easton shied a bit from the compliments.

"I'm proud of you. I'm proud of both of you. Barely out of training, and you faced combat with courage." Gray thought to himself, *I don't know how, but someday I'm going to make Easton's mother say that to him.*

Gray went to young Parker's bed. Several bloody bandages covered his unconscious body, accompanied by tubes and leads and noisy machines. Gray talked to him for a while. He held his hand, told him he was proud of him, and knelt beside his bed in prayer. Gray looked in on Jax, but she was asleep. Maya reported she had received the antidote on time and would recover in a couple of days.

He went back to his brother. He too was a mass of medical tubes and machinery, humming, beeping, and swishing air. He thought back to Jilly. He had his head on the side of the bed and was praying when Jilly came into the room. She sat down beside him and put her arm around him. She wanted to be strong for Gray, but the thought of losing Axle was unthinkable.

Bannon took over the negotiations, and he went to the legislature with the proposal at midnight. It provided the Guard, as it was officially named in the bill, with the following provisions and privileges:

- access and residency to all four Hold buildings
- the agreed-upon supplies
- an agreement of peaceful interaction
- continued communication
- reciprocal military assistance as circumstances allow

Most of the legislators disliked the bill. Bannon asked if Gray was available. He hated pulling him away from his brother, but a few words from him could make the alliance happen. Gray headed over to the Town Hall. Though still reeling from the loss and injuries to his soldiers, his brother. He quickly went over in his head how to say what he knew in his heart.

"Mayor, senators, representatives, I understand your apprehension. We don't know this group. The thing is, we can give our permission for them to be at the Hold, but they already have possession of it. And yet they ask anyway. We can request that there be peace and communication between us, but they have already offered it. And yet they ask. We can give them the supplies to help them through the winter, or with the militia they possess, they can take it, and this place. And yet they ask. I'm not sure what the debate is about, but I do see the risk. What I don't see is how we can deny that we are on the map. We need more defenses than we have. We need allies. Are these the right allies? I pray they are because I don't see any other offers. Now, unless you have any questions, I need to return to the hospital."

The legislators passed the bill unanimously. Gabe and Dewy took over for Gray. They presented the signed contract and got William's signature in return. They gathered the supplies and a couple of transports to deliver them and their supplies back to the Hold. It was late that night, and Gray was sitting with Axle. Jax came to, hearing their conversation.

"I'm sorry, Gray. He's gone. We did everything we could. He was a good man. He'll be missed."

She heard Gray sigh, and little sobs came from behind the curtain. Jax wanted to wake up, but she was too groggy. A nurse came in and, seeing her distress, she upped her meds, and she was out again.

Chapter Twenty

Jax woke up in the dead of night facing the fearsome specters that prowled her dreams. Her nightmares had become bizarre with the medical treatments battling inside her. She sat up, trying to clear her murky brain. The mélange of drugs in her system, combined with the shadows of a dark memory, demanded she surrender back to the comfort of the bed, but the lioness side of her fought back. She would not lie helpless in this sterile, pre-coffin cradle for the weak. She had to see for herself. She had to know where he was.

Holding on to the bed rail, she reached for the adjoining curtain and yanked with more force than she anticipated. She regained her balance only to lose it again upon seeing the empty bed. It was unmade and still bloody. She pulled herself up and reached for his bed's railing, and sank her face into his pillow. It still smelled like him, and she held it to her. Clinging to the pillow with one hand and grabbing her rail with the other, she made her way back to her bed. Curled up with his last breaths, she sobbed herself into sleep.

She was awakened by the curtain being swung back, and this time, she easily cleared the fog from her head.

"What the hell, you think I'm dying so you steal my pillow?"

Jax was speechless. "How... I heard them talking. They said you were gone. And I saw your bed empty."

"Well, I guess you at least waited until you *thought* I was dead to grab my shit."

"Ax, I...need a moment." She stood up with more stability than last time and closed the curtain. She couldn't let him see her tears.

He heard her trying to stifle her quick little shuddering breaths. "Jax, I'm sorry. Talk to me."

She wiped her tears away and opened the curtain. "Last night, I heard Maya tell Gray you were gone."

"Parker died last night. Maybe they were talking about him. I guess Ged died too, in the yard from a mini sticker bomb."

"Oh, that's sad," she whispered in a sniffly voice. "I remember how bravely they fought at the Hold. But why was your bed empty? Where did you go?"

"They were removing some drain thing and my ventilator because I had stopped leaking shit and could breathe on my own." He paused when he realized the depth of her sincerity, and it moved him.

"Look, I'm sorry. I guess we need to work on having real moments without saturating every statement with sarcasm. Some things should be handled with more sincerity. Hannah and I used to promise each other before every engagement mission that we'd come back. I couldn't believe it when she didn't. I can't stop hearing her call my name into her helmet com as she was dying while I stood there helpless in the monitor room. It was the last thing she said, and it kills me. I know how hard it is to lose someone, and I don't want to hurt you or be insensitive. I fought to come back because of you. I couldn't let you down, and I couldn't let you go. I think I might kinda like you or something, and I want more, a lot more."

She pulled her IV pole over to him and crawled into his bed. "I hate that we lost Parker and Ged and that you lost such a dear friend, but I'm glad I didn't lose you."

He moaned a little from the painful jostling, but he quickly curled around her, and they both were sound asleep when Gray and Maya came in.

"I kinda figured they'd either keep fighting or start..."

"Yeah, I think I can finish that sentence on my own. Not to be a killjoy, but they can't stay like this. We need to take vitals, check his wound and dressing, and we can't have their lines get tangled or pulled out."

Gray looked at the peaceful look on his little brother's face. He looked like that scrawny kid again. He thought back to the day his dad brought Axle home and said he was going to live with them. Gray's aunt and uncle had just left with their brood, and he was enjoying having his own room again. He had just turned eleven, and he liked having his dad and his home to himself. Axle was about six, they guessed, because he didn't know for sure. He had been living at the city dump, snatching out a pitiful existence one piece at a time. He was terrified, but he was thankful for the food and a roof.

Axle fought Gray and his dad when they gave him a bath. He finally gave in to the warmth of the water, but he fought like hell when they scrubbed his wayward curls of filthy hair. He had a fighting spirit that Gray admired, but later that night, he heard him crying. Axle was standing over him, looking so scared. Gray let him sleep with him, and later, moved his cot from the kitchen into his room. The two became brothers and had mountains of memories and fierce loyalty to each other. Gray couldn't have prayed for a better family.

"They're cute though," cooed Maya.

"Say that, and they'll probably leap into their own beds. Well, maybe, maybe not."

The town was in an uproar after word of the alliance came out on the news feed. They were especially angry that half a year's worth of precious supplies and even two of their backup generators had been given away. But committing the town's Defenders and weapons to other factions' wars was unthinkable to everyone, especially the parents of the newly emancipated young recruits. Who decided they had the right to sign this bill? They were never notified, and their opinions were unheard on the most significant and precarious legislation ever passed. Signs and shouts of "Down with the Corporate liars" and "We need new representation" were filling the air.

Workers filled the streets, abandoning their occupational stations. The already weary Defenders were on full duty to keep the peace. The volatile situation was filled with unstable emotions, and an accord had to be reached soon before their destructive appetite ruined them all. Bannon sat with Gray and Ari in his office.

"They've called for my resignation as well as all the other legislators, too," sighed Bannon.

"They don't know what they want right now. "They're too angry to go through a logical process. I think they're scared, and their feelings are hurt. You think they don't believe in you, but they don't think you believe in them. They don't care that the storm caused us to rush the decision. They only know they were bypassed and run over." When Ari finished speaking, she started pacing the room. She was a day past her due date, and sitting for too long made her uncomfortable.

Bannon gave his wife a concerned look, and she waved him off to assure him she was fine. Bannon turned to Gray, "I offered this whole little world freely, and I would do it again. No one owes me anything, and I'd run away from this office if I thought the next person understood the point of it all."

"I think they need to be reminded of what that purpose is. In every occupation, we devised a mission statement to serve as a compass for success and progress. Maybe the town needs one," Ari said, looking more and more uncomfortable. They were following her pacing and seeing their concerned looks, she quickly answered them. "Yes, I feel uncomfortable, and these Braxton-Hicks contractions are miserable, but they aren't regular or hard enough to take any action, so settle down."

"Maybe you're right. We need to make them feel connected again. Remember the positive energy after the naming event? Maybe we should allow them to have input on the mission statement. Chances are they will realize that the bill we just passed is truly in the best interest of the town."

"I'll set up a live feed, with a series of debates from each section to follow. We'll do them on different nights to allow the Defenders to implement crowd control. But we need people to go back to work. This street rally is going to go wrong at some point." Gray was exhausted and had not slept much since the night before the battle. He was slouching in the comfy padded chairs, and his thoughts drifted to holding his wife in his arms and sleeping in. Many were fighting the fatigue of battle trauma, and many continued to work to put the town right again. So he straightened his posture to do the work to get home.

"I need to address them," Bannon realized. "I need access to the tunnel intercom."

"Actually," Gray stated while looking at Ari, trying to manage her pains, "I think you need to get your wife to the hospital. It's highly likely that as an engineer, she is not qualified to determine the onset of labor."

Bannon called for a cart and helped Ari downstairs. Gray got on the intercom to address the residents.

"Residents of New Haven, it is plain to see you love your town, and we acknowledge your valid concerns. A time and place will be arranged to hear your grievances. A news feed will be sent within two hours to explain the goal and schedule for the town forums. Please make your way to your jobs, homes, or activities. I ask you to respect this request on behalf of our Defenders. They are weary from battle. We have lost two Defenders, and we have four more recovering. They are, they were, our friends, family, neighbors, and citizens of New Haven. We all need to take a moment to slow down to grieve. It is the respectful thing to do for now."

He paused to read the crowd for compliance, and most seemed calmer, but a few agitators appeared to be ramping up again. "However," he said with a commanding tone, "not complying with these orders will result in your arrest, credit fines, and a disorderly conduct record." Though mumbling and still charged with disdain, the crowd dispersed, going in various directions.

Twelve hours later, a healthy, seven-pound Sebastian Tomas Vogel was born. Bannon looked down at his son. "This is why I decided to dream this world into existence. It is for these precious moments that we are willing to endure a world of despair. He is God's gift to prove there is hope. Love is why we risk, fight, and even die for the right to dream into reality a better future."

"I think you just wrote the opening statement of your speech." Ari patted the bed for him to sit with her and admire New Haven's newest citizen.

It was six days later before the storm had cleared enough to send a drone to the Holds. Bannon wanted to check on the Guard before he gave his report to the citizens at the meeting tomorrow night.

"William, glad to see you made it through the storm. How are those two generators working out for you?"

"Just call me Will. Bannon, those are sweet. We'll have power for a couple of decades with the energy-efficient systems here. Can't thank you enough. We got into a skirmish on the way back. We engaged seventeen Drangers heading up the mountain. I guess they don't know how to read the weather. Some we took out, and several others were already dead from hypothermia. We have the survivors locked up. As hungry as they are, I'm sure I can turn them. It's how I've gotten several of my recruits."

"How crowded are you out there?"

"I think we're just over 230 troops in the Hold, and we've got a couple of dozen encampments scattered within the surrounding fifty miles with a couple hundred more soldiers. We've dedicated one of the Hold buildings as an occupational section. The yards, as you call them, are used as combat training areas. Each building had an animal area, so we're using those the same way. We also set up greenhouse areas on the edge of two buildings. That biotechnology that hyperclones the food will help us feed a lot of people. Thanks for the dirt additives, too. The soil around here is pretty acidic. Everyone here is elated about our new alliance. How is your town taking it?"

"They're adjusting. We have a big meeting tomorrow. I wanted to touch base with you so I could assure them."

"Will, Gray here. Can you give me any news about the outside? We feel blind without the satellites, and drones can only go so far."

"The bigger factions are starting to crumble. Little groups are starting up and offering benefits to recruits, but then they turn into slave labor camps. Tech weapons are hard to sustain, so bullets have come back in style. Steel barrels last a long time with simple maintenance. We build our own guns and reload our ammo."

"How about long-range weapons like toxbombs?" Gray asked.

"They're less attractive because human labor has become a valuable commodity as well as livestock. Human trafficking is sky-high, though. No one can go out without an armed team."

"How are your defenses? I can help you learn to operate the stealth technology still in the Hold." Gray was sure he hadn't uncovered the subfloor hide, and there were some supplies still in there. They left them because they were old-school technology, but it sounded like it would be useful to them. Gray and Will talked for a while longer, and Bannon waved goodnight.

Jilly was over at their house holding Bastian while Ari played with Ellie and her kitten, Nikka. Ellie was in second grade now, as well as Zoey and Meshka. The three were inseparable, and it was fun watching them play and run up and down the street carefree. Jilly wished every kid lived this way. She was starting to get baby fever a little with Katie next door and now Bastian. She wondered what Gray's thoughts were.

Bannon came home, and Jilly was baby-talking with his infant son. "You're good with babies. You'd be a good mom."

"Well, we haven't made any plans other than someday we might. All these new little cutie pies around town have me thinking, though."

It was a week later that Bannon held the town meeting, talking about how fortunate it is to be in New Haven. He stated that with the supplies, recycling programs, and their small manufacturing plant, they would live the same for the next year and a half.

"After that, some things will start running out. Many pharmaceuticals have a shelf life, and there are some whose dates are within a year. But the most important thing to consider is this: We have been discovered. Defending this town and this base is not going to get any easier."

"We, your elected officials, voted unanimously to support the Guard faction for three reasons. First, we cannot survive another summer without an ally. We may still be overrun, but it will be harder for our enemies to overtake us if our armies are united. Second, he has more than twice the number of soldiers we have. Hell, he could have easily overrun us at that battle if that was his plan. Third, they manufacture weapons and ammo. It's old technology, but still effective. They have connections for trading and gathering supplies, and they're willing to trade with us."

It was Gray's turn to talk. He reported the news from Will and re-iterated Bannon's message of the battles to come. "Will has Guardsmen on both sides of the tunnel. He has underground connections in Central City on the east, and with the Hold and access to our drones, he can monitor the west. He is a strong first line of defense. I just hope we have as much to offer them as they have to offer us."

The hands went up for question time.

"How can we trust him? We don't know him."

"How can we not? If he wanted our town, he could have it," Bannon answered.

"Why didn't you even consult us?"

"They had to leave by morning to beat the storm. We couldn't know how bad it would get, and it ended up taking six days to clear out. It was a decision made in combat. The legislators have that authority in circumstances when the danger is high, and there isn't enough time to go through legislation. They never breached our walls, and they still don't know what we have. But that day will come, eventually, and we need to plan for it." Gray saw many nods, and they seemed a bit less agitated.

Bannon spoke again. "Our creed has been like our mission statement. We protect the town and its location by sacrificing our freedom. We relinquished our freedom to travel where we will and seek out new friends and adventures outside of the tunnel, and the freedom to own our own homes. I tried like hell to provide a safe place for new opportunities, career choices, and supplemental income, but I know it falls short of the true goal of New Haven. This is just the beginning. It's time to expand our world and rethink our purpose and our goals. I have something to tell you. There are more towns like this out there. I know of many other business owners who created places like this. I don't know where they are, and I never divulged our location to them, but I can only hope someday we can work together."

"We abandoned the rest of humanity to find our own. I pray we are forgiven, but I still believe it was the right thing to do. I can only hope we had it long enough to treasure it, teach it, fight for it, and keep it alive." Bannon paused, then looked up again. "Work together to come up with our new town mission statement. Does anyone have any ideas of what we should include?"

The suggestions poured from the crowd, overlapping one another in exuberance.

"We need to make more things."

"We need to help people on the outside."

"We should share our educational programs with the children of the Guard."

"We still need to stay in here and protect our town until we can't anymore."

"What kinds of supplies do we need?"

"How can we find those other towns?"

The residents were asked to write out their mission suggestions and send them to the notebook suggestion address. Bannon felt good about the meeting, and no one brought up recalling the elected officials. He and Ari stopped at the park on the way home and watched Ellie swing while tending to the baby in the stroller.

"You know," said Ari, "the citizens of this town started out isolated and lost in their hideaway homes, but they clung to a desperate hope. They gambled everything on a future offering more than their brutal existence. They came to the Hold broken and scared. You provided them with skills to navigate a working community, you opened their minds to the forbidden knowledge they had been denied, and you taught them how to trust others. They embraced this place, and now they're making their own way."

He smiled at her. She had a way of putting things into perspective that allowed him to step back and reevaluate his point of view. After weeks of whittling down the suggestions into a few versions of the declaration, a new mission statement was voted into law.

It is the mission of New Haven to create and maintain a town that can: generate and allocate supplies within a healthy environment, train and provide employment for all citizens, provide a strong defensive military, and maintain and seek out mutually beneficial relationships with outside allies.

Many suggestions were too specific to be in the mission statement, but were adopted as tasks to fulfill it. The list included: finding the other sanctuaries, setting up trade, creating manufacturing plants, using the Hold as a training camp for soldiers, recruiting more people to join them to create a new nation, learning about and locating medicines available in nature, arranging hunting and gathering parties, recording their history, and so much more.

Gray and Jilly sat in the west yard looking up at the late October stars and the slightest sliver of a moon. It was a cold, clear night, and they huddled together under a thick quilt. The tunnel would close permanently soon with the frigid temperatures and more blowing snow on its way. They couldn't believe it was fall, and they were beginning their second year in the tunnel. Billie and Gabe were expecting a child in May. Bannon, Ari, and their two children were growing happy and healthy. Dana and Indy were dedicated to challenging Zoey, whose extraordinary musical abilities were recently confirmed.

Aniya was preparing to travel to the Hold to run their ranch and farm. She had a natural gift for dealing with animals and growing things. The education department shared its programs and curriculum files with their allies at the Hold, so she could continue her studies of horticulture and animal husbandry techniques through New Haven University.

Lana quit the Defenders to head the newly adopted historian division. She interviewed and gathered historical information from the people of the town. That endeavor would take a lot of time, but she hoped to get a couple of assistants, so she could expand the compilation to include stories from their allies. The combined citizens were now the United Citizens of Free America.

Tanya had been working feverishly on her book, The Lost and the Found. It was about her introspective journey on what she had observed and learned in New Haven. She had also trained to be a minister, and Haru said she was his best student. She was preparing to sell her book for credits on the feed. With her exemplary behavior and credits to pay off her fee, the parole board might shorten her sentence. When released, she planned on becoming the permanent religious guide at the Hold.

"I love this quote she sent out," said Jilly. She pulled out the paper she had copied it on while shivering at the cold air replacing the warmth that surrounded them.

"Struggle gives us purpose, but freedom gives us the power to serve that purpose. The tunnel has been our nursery to reflect on what humanity means, to solidify our beliefs, and to discover who we should be. And now, we are called to *be* what we believe."

Gray thought about the last sentence. Tonight, they were safely wrapped in their blanket under the stars, but contrasting this idyllic moment was the threat of war. Just like the disaster that brought the planet to its current state, its approach was silent. But its arrival would unleash a fierceness that could reduce their home to dust. They had one chance to avert the coming invasion and its insurmountable odds.

A select few were being sent out to do what was required to save New Haven, and he was one of them. He wondered how much of the plan Bannon would share with the residents. Soon, he would have to let Jilly know he was leaving and might not be home for a long time. And maybe never.

Lion's Creed

Book 2 From Darkness

William Alexander sat up abruptly, his heart racing, his breaths rapid and heavy. Beads of sweat soaked through the cheap oversized t-shirt that twisted and gnarled around him. The recurring nightmare of dandelion seeds swirling in a red mist was tangled in his new dilemma. When he woke up bandaged and hazy, he recalled the events of that day and realized his stellar reputation as a soldier had been reduced to a deserter and a traitor. He had spent the day running from heavily armed, well-trained men who outnumbered him. How had his life gone so wrong?

As a boy, he understood his purpose, to stay alive, and that had been hard enough. But that all changed when, in a desperate moment, he was given a relic. He had heard of it, but it was just a myth. Now, he was caught up in its destiny. The next thing he knew, the one person who would have explained what was expected of him was gone, and he was alone with a purpose that was a complete mystery. Over a decade passed without destiny pressing on his mind. To him, it was all just a desperate whim, a childish myth. Though he didn't believe in magic, he did believe in hope, but it was the kind that got one out of tough spots. No item, or person for that matter, contained enough hope or magic to set this land free.

But it all came back, and hope was all he had left, This morning he was drugged, kidnapped, and woke up in the presence of a man from his past. It was a man he honored and respected, and he was dying. Again, he was told he must fulfill his destiny. Will never told anyone about the talisman or the person who gave it to him, so how could he know about it? The information he shared was muddled with ambiguous tasks and sketchy details. But the moment left no time for questions because his friend handed him a crude map and a backpack with one hand while he pointed with the other saying *RUN*. Will ran for hours through the roughest terrain he had ever seen. He felt physically depleted, utterly lost and alone, and failing to do... something.

His injured leg ached as he reached for a dry shirt from the backpack and added his coat to the blanket over him. It was all he could do to keep from freezing in the temporary earthen shelter. He needed sleep to continue his escape, but old ghosts strangled his thoughts, and his new burdens further tightened his mental noose. It was always a struggle to put his nightmare away. He knew nothing good could come from reliving it. It was a time past, a deed done, and no redemption to be had. He accepted this in his waking hours, why couldn't his dreams do the same? The undisciplined side of his brain kept drudging up phantoms of futile memories that could not be changed. The dead could not be raised, nor could the answers that died with them. He shook his head and grabbed his canteen from the floor near his bed sack. The cool water soothed his parched throat, and he settled back into a restless cold sleep.

His early recollections as a young boy held loving memories of his father, Ben, being protective and kind. Like all workers on the lowest rung of the caste system, Dailys as they were called, life was difficult and hunger was a familiar feeling. They lived a bleak existence under the domination of the Corporates and their nasty Neighwah soldiers and the efficient mercenaries called Drangers. Even though his world was precarious, it was all he knew, and he trusted his father to keep him safe with naïve innocence.

Will was too young to remember the meteorite strikes that lasted seven days and devastated the entire planet, but the stories prevailed. The governments fell and the most basic of resources dried up for the unfortunate common citizens. As people became ill with the thick, acidic dust, the bodies began to pile up causing more illness. During those tragic years without proper medical diagnoses or interventions, every affliction was called a meteor sickness. Will's mother died of meteor sickness when he was six years old. He struggled to recall her, but he remembered she looked like him. She had dark coffee skin, big brown eyes, and a smile like sunshine. His dad's skin was a gentle bronze, and his eyes were a haunting green. Will's eyes were brown with green mixed in. His father was tall and strong in muscle tone and heart. His parents were both stunning people, and though Will had a mixture of their traits, he felt he was awkwardly pieced together.

Their close friends, Tim and Rita, lived nearby and were kind and supportive after his mother died. Rita worked evenings at home as a computer technician, fixing minor low-security software problems remotely. This allowed her to care for Will and other children under nine during the day in exchange for work, items, or credits. Her children were grown and on their own, but she loved being a mom, so it was a good fit for her. But it was a temporary solution. All Dailys over twelve were required to work, or their food rations would be cut off. But eventually, she would have to go back to the computer lab.

It was fall when Will was almost eight years old, his dad, Ben, and Tim went out to hunt antelope while Will stayed with Rita. Hunting wild game with anything more than a snare was illegal since it required weapons that Dailys were not permitted to own. Ben fashioned a bow and arrow set and disguised it to look like a walking stick. The flexible bow was made sturdy and straight by wrapping the untipped, and un-fletched arrows around it with the bow string. It was simply an interesting walking stick until he assembled it. The stick was stored in plain sight, leaning against the wall in his room. When hunting, the fletching, and arrow tips were concealed in a pouch tied to his leg and under his boot. At his home, he kept them hidden under a floorboard in his room with his cache of prohibited items.

When they came back from their trip, they had the quartered antelope draped under their jackets and a young woman walking between them. She was extremely thin and showed signs of physical abuse. They found her where she had collapsed from severe dehydration in the badlands. Ben decided to care for her, and in return, she would watch Will until he was old enough to be on his own according to Corporate rules. To the Corporates, the kids represent future workers, and they didn't want to invest time and credits only to have them die of neglect.

Will's father planned to tell the authorities she was an abandoned hostage of Fringers. Fringers were bands on the run who lived on the fringes of the settled areas. The story would be accepted because it was rumored the rebel bands were marauding criminals, and kidnappings were among their offenses. No one cared about keeping detailed records on Dailys, and young able workers were very valuable to a township. So as long as she could work, she would be registered.

Ben explained to his son that he didn't know where she came from because she lost her memory. But Will had an uncanny ability to read expressions and body language. Will watched her as his father recited the questionable tale of her journey. He didn't know her, but he heard enough covert stories from Dailys with secrets to hide. He was certain she remembered more than she was saying. He also suspected she had escaped from something important and dangerous, and taking her in was a huge risk. His father and Tianna were married in a small ceremony in their house with Tim and Rita in attendance.

Will didn't remember much about his mother, but he did remember Tianna. She was a gentle woman with soft light skin, golden hair, and twenty or so freckles dusted across her cheeks and nose. She had pretty, delicate features, light blue eyes, and a warm, kind smile. Will was the very contrast of her with his rich cocoa skin, thin gangly limbs, tall stature, and brown eyes streaked with green highlights. He was in that awkward stage of growing and not being in proportion. But she always boosted his confidence and called him her handsome warrior.

Though both he and his father treated Tianna with tender kindness, she was quick to startle, had a timid nature, and experienced random panic attacks that were followed by profound sadness. Even young Will knew something horrible must have happened to her, but whenever he probed, she would just fall back on her loss of memory claim. But she seemed to have a complete recall of her extensive education, and she was extremely bright. Will knew there was more to this worldly woman, and that she hadn't lost her memory. She probably remembered everything, but he didn't care. He just hoped the world wouldn't invade their home and take her away.

Acknowledgements

Writing this book was one of the most enjoyable of all my professional careers. I attribute much of that to the support I received from my beloved family, friends, and business partners.

In loving memory, I thank my parents, Harold and Carolyn, for providing me with a loving home to grow up in and for their inspiration to always learn.

I thank my husband, Bryan, for taking on more than his share to give me the time and space to write, encouraging me, reading and rereading everything, and for being my business manager. But I thank him mostly for being my biggest fan and pushing me to publish.

I thank my children, Russ, Aaron, Garrett, and Corrin, for engaging in hours of reading, reviewing, researching, and the meaningful dialog that ensued. I thank my sisters, Carol and Lorraine, and my brother, Richard, for reading and encouraging me throughout this journey. And thanks to my in-law family for reading, encouraging me, and giving loving advice. I love you all so much. I am blessed with the best family ever.

I thank my cousin, David, for his honest and kind evaluations, professional research, and help with my creative science.

I thank Laura Jones, my agent at Fulton Books for her endless patience and quick responses to my many questions. I thank the Fulton Book staff for all their work to get my book ready. I especially thank the editing staff.

I thank all my friends, Brenda, Terry, Lindy, Erin, Becky, and many others who have offered their time and support over and over again.

I thank Fay Wright, my college literature and writing instructor, for pushing me and believing in me as a writer.

But mostly I thank God for his guidance, forgiveness, love, and a compassionate place to rejoice and cry. I have been blessed with a wonderful life full of good people. Amen

About the Author:

Roxanne Ward has always loved putting her thoughts to paper. She was heavily influenced by her father, a college administrator, and his love of literature and fascination with science. She spent six years in the Air Force Reserve before she returned to school to pursue a degree in education. She earned her MS in education from the University of Idaho and taught middle school classes in language arts, and science. Fostering a joy for the art of language and the thrill of learning stretched beyond the classroom to her children and grandchildren. She retired from teaching after twenty years and began her writing career. She lives in Northern Idaho on five acres with her husband of forty years and their border terrier Nikki.

Roxannewardauthor.com